SWIMMING IN THE SHADOWS

SWIMMING IN THE SHADOWS

Diane Janes

severn House

This first world edition published 2014
in Great Britain and in the USA by
SEVERN HOUSE PUBLISHERS LTD of
19 Cedar Road, Sutton, Surrey, England, SM2 5DA.
Trade paperback edition first published
in Great Britain and the USA 2015 by
SEVERN HOUSE PUBLISHERS LTD

British Library Cataloguing in Publication Data

Janes, Diane author.
  Swimming in the shadows.
  1. Murder–Investigation–England–Yorkshire Dales–
  Fiction. 2. Anonyms and pseudonyms–Fiction. 3. Romantic
  suspense novels.
  I. Title
  823.9'2-dc23

ISBN-13: 978-0-7278-8431-2 (cased)
ISBN-13: 978-1-84751-536-0 (trade paper)
ISBN-13: 978-1-78010-581-9 (ebook)

Typeset by Palimpsest Book Production Ltd.,
Falkirk, Stirlingshire, Scotland.

ONE

Susan McCarthy gave me life.

She was not an anonymous donor, for I had known Susan McCarthy, with her long dark hair, her ready smile and the mole on her left cheek, round and dark like a beauty spot. I knew something of her family, parents, brothers and sisters; a warm, close-knit circle, for whom her early death must have been a heavy blow. I never rejoiced that Susan had died, consigned to oblivion on a road in southern France, but I suppose somewhere, deep down, like the recipient of an organ donation, I couldn't help but be grateful that she had died at such a convenient time and place for me.

I don't know if Susan carried a donor card, but even if she had, there was no question of her giving advance consent for my posthumous operation – nor had approval been sought from her relatives, for when I took Susan McCarthy's name and the precious paraphernalia of her identity, I worked alone and secretly; not at all like the messy transplant of organs, attended by an orchestra of operating theatre staff, cutting and snipping around warm, blood-bathed heart and lungs, with perhaps the addition of liver and kidneys, carrying their uneasy butcher's shop connotations or even more squeamishly, bits of eyes. Eyes, the mirrors of men's souls, sliced away with shiny scalpels that chink on silver trays: the very thought of it jarring, as hideous as the screech of nails on a blackboard.

Once or twice I caught myself wondering whether Susan's organs might have been transplanted. Whether there was, somewhere, a physical part of the real Susan living on as part of someone else? It was a dangerous avenue of speculation to follow. I didn't like to think of Susan McCarthy or even a part of her suddenly confronting me, Jennifer Reynolds, the thief of her identity. At moments like these I forced myself to remember that it was just a name – a label of convenience.

Like those other names, Louise Mason, Jane Smith, Elizabeth Wilson, which had each served for a time, though they were different somehow because they were made-up names. With Susan McCarthy I had entered different territory, taking a real person (albeit a dead one) and using the bits of her I fancied, discarding any useless, cumbersome pieces that did not suit my purpose as callously as any transplant surgeon had ever done.

I tried to reassure myself that none of this could hurt the real Susan's family. So long as I was careful, they would never find out, and as for Susan herself, I didn't really believe in ghosts. And anyway, if Susan's restless spirit lurked anywhere, surely it would be in France? I had pictured the scene many times, Susan and her fiancé driving in an open-top car along some dusty sunlit road, surrounded by the fragrance of spring blossoms like a snippet from a travel show. Her long dark hair would be streaming out, her sun-bronzed arm resting on the windowsill, and on the back seat there would be a basket from which a baguette protruded alongside a bottle of blood-red wine, with an edge of cheese peeping from beneath the folds of a checked tablecloth. Their last cliché-ridden moments preserved forever, oblivious to the impending disaster around the next bend. In my mind's eye I saw it all: the sporty car with its roof down, the sunshine, the picnic basket – other people's lives, events of which I had only scant knowledge. The reality may well have been completely different: it did not matter.

It was easy to believe in these imagined details of Susan McCarthy's final journey, because with the passage of time they had merged into the genesis of that other Susan McCarthy – the self-invented Susan, resurrected back in 1986, whose life was carefully recorded in an exercise book in the drawer of my kitchen dresser – the life which I had by then been living for more than three years, with its fictitious past that I had half come to believe in.

If this new Susan were to marry Rob, that exercise book would have to go. No one could offer their spouse a rational explanation for keeping a book which carefully set out their autobiographical details in the way my exercise book did. I had almost persuaded myself that I didn't need the book any more. I was word perfect in Susan McCarthy. Those notes had served a vital purpose in the beginning, providing me with a script from which to learn my part. I had never been much of an actor in my previous life, but maybe I was good at this role because all I had to do was be my new self – a part I had been waiting to play my whole life.

In posing as the unmarried only child of two deceased only children, I had managed to deflect any awkward questions about my lack of visible family. Yet this complete dearth of relations, friends, ex-colleagues – nay, any person who belonged to the period of my life before I came to live in Lasthwaite, until now a minor problem which I had bluffed through successfully – was destined to become a paramount difficulty if I married Rob.

Every bride has someone to give her away; someone to sit on her side of the church. No woman can reach thirty-four without accumulating a few wedding guests along the way. Worse still, I had already made a critical mistake – the direct result of trying to be too clever. Thinking to defuse any suspicions which might be aroused by the complete absence of past acquaintances, I had foolishly augmented the cards I received at Christmas from current friends and workmates with several fraudulent missives from distant theoretical friends. Rob had seen these cards on my mantelshelf, and while he had obviously not committed their senders to memory, he was nonetheless under the impression that I was on Christmas card sending terms with several persons from my fictitious past, including an old friend called Maggie, who supposedly lived in London and with whom I allegedly corresponded on an occasional basis. Excuses would need to be invented against inviting Maggie to the wedding. Lies would need to be told and I hated myself for lying to him.

Time after time I had come within a breath of telling him the truth – but where to begin? And once he knew the truth how could he ever trust me again? How could he marry someone whose whole existence was based on an enormous lie? In my heart I knew that honesty could only be self-defeating, because if I abandoned Susan McCarthy, I would effectively be abandoning my chances of marrying Rob. The fact was that I *could* only marry Rob as Susan McCarthy – my other self being inconveniently married to someone else.

I wasn't entirely sure how the assumption of a false identity stood in the eyes of the law. At the very least it must constitute some kind of fraud. I did know that to remarry, albeit under a new identity, was most definitely illegal. It was bigamy – an ugly word, suggestive of a large, noisy crime. My choices appeared clear cut: to carry on as Susan McCarthy, maintaining the deception to the bitter end, or to lose Rob.

It was not as if I had originally set out to trap or deceive him. I hadn't intended to fall in love with him, or dedicated myself to making him fall in love with me, but the thing had happened, just the same. Before I had time to think about the consequences or even realize what was happening, he was there in my life – an unplanned diversion from the anticipated route. Up until that moment I had mapped my way so carefully, painstakingly building a good solid road from which it seemed impossible to falter. Only now I had faltered. I had blundered off the secure causeway and out on to the marshes. In no time at all I had lost sight of the safe path and didn't know how to return to it. All around me lay the fatal stinking mire of my own deception. Lately I had been no more than hopping desperately from one uncertain piece of ground to another, never quite sure which lie might be the one to give way beneath my weight and draw me down. Dark oily waters, little pools of uncertainty, swirled and eddied at my feet. Every new lie seemed to undermine my footing a little more.

I knew that it was wrong to marry Rob. Not just in the eyes of the law, though the legal technicalities did not trouble me overmuch – what's one more document, fraudulently obtained? No, it was my own conscience that argued against it. Marrying Rob meant entangling him even further in my net of deception – and yet not marrying him represented a cruel rejection which would hurt him deeply. He would not understand why I had changed my mind when we were so happy together, so . . . right. He would want an explanation, but if I told him, if I explained the truth, what then? I had painted myself into a

corner, stitched myself inside a straitjacket of my own manu-
facture. All I knew was that I wanted Rob. I wanted to bear
his children. Was that so terribly bad? Isn't everyone entitled
to a shot at happiness?

TWO

Some people would argue that there is such a thing as a good lie, but where to set the dividing line? How about the deceits in which I had engaged with my mother as she endured the living death of her final year?

'I have a daughter, you know,' she told me one day, leaning forward, patting my hand in the attitude of one sharing a confidence. 'Her name is Jennifer.' She had articulated it carefully – 'Jenn-if-er' – as if it was an exotic name of complicated pronunciation.

'Mum, I am Jennifer,' I had replied as gently as I could, stupidly expecting cognisance to dawn.

'No you're not.' Her thin, high-pitched voice was embarrassingly loud in a room full of mumbles. She repeated the words more loudly, over and over again, rising to a shriek which reverberated against the window panes, bounced around the pelmets. 'You're not Jennifer!' Then she had begun to wail, a terrible keening sound, occasionally repeating it: 'You're not Jennifer. You're not Jennifer.'

The old woman in the chair next to my mother's had begun to wail in sympathy, and when a couple of the others joined in, the staff arrived in force, suggesting with as much tact as possible that the visit be cut short.

'You're not Jennifer,' my mother had said. Well, curiously enough, she had had her way in the end. I was not Jennifer any more.

I had been careful never to repeat my error. From then on I was prepared to go along with whatever my mother said. Mostly she was convinced that I was called Julia. I never found out who Julia was. A childhood friend? Some long-forgotten relative? I was equally unenlightened about Aunt Cicely, but tentatively played along whenever Mother stated that it was her intention to go to Aunt Cicely's for tea.

'Shall we go together?' she would ask.

'Oh, yes,' I would say, with all the enthusiasm I could muster.

This train of thought quite often kept her cheerful for several minutes at a time, musing greedily about the possibilities of crumpets and angel cake. I tried hard to believe that my mother derived some pleasure from the days when I assumed the part of Julia, endeavouring to keep her chatting happily and well away from the subject of bridge.

She would spring it on me suddenly, the arrival of the thought as random as the cherries and bells falling into line on a seaside slot machine. 'Do you play bridge?' I knew it would end in tears whichever way I answered. Sometimes she would repeat the question, asking again and again like a record stuck in a groove, her hands fluttering for possession of imaginary cards, or else she would begin to rant nonsensically about tricks and bids, her hysteria increasing as I, her partner, failed to come up with an appropriate response.

At other times she would ramble from one idea to another, often stopping abruptly and fixing me with a stare. In her youth it would have been cool and piercing, wilting in its path any social upstart who had presumed upon her acquaintance, but now it was merely pathetic, her mouth trembling and her watery eyes struggling to focus. 'Do I know you?'

No surprises then that Rob's announcing it was time I met his mother not only awoke these uncomfortable memories but also provoked an inner panic. Up until then the fact that his mother lived in a retirement flat in Devon had ensured sufficient distance to render any casual social calls impractical. Now, however, Rob wanted to break the news that we were getting married: 'And obviously she's going to want to meet you.' Not just meet me, I thought, but find out all about me. Subject me to the kind of quizzing about my family background and antecedents which my own mother would certainly have indulged in had she been in the role of prospective mother-in-law. Worse still, we were 'making a weekend of it' – something of a given when travelling down from Yorkshire. Rather than being able to limit ourselves to a quick get-together over tea and cake, we were going to be in his mother's company for an entire

day and a half – more than enough time for her to pose all
kinds of searching enquiries.

By the time Rob collected me for the long drive south, I
was already sick with nerves. On top of this it was not an
auspicious night for travelling. Light drizzle during the afternoon had turned to lashing rain, and the Friday evening
traffic was heavy. Rob was quieter than usual, concentrating
on the road, and I matched his silence, preoccupied with
concerns of my own.

Under normal circumstances I would have enjoyed the
journey. Rob handled the car well, instilling me with confidence in spite of the testing conditions, and our love was still
new enough for me to thrill at being alongside him in the
dark, close intimacy of the car. I loved the sense of his large,
comforting presence only inches away, but all this was spoiled
because I couldn't forget that every passing mile brought his
mother a little closer. With a hundred miles still to go, I began
to lay the ground for an early night: yawning theatrically and
mentioning several times how tired I was, since I reasoned
that the best way to avoid an interrogation was by being
tucked up in bed.

The traffic gradually dissipated and the weather improved,
so that by the time we were south of Bristol, the clouds had
rolled away and stars peppered the sky. Weariness remained
my trump card. 'You must be shattered,' I said. 'I wish we'd
done something about the insurance so I could have shared
the driving.'

'I can't say I shall be sorry to get into bed.' His left hand
strayed from the steering wheel to squeeze my thigh.

'Your mother must be a good deal more broadminded than
mine,' I said. 'Do you know, I'm sure she would never have
let us share a bed, however old I was and whatever our ultimate
marital intentions.'

'My mum's all right – you'll like her. Anyway, convenience
is a great incentive to turning a blind eye. There are only two
bedrooms in the flat and I'm sure she'd much rather have us
staying with her instead of putting up in some B and B.'

At that moment I could not help wishing that Rob's mother
had been as straight-laced as my own. An escape to a B & B

would have cut down enormously on all that togetherness which lay ahead of us.

It was after ten when we arrived. The flat was in a modern block with a parking area near the main doors. Rob's mother buzzed us in through the intercom and he led the way along a corridor to where his mother awaited us in the doorway of her flat. Everything about her was small and neat. She was a bright-eyed, white-haired lady wearing a red knitted dress and pearls. Her hair was permed and discreet eye shadow and lipstick had been applied; not just for our benefit, I thought, but because she was the kind of woman who would have felt undressed without them.

Rob looked enormous alongside her. He put down the bags, gave her a bear hug then stepped aside while she took both my hands in her small ones and kissed me on each cheek. 'It's lovely to meet you, Susan,' she said. 'Come inside, you must both be exhausted.' Rob had yet to tell her that we were getting married, but I saw the swift appraisal all the same, the relief at finding that I did not have a nose ring, or bright pink hair, did not look like a bimbo or a tart. I reflected that she probably didn't get to see many of his girlfriends – he lived too far away – so when he told her that he was bringing someone down she must have guessed there was something in the wind.

The flat was extremely tidy, like its occupant, though she had made the room bright with pictures, pot plants and cut flowers. Rob and I sat together on the settee while his mother bustled in and out of the kitchen, making hot drinks. I took care to let him see me stifling another yawn. There was an inevitable interlude of enquiries about the journey – which way had we come down and how had the traffic been, but then she said, 'You must be very tired after the drive. I expect you want nothing more than to get to bed. Don't feel you have to sit up just to be polite.'

I was only too delighted to take my cue: 'I must admit, I am really whacked . . .'

'You go and get your head down, dear. Your room is the first door on the left and the bathroom is right next door.' She smiled. 'There will be plenty of time for me to find out all about you tomorrow.' She turned to Rob, mercifully oblivious to the way I had all but choked on my last mouthful of tea. 'Now, I know you like a lie-in on a Saturday, so I thought rather than make a big thing of breakfast, we could all go out for lunch. The Riviera Hotel is very nice – do you remember it? The big one on the Esplanade?'

As I settled beneath the duvet I realized that I was genuinely weary. Even so, I lay awake for some time in the unfamiliar bedroom. I knew that I was being ridiculous – investing her words with suspicions which simply were not there. She was just a harmless old lady. I had maintained my deception for years in the face of all-comers and there was no particular reason why she should present a problem. All we had to do was get through a day (half a day if I could hang out the Saturday lie-in for long enough) of chatting and exploring whatever Sidmouth had to offer. Then, first thing on Sunday we would be back on the road again, our engagement announced, her curiosity satisfied and me safely off the hook until whenever we met again – which given the distances involved wasn't going to be any time soon. So why was I losing sleep? Was it just that I had worked myself up to expect a problem? Or did I genuinely have a bad feeling about this whole enterprise – a feeling in no way diminished by my first look at the little old lady in the red dress, with those bright blue eyes which seemed to see right through me?

THREE

Sometimes I even tried to deceive myself. I told myself lies about Rob, saying that I had not wanted him to fall in love with me. I always knew that a relationship with Rob represented too much of a danger, so *of course* I never wanted him to fall in love with me – but it wasn't true. I wanted him desperately. I wanted him to love me back for real, not just as a passing romance but for keeps. Children would call it pretending. Let's pretend that you're a knight and I'm a beautiful princess. The gentle art of self-deception. Let's pretend that I'm not really married to someone else.

All this I thought about as I lay in Rob's mother's spare bedroom, where the morning sunshine was forcing its way through the floral-print curtains.

'Penny for them?'

I realized then that he was awake and had perhaps been watching me for some time. I turned to him and smiled. 'I was thinking how happy I am – and how lucky I am to have you.' I kissed him, one kiss leading to another until we were making love, the whole business conducted in furtive silence out of unspoken respect for his mother, whose walls were thin and whose spare room door did not quite meet the beige carpet. It *may* have been this concern for her finer feelings which prompted me to say afterwards, as we continued to lie in bed, disputing half-heartedly about which of us would use the bathroom first, 'Do you think it might be better if we didn't mention getting married this visit?'

'Why not?'

'Well, it's a lot to spring on her, isn't it? The first time she's ever met me – in one breath, "Hey, Mum, this is Susan," and in the next, "Oh and by the way, we're getting married."'

'You're not having second thoughts, are you?'

'About telling her this weekend – yes.'

'About getting married?'

'No, of course not.'

Yes, yes, a thousand times yes. It would be so much easier if we could just live together like everyone else does – but if I say this now you will feel rejected and I can't bear that.

'I just feel as if it would be – I don't know – good manners to let her get used to me for a while. It's not as if we've set a date. There will be plenty of other opportunities to break the news.'

'Not exactly plenty . . . It's not as if we're down in Devon every other weekend.'

Her knock on the door startled us both. 'Hello in there – I heard you talking, so I know you're awake. Would you like a cup of tea in bed?'

'Cheers, Mum, but we're getting up now.' As if to make good this statement, Rob scrambled out of bed and wrapped himself in his big blue dressing gown.

'It's no trouble,' came the disembodied voice from the hall, but he was already opening the door en route for the bathroom, our discussion about whether or not to break the news left unresolved.

It stayed that way for the rest of the day. She provided us with a late breakfast of croissants, juice and coffee, after which we went for a walk along the Esplanade. The wind was coming in from the Channel, pushing foamy waves up the shingle beach, tossing cascades of droplets into the air where they caught the sunlight and turned into a million tiny rainbows against the clear blue sky. The conditions made conversation difficult, but I sensed the likelihood of a grilling once we sat down to lunch.

The waiter at the Riviera Hotel obviously recognized Rob's mother. She probably lunches here regularly, I thought. I had been steeling myself for the interrogation to begin at once, but I had forgotten all the fussy little preliminaries, the removal of coats, the aperitif in the bar, decisions over the menu – and just when the gentle dispute between Rob and his mother about whether he had eaten there with her before had run its course, the waiter arrived, ready to show us to our table. Then there were our starters to be tasted and commented upon, someone noticing that it had begun to cloud over and might soon begin to rain, questions about Rob's cottage – had he got that problem with the central heating boiler sorted out? I knew it was only a postponement, not a reprieve. At any moment now Rob's mother, while managing to stay on the right side of polite, would start to pose a variety of enquiries about where her son's new girl-friend came from and who her family were. Yet all through our main course Mrs Dugdale confounded my expectations by keeping her curiosity politely under wraps, making easy conversation about anything and nothing.

The time came to choose our pudding. 'If you like pavlova, Susan, you should really try theirs – it's absolutely heavenly.'

'Hang on a minute,' Rob interrupted. 'Before we commit ourselves on this, you'd better come clean. It isn't fair to encourage Sue to fill herself up at lunchtime, then produce some sort of gargantuan gateaux you've made when we get back to the flat.'

'I'm sure Susan has a very healthy appetite . . .'

'So you have baked a cake. I might have known.'

'Well of course I have. You know I always bake when you come down.'

'The trouble with you, Mother, is that you always think everyone needs feeding up.'

'Do have a pudding, Susan, and take no notice of my son. You are under no obligation whatsoever to eat any cake later if you don't want to. And don't think any of it will be wasted, because what you don't eat I'm going to wrap up for Rob to take home. Not that I want you to think I'm the sort of silly woman who sends her grown-up son home with food parcels,' she added. 'But I know very well that in spite of his protesta-tions, he is extremely fond of home-made cake.'

'It was very kind of you to bake specially for us,' I said. 'And I love cake, so I'm sure I can manage to eat some pudding now and some cake later.'

'It was a pleasure,' said Mrs Dugdale. 'Visitors provide me with a good excuse to keep my hand in. Do you enjoy baking or are you too busy with your job?'

'I never really got into baking,' I said, 'living on my own.'

'Mum is an absolute demon,' said Rob. 'She does about six Christmas cakes for various people every year. If I were you, I'd get your order in now and she'll put you on her list. The whole operation starts sometime around June.'

'I do mince pies too.' Her blue eyes lit up. 'For the Christmas bazaar, and for friends.'

'I'm afraid my mince pies usually come out of a box,' I said.

'Mince pies out of a box.' Rob pretended to chide me. 'Mentioning that in front of the Kitchen Crusader is like telling Batman that the Penguin's on the loose in Gotham City.'

Mrs Dugdale smiled her twinkly smile again, completely disarming me with all this inconsequential talk of seasonal confectionery, before saying, 'You know, Susan, ever since you got here last night I've been trying to place where I've seen you before.'

I was caught completely off guard. A mass the size of a Christmas cake abruptly took up residence in my chest, where it tried to force the air from my lungs while my heart beat against it in thunderous protest. I couldn't risk one of those 'did you ever live here' or 'visit there' conversations, so I tried to cut her off with: 'Well, I expect it was when you were still living in Richmond. We could easily have seen each other there.'

'No dear,' she said. 'It can't have been in Richmond, because I moved down here long before you went to work in Lasthwaite – and didn't Rob tell me that you lived somewhere in the Midlands before that?'

I maintained a fixed smile while cursing the fact that Rob had never bothered to mention his mother was some sort of female Sherlock Holmes, who apparently committed every little detail she was told to memory, so that you couldn't gloss over anything without tripping up.

'Actually,' she continued, 'I was going to ask if you had a sister. I've been thinking about it all morning – trying to remember where I'd seen you before – and when the waiter brought the menus across just now, it suddenly came to me. You look just like a girl who used to work in a hotel that a friend and I stayed at in Keswick.'

'I don't have any sisters.' Keep smiling, keep it light. Keep breathing steadily, in and out, in and out.

'Sue's an only child,' Rob volunteered.

'And I've never worked in the hotel trade.' Might as well throw in a lie for good measure.

'How funny,' said Mrs Dugdale. 'I've generally got such a good memory for faces. Not that you would normally remember someone like that, but there was a problem over our bathroom, you see. We had to change rooms and this girl who served the meals at the hotel helped us with our luggage. She looked so like you, and I remember her voice was similar – another girl from the Midlands – it could almost have been you. It was at the Heather Bank Hotel in Keswick.'

'A doppelgänger,' I said. 'They say everybody has one.' I managed to sound interested, but not *too* interested.

'Did you see that thing in the papers last week?' Rob asked. 'About those people who look like famous celebrities? They get paid to turn up at parties, pretending to be Marilyn Monroe or the queen. There's a special agency apparently. What a weird way to make a living.'

I blessed him for providing a diversion. Hotel guests fell into two categories: those for whom the staff were part of the fixtures and fittings and therefore completely unmemorable, and those much more dangerous guests who were capable of recognizing the person who had served them their dinner, or helped them move their luggage, when they ran across that person again years later. Mrs Dugdale evidently fell into this latter category. For my part, I could honestly say that I did not recognize her from my time as Louise at the Heather Bank Hotel. In small hotels there was always a multitude of white-haired old ladies who all merged into an amorphous crowd – if not before their departure then very soon after it. Moreover, the odds were stacked in favour of the guest: there were only a handful of staff and thousands of little old ladies. Inwardly I cursed my bad luck – of all the hotels in all the world . . .

Nothing more was said about the hotel in Keswick, and whether I had satisfied her curiosity or not, I managed a bravura performance as a prospective daughter-in-law, complimenting her on the cake, insisting on helping with some washing up, admiring old photographs of Rob and taking an interest in anecdotes about his childhood, his late father and his sisters.

'She really likes you,' he said as we lay in bed together that night. He had said nothing about our getting married and Mrs Dugdale was too polite to fish – not even asking anything about our living arrangements – although perhaps it was obvious from our conversation (she was ruddy Miss Marple, after all) that we still maintained separate establishments. 'I'm glad,' I said. 'I like her too.' Which would have been completely true if she had not been so infernally sharp.

'I've been thinking about what you said this morning,' he said.

We were both keeping our voices low – consideration lending a touch of conspiracy to our conversation. 'What about?' I asked, in little more than a whisper.

'About not telling her that we plan to get married, and I think you're right. Telling her this weekend would be like a *fait accompli* – not that she's really got any say in the matter, but if we come down again in a couple of months and tell her then it will be nicer, somehow. Not so in your face.'

'I'm sure that would be better,' I said. I imagined her a few weeks hence, lunching with friends and telling them that Rob was bringing me down again. 'It sounds serious,' one of them would say, and another one would add that it was about time too. They would all be the sort of women who wanted their children to have nice weddings: everyone in big hats, with the grandchildren who had already been provided by other offspring acting as page boys and bridesmaids. I pictured the empty pews on my side of the church and felt slightly sick. No relations. Who on earth can claim to have *no* relations? Alongside me, Rob was saying something about introducing me to his sisters soon, while I made non-committal 'mmm' noises, and thanked my lucky stars that neither of them lived near enough to have joined us in Sidmouth for the day. Always with new people there was that chance of recognition – not from the hotel work, an unlucky, million-to-one coincidence, but from the newspapers who'd printed my photo after my disappearance. Sooner or later someone was going to spot my resemblance to Jennifer

Reynolds, and if a good memory for faces ran in the female side of Rob's family . . .

It seemed to me in that moment that if one of us was rather short on relatives, Rob had more than enough for both of us.

FOUR

We set off for home after breakfast on Sunday morning. Rob's mother kissed me goodbye – one on each side, lips brushing my cheeks so that I caught a hint of her discreet floral perfume. She was so petite, so utterly *Good Housekeeping* and Elizabeth Arden that I found myself wondering how on earth she had ever produced a hulking, outdoorsy type like Rob, but perhaps he had taken after his father's side of the family.

Our journey home was uneventful. We listened to the radio and talked. Normal, safe, unimportant topics. Nothing more was said about doppelgängers or hotels in the Lake District, so I was able to relax in the happiness of the moment: Rob and I travelling together, not looking to the future nor troubling over the past. When we reached my cottage, he insisted on carrying my small weekend bag to the door, although he declined to come in. I didn't press him, because I knew that he had a stack of Year Nine projects waiting at home which had to be marked by the morning. He kissed me goodbye and I stood on the doorstep, waving him out of sight down the lane.

Heb's Cottage had been the only property available for rent in the district when I had been offered a job in Lasthwaite the previous year. It was a typical Dales cottage almost a mile from the village, out of sight of any other habitation, but in many ways the isolation suited my purpose and the place had quickly become 'home'. By the time I unlocked the door that afternoon the central heating had already switched itself on, so the place felt warm and welcoming. Casual visitors might have thought the furnishings rather spare, the style bordering on minimalist, but to my eyes it was a safe haven, comfortable and uncluttered.

I went straight through to the kitchen to make myself some coffee, and as I waited for the kettle to boil I thought about

Rob and his mother, and the way her kindly, uncomplicated welcome only seemed to make things even worse. Why on earth had I agreed to marriage, with its inherent legal complications? Why hadn't I decried the whole institution as outmoded, stood firm as an independent woman at the start of the nineties surely should and told him that it was just a worthless piece of paper? Because secretly, said a treacherous voice inside my head, you adore the romantic in him. The very fact that he *wants* to marry you is dangerously appealing. He proposed with roses and champagne – how the hell could you refuse?

Yet here was the dichotomy. He was my lover, my future husband, my best friend – but when it came to the biggest single issue in my life I could neither confide in him nor solicit his advice. There was no one I could talk to. No one else knew that I was really Jennifer. Not even my alter-ego, Susan . . . Not unless the dead can watch the living. I shut that silly thought straight back in its box. When you live alone in a cottage on the edge of the moors, there are some ideas which need to be banished before you can finish articulating them. I quickly put some bread in the toaster, just to have something to do.

I took my toast and coffee into the sitting room, then rifled through my small collection of music until I located the Carpenters *Greatest Hits*. Sitting cross-legged in the window seat, I could look out beyond my reflection to where the folds of the dale faded into one another in the dusk. Secure familiarity wrapped itself around me. The lyrics were comforting, not because they reminded me of happier times, but because I knew every word. *Yesterday Once More* was a soothing mantra, but not a wish.

When I had finished my toast, I began to look through the bundle of Sunday newspapers picked up at the service station where we broke our journey. In the car I had merely glanced at the headlines before tossing them on to the back seat, but now I worked my way through the royal family gossip and the latest political scandals, skimming a lot of the so-called 'news' until an item on the inside pages caught my eye. A couple of lads out fishing had discovered a woman's body,

half submerged in their local lake. There was no firm identification and the police were saying very little, but the spot
was well frequented by anglers so it was considered unlikely
that the body could have stayed undiscovered there for long.
The lake itself was not far from the A456. I found myself
automatically calculating how far it was from Nicholsfield.
Old habits die hard.

With a shiver I turned over the pages until I reached the
TV guide for the coming week. I had never been an avid TV
viewer and the poor reception in the dale had not exactly
encouraged me to increase my consumption, but I glanced
through the forthcoming programmes to see whether anything
took my fancy. Alongside the listings for each day, three or
four programmes were picked out for more detailed description in a column at the side. As I read the recommended
programmes for Thursday evening, my whole body went icy
cold.

BBC1, 9.30 p.m. DISAPPEARED!
In 1968 Deidre Lazenby went out to the corner shop but
never returned. Shirley Wallingforth has not been seen
since she waved goodbye to her children three years ago,
as she set off for a night out with friends. Jennifer
Reynolds vanished from her home in Nicholsfield in 1983.
What happened to these and others like them? Martin
Bullock investigates Britain's legions of missing persons.

I sat as if frozen, half expecting an immediate knock at the
door or the shrill demand of the telephone. I must have stayed
like that for several minutes while the Carpenters carried on
with their greatest hits as if nothing had happened. Then, like
a sleepwalker, I crossed the room to silence them. It was
suddenly very still.

I returned to the window seat and read it again. Why me?
There were thousands of missing persons – 'legions' was the
word used in the paper. Why did bloody Martin bloody,
bloody Bullock have to pick on me? I felt persecuted and
angry. He had no right. Absurdly I found myself thinking
that the BBC ought to have obtained my permission in

advance, before remembering that this was hardly an option in the circumstances.

Then – oh God, another stab of fear – had the sensation-seeking Mr Bullock actually tracked me down? Had he secretly filmed me operating under my new identity, ready to expose my duplicity to the world? In spite of telling myself that this was a ridiculous idea, I took the precaution of drawing the curtains against any inquisitive cameramen who might be lurking unseen behind the dry-stone wall. I couldn't bear the thought of disclosure. I couldn't stand the curiosity, the sideways glances, the questions. I did not want to provide explanations – I was not even sure that I could.

When I finally went upstairs I took a last look out through the bedroom window. There was a pale moon, enough to make out the shadowy edges of hills and trees – a series of darker outlines against the night sky. The silvery pinpricks of all the stars lined up in their usual places were strangely reassuring, like an astral Carpenters *Greatest Hits.* For some reason they reminded me of the nights I had spent in the beach hut. The stars had not seemed so sharp there, where they had to compete with the promenade string of coloured lights swaying in the evening breeze as if dancing to the continual song of the waves, whispering or roaring dependent on their mood, a constant advance and retreat, that incessant routine of time and tide. In and out. In and out. Boring and predictable, like the tables I had served at the Seaspray Hotel.

'Cornflakes for three, please. Then two full breakfasts and a lightly boiled egg for Mother. Have you got that, dear?' Kindly, middle-aged guests giving me their orders slowly, repeating things unnecessarily because my pad and apron marked me down as a waitress, and therefore by definition not very bright. Waitresses are not suspected of brains or qualifications.

At the Seaspray I had been a waitress and safe from suspicion, holidaying car workers from Coventry and store supervisors from Cambridge never suspecting for a moment that I was Jennifer, health centre manager, headmaster's daughter and one-time school swot. For them I was Louise, the waitress who was better than the girl they had last year, who had been forever getting the order wrong and was a sullen little madam to boot.

At the end of their stay they used to slip me a fiver or a tenner, and sometimes, when they thought I was out of earshot, they told each other that I was a nice girl.

Here in the dale, I thought, they don't know about Louise or Jennifer. Here I am Susan . . . until Martin Bullock tells them otherwise.

FIVE

In that dim no man's land somewhere between sleep and wakefulness, I dreamed that Martin Bullock was approaching the end of his programme, drawing in the loose threads ready to astound the rapt viewing public with a rabbit out of a hat: he was a smart-ass in an expensive overcoat, his serious expression not quite concealing the smugness of a presenter about to reveal that BBC researchers had succeeded where the police and others had failed.

'. . . and against all odds, we have tracked down Jennifer Reynolds . . .'

My lungs wouldn't work and I had to fight for breath. Then she appeared on the screen, this Jennifer Reynolds – not me at all but a woman who had stolen my identity, someone pretending to be the real Jennifer Reynolds. The picture faded and I realized that I was awake, struggling for breath, clammy with sweat. I lay still for a few minutes, trying to make sense of what was real and what had been a dream, but the frail hope that Thursday night's television schedule was no more than a figment of my imagination didn't have time to gain a foothold before reality set in.

The familiar morning routine helped to reassert some sanity. I reminded myself that no one had any suspicions. Only I knew about the telltale notebook in the drawer of the dresser. No one up here in Yorkshire would have taken much interest in some woman who had disappeared from Nicholsfield six years ago. No one but me would have seen anything in the television guide which could be remotely connected to Susan McCarthy, the woman who was the manager of the health centre. As for *Disappeared!* – well, hopefully there would be very little about Jennifer Reynolds and with a bit of luck the programme would arrive at some ludicrous conclusion – abduction by aliens, for example – thereby forfeiting the interest of anyone intelligent enough to put two and two together.

Dark clouds scudded across the sky as I left for work that morning. The wind had risen during the night and when I went outside it whipped at the edges of my jacket and threatened to slam the car door before I was safely inside. A stray twig ricocheted across my bonnet as I drove down the lane. I knew every inch of the road as it descended into Lasthwaite. I knew just where to expect the tanker driver and where I would see Mr Henderson, on his way home with the morning paper, his little terrier Jeff straining ahead on his lead. This morning, in spite of the weather it all seemed doubly precious – my treasured new life which was about to be snatched away.

Heb's Cottage had been my home for almost a year by then. It stood on a single track lane, so little frequented that some days I saw no passing traffic at all. The nearest building was several hundred yards down the lane – a working farm called Rosecroft. A pretty name somewhat belied by the reality: an austere house, half hidden by the semi-ruined outbuildings which surrounded it, most of them roofed in rusting corrugated iron, with hardboard stopping up the numerous broken window panes.

Rosecroft's inhabitants, Jim and Bob Fox, were gruff local men: brothers of indeterminate age, who despite the squalor of their farmhouse always appeared well scrubbed and neatly attired in collars and ties for their evening pint down at the village pub. Jim and Bob were not talkative. Communication with me seldom extended beyond friendly nodding, although during the heavy snows of my first winter at the cottage they had unexpectedly appeared at my front door with firewood and fresh milk, talking around me rather than to me, in a curious, half-embarrassed double act.

'Mek sure t'lass is areet for coal, our Bob.'

'Aye and if t'lass wants a lift down t'village on't Land Rover, she've ownee t'ask.'

Jim and Bob never directly alluded to the woeful inadequacies of a Ford Fiesta in the Yorkshire Dales, probably assuming that being a foreigner (from outside Yorkshire), I had failed to realize that my vehicle would be useless when the lane was snowbound, a not infrequent occurrence.

It was said by some that the Fox brothers were 'not quite

right'. Older residents added, for good measure, the claim that their mother had been 'a bit strange, like' and that an uncle had been 'put away', but as a newcomer who was not conversant with the ins and outs of whose cousin had been slighted by whom in a dispute over the seating arrangements for the last Coronation party, I was inclined to dismiss these intimations of the Fox family's alleged deficiencies as no more than old tabbies' gossip.

Besides which, what family did not have its secrets, its quirks and abnormalities? What appears to one family as entirely normal may to another be the height of eccentricity. Children accept their parents' foibles because they have no yardstick to measure them by. Thus I had assumed throughout my childhood that affection and approval were carefully rationed commodities, and that children who received the unqualified affection of their parents were 'spoiled'. In their joint determination not to 'spoil' me, my parents had maintained an emotional distance, raising a lonely only child who found it difficult to form relationships with others and was intimidated by those of my peers who pushed themselves forward and stuck up for their own opinions – confident that if they got knocked down, their fall would always by cushioned by the certainty of family love. In our house 'love' was something you wrote on a gift tag at Christmas, the word seldom otherwise mentioned.

There was of course that other kind of love – the romantic love which filled so many of the books I devoured in my teenage years. I coveted this more than anything, while at the same time wondering if it genuinely existed outside the covers of fiction. Did people really fall wildly, madly in love – or was it like so many things in books, the imaginative licence of poets and writers? None of the occasional teenage boyfriends with whom I exchanged gropes and kisses in darkened cinemas evoked anything close to the engulfing tidal wave of fictional love. Alan had been different, of course. The mature, analytical Susan could see at once the impact that a man like Alan would have had within the emotional vacuum that was inexperienced young Jenny's life.

There had been no tidal wave with Alan, but he was older,

smarter, and had the ability to flatter. I mistook age and experience for sophistication and wisdom, affection for attraction, and a passport out of my parents' house as a passport to freedom. Everything happened so fast. Alan not only won the daughter but swiftly gained the approval of my parents too. To them he had appeared safe and sensible – and since I was never going to be the blue stocking academic that my father might once have hoped for, my parents enthusiastically propelled me towards their only other approved alternative – the good little wife. An outcome which may have secretly been my father's preferred option, since it maintained his own intellectual supremacy within our household.

From my earliest schooldays, my father had also been my headmaster: an imposing figure on the platform taking assembly, or else closeted in the Headmaster's Study, a place of mystery and fear with which naughty children were threatened. At home my father also spent time behind the closed door of a room known as his study, where he retired to engage in suitably learned activities and probably also to get away from his wife and daughter.

It was an era when head teachers still inspired the respect of staff and pupils alike. The idea of my father joining in any activity which involved entering the school premises without the safe uniform of his dark suit, complete with collar and tie, was unthinkable. At home he might go so far as to roll up his shirt sleeves in the garden, but for the most part he disliked what he termed 'sloppiness' in dress.

My father had a narrow, uncompromising outlook on life: academically he was a snob, who despised popular music (and by association me for listening to it), condemned as worthless most modern writers, and deplored almost everything conveyed into our home via the television set. My mother's addiction to trashy romances, light musical comedies and *The Archers* provided him with a source of persistent aggravation, but this was mitigated by their shared petty snobbery: an obsession with table manners, the niceties of pronunciation and an overriding concern about what the neighbours would think gave them a lot of common ground.

This kind of quiet domestic tyranny has been the breeding

ground for many a Wild Child, but I was as colourless as they were. A dull, biddable child, who always hoped (in vain) to please. In marrying Alan, I for once achieved a modest success. The traditional white wedding was my mother's finest hour.

I could never have explained to them my slowly dawning realization of how unhappy I was. True happiness was not a concept they understood.

SIX

There was a little plaque on the door of my office: S. McCarthy – Centre Manager. A comforting daily confirmation of my identity. Lasthwaite Health Centre, also known as Belsay House, was a substantial Victorian property to which a modern extension had been added, but my room was in the oldest part of the building, and retained the original high ceiling and lancet windows reminiscent of a church.

Dales folk had been seeking advice and treatment at Belsay House for generations and the premises were still universally known as 'The Doctor's' – the term 'Health Centre' having yet to gain popular currency. Many of our patients had been registered there all their lives. There were some who could still remember Dr Bagshaw, a man who, uniquely among medical practitioners, had legible handwriting. The notes of some older patients still bore witness to his precise longhand, although he had been dead for half a century. Dr Bagshaw had been pre-World War II, pre-National Health Service, pre-free prescriptions. He had lived in the upper rooms of Belsay House, as had doctors before and after him, for not until 1968 had the last vestiges of domesticity finally been expunged from the building. That was the year when the elegant drawing room had been partitioned into extra consulting rooms – and several long-dead doctors' wives had probably spun in their graves.

These days telephones and bleepers summoned doctors where once a lion's head doorknocker had sufficed. Yet in spite of the computers and the modern office furniture, there was a pleasing sense of continuity about the health centre and I had become quietly absorbed into it.

Any initial nervousness on my part had soon worn off. I knew my job and enough about the way GP practices worked to proceed carefully until I had the measure of my colleagues. The senior partner was Dr McLeary and I quickly decided that he was a real sweetheart; a tall man, with a mane of white hair, and shrewd blue eyes which shone behind steel-rimmed spectacles. Dr Mac really cared about his patients and they seemed to return his affection in equal measure. Then there was Dr Hindmarsh, whose slightly abrupt manner belied a good heart, and whose only weakness was the need to believe that any changes were his own idea before he could accept them. The youngest partner was dashing Dr Woods, beloved of all the female patients but horribly disorganised behind the scenes.

Our regular trio of doctors had recently been augmented by a GP trainee, Terry Millington, who was still something of an unknown quantity, though from the outset of his placement I observed that he belonged to the Dr Woods School when it came to systems and paperwork. More troubling whispers had reached me regarding the amount of time he appeared to spend propping up the bar in The Bull, but there had been nothing tangible enough to pass on to the doctors, and essentially Dr Millington was their responsibility.

The reception team were a good crowd, and I soon gained a rapport with the health visitors and district nurses, but the most difficult nuts to crack were the trio who provided clerical support, Kathy, Maureen and Hilda, who in a particularly exasperated moment I had privately christened the Three Ts: the Trollop, the Tragedy Queen and the Trainspotter respectively. All longstanding members of staff, they worked to an entrenched, but not particularly efficient agenda, opposing all change on principle, though lately I felt I had begun to make headway in getting them onside.

Assessing the risks posed by *Disappeared!*, I feared the Three Ts the most. They were incorrigible gossips and since the Trainspotter watched television every evening, she was the person most likely to catch the transmission on Thursday night. If *Disappeared!* was scheduled against any of the soap operas, I could be reasonably confident that she would ignore it, but if it was up against sport or anything political, the odds were well stacked in favour of her watching the wretched programme.

And what about Rob's mother, Mrs Dugdale? She was an elderly woman who lived alone and therefore might watch a lot of television – suppose she watched the programme? If

they showed a photograph of Jennifer Reynolds – who was I
kidding – *when* they showed a photograph, wasn't it inevitable
that she would think it was one likeness too many? It didn't
take a genius to join up the dots and make a trail from
Nicholsfield to Lasthwaite via the Lake District. She was
already a bit suspicious . . .

Stop it. *Stop* it. There isn't anything to connect the Heather
Bank Hotel to Nicholsfield. They're a cool two hundred miles
apart. Besides which, hadn't Mrs Dugdale said she went to
the W.I. on Thursdays – or was it Tuesdays? Why, why, had
I not paid more attention?

I took a deep breath and reminded myself that whatever
happened I had to carry on as normal – if anyone at work did
watch the programme and remarked on my similarity to any old
photographs, then a laughing denial ought to dispel any suspicions. I tried to put the whole thing to the back of my mind
while I wrestled with the quarterly budget.

Rob rang me at eleven fifteen. Mid-morning break. A respite
from GCSE Geography. 'What do you say to dinner at mine?'

'Yes, please,' I said.

'Do you fancy a stir-fry?'

'Anything you like.'

I knew he would make a detour to raid the supermarket on
his way home. School was finished by four, so even after
calling in for some shopping he would certainly be at his
cottage before me. By the time I arrived there would be piles
of neatly chopped meat and vegetables, ready for the wok. He
would cook without fuss and produce a good meal without
the flourish which had been an inevitable accompaniment to
masculine culinary efforts in my previous experience.

On the rare occasions when he had prepared us a meal,
Alan had always adopted his see-how-clever-I-am look. Not
that my own efforts in the kitchen were expected to elicit
praise or wonder. On the contrary, they were up for whatever
criticism seemed appropriate: 'A bit tough, isn't it, Jenny?'
For years I had accepted this without question. It had never
occurred to me to do otherwise.

Rob never seemed to criticize anything I did, but that was
not why I loved him. It was something much more fundamental

than that. I was in love with him long before I found out about his uncritical nature. In fact, I was a little bit in love with him from the first moment I set eyes on him.

It happened not long after I arrived in Lasthwaite to take up the job at the health centre. Since I was a newcomer to the district, the doctors and their wives had conspired to involve me in local life, so that I would meet people and make new friends – an alarming initiative which filled me with horror, until I realized that it was the best possible way to become accepted and blend in. The local people seemed to fall into three distinct, yet overlapping groups. At one extreme was the beer and bingo brotherhood, and at the other the rather smart dinner party set to which the doctors and their wives naturally gravitated. Between these two there was a middle ground of people who belonged to neither group but mingled with both – a community loosely bound by the churches and chapels, the Young Farmers and the various hobby classes which took place at the institute; the cricket club and the pub quizzers, all of whom were likely to be encountered at the summer barbecues and bonfire night held by Friends of the Hospice.

One popular annual fixture was a barn dance held by the Metcalfe family (pie 'n' pea supper, all the proceeds going to the Church Restoration Fund). The 1989 dance took place within a fortnight of my arrival and the McLearys insisted that I accompany them to it. When we got there it seemed as if the entire population of the dale had turned out and the McLearys appeared to know everyone. I must have been introduced to scores of people, but the only one that really mattered was Rob.

I immediately fell for his smile, his open, easy-going manner. I liked his deep voice, his brown eyes and the way his hair jostled the back of his collar when he turned his head. Since he appeared to be about my own age, I expected a wife or a girlfriend, or perhaps even a boyfriend to turn up at any moment, but that didn't happen. When I wasn't being whisked around the floor in a series of hectic eight-somes, we sat together chatting between dances. He wasn't the sort to pour out his life story, but by the end of the evening I had gleaned the information that he taught geography at the local comprehensive and that he lived alone, on the opposite side of the village to me.

I had absolutely no intention of becoming romantically involved. Even overly close friendships had the potential to end in disaster, so I had developed a strategy for keeping all-comers at arms' length, which included greeting any suggestion of a date with a polite refusal. Thus if Rob had suggested meeting up for a drink, or issued some similar invitation on the evening of the Metcalfes' barn dance, I would have made an excuse and our relationship would have faltered at the first hurdle. If he had courted me ardently, I am almost certain that nothing would have happened between us – but of course he did not. Each time we met he continued to treat me with no more than the ordinary friendliness one might accord a casual acquaintance, and in this apparent lack of interest lay the seeds of my downfall.

After the barn dance I caught myself thinking about him constantly. It was foolish, like a schoolgirl's crush. Yet it persisted. A glimpse of him in the village store set my heart racing. When he smiled at me my stomach did a back flip in sheer delight. And since I knew that nothing could possibly come of it, I thought that I was perfectly safe to allow myself the indulgence of these feelings, secure in the knowledge that Rob had no interest in me at all. Every local event became coloured for days in advance by the possibility that he might be there, culminating in joy if he was, desolation if he failed to show. All of this studiously concealed from everyone else of course, because so long as no one ever found out, so long as *he* never found out, I was perfectly safe to indulge in my secret obsession.

As those first weeks passed, I reminded myself several times a day that I had not fallen in love. That could not happen, because falling in love could not be countenanced under any circumstances. Falling in love represented a dangerous loss of control. I knew the feelings which swept through me were not only delicious and wonderful, but ultimately dangerous. It was a tidal wave which could sweep away my very existence; carry before it the fragile foundations on which my life was built, like a shanty town collapsing before the weight of a hurricane.

And even on the rare occasions when I admitted to myself just how besotted I had become, I still knew that I was safe – because Rob had shown no interest at all. It never occurred to me that whereas chance meetings in towns and cities call for quick action on someone's part, before a would-be date vanishes from view forever, in a community as small as ours, Rob could simply bide his time, knowing full well that we would bump into each other again and again.

At the beginning of December I received an invitation to pre-Christmas drinks at Dr Woods's house. Malcolm and Penny Woods lived in a spectacular barn conversion, whose interiors looked like illustrations from *Home and Garden* magazine. By the time I arrived there were already at least a dozen cars parked in and around the courtyard and, glancing at some simultaneous arrivals, I was glad that I had donned a posh frock made of black velvet with sparkly bits on its low-cut bodice, having fortunately been tipped off in advance about the form.

Once inside I followed the established rituals of such events, sipping a drink and answering enquiries about whether I was 'ready for Christmas', filling any silences which developed by admiring the elaborate Christmas decorations which festooned fireplaces and dripped from wall lights. After about fifteen minutes of this, as if from nowhere I found Rob beside me. The press of people forced us to stand close together and I found myself looking up into his eyes, fixated by his physical presence. The attraction was so strong that I had to concentrate in order to hear what he was saying – something inconsequential, the latest proposal for a new curriculum, or the forthcoming Christmas carol service – while all the time I experienced an overwhelming urge to touch him. In that moment I understood for the first time in my life what it was to desire someone so wildly, so desperately, that any kind of madness seemed possible. Yet somehow I kept my voice steady, managed to carry on chatting and smiling as if everything were perfectly normal. More people drifted across to join the conversation, and then Penny Woods eased herself between Rob and me, proffering a tray of nibbles in each hand, and in the general re-shuffle which followed, I somehow found myself edged out of our group and into another, where Dr Hindmarsh was making some kind of joke about whether the nineties would turn out to be the Naughty Nineties – and all the time I could think of nothing except how I might contrive to manoeuvre myself next to Rob again.

More and more guests seemed to be crowding into the room; groups converged and dispersed, borne along by the ebb and flow of chatter. I tried to concentrate on the small talk while I cast around in search of Rob, but I was too short – even in my heels – to see beyond the tall, red-faced rugger buggers who had gathered to my left. I caught a glimpse of Dr Woods over by the fireplace, topping up glasses and flirting with all the women, while there by the front window was Mrs Woods, tall and slim, a gracious hostess to the tips of her manicured fingernails, soaking up the compliments of all the lady guests who wished that they had such a knack with evergreens and baubles. Dr McCleary was at the centre of a laughing crowd away to my right, but where on earth was Rob?

The tide drifted me alongside the Christmas tree: a giant Scots Pine, whose twinkling white lights and decorations looked new and expensive. It took more than mere talent to make a room look that good. Mrs Lindsay-Scott, who owned the riding stables half a mile outside Lasthwaite, caught my eye.

'The grandchildren dress our tree,' she said. 'We've been using the same decorations since 1952, give or take the odd fir cone.'

I smiled in unspoken acknowledgement of a shared thought. The Lindsay-Scott grandchildren probably got a lot more fun out of their tree than the Woods children did from their look-don't-touch version. Suddenly as if by magic, Rob was standing beside me again, sharing the smile, although he couldn't possibly have known what it was about.

'I hear you're going to open your garden again next summer, Mrs Lindsay-Scott,' he said.

'Well, yes, we are. It is in a good cause and people seem to enjoy it. It's mostly the locals who come, of course. One or two from a bit further afield . . .' She boomed on for a while about her roses before abruptly cutting herself off short

as she spotted some other acquaintances on the point of departure. 'Do excuse me,' she said. 'I must have a word with
Norma about the Christingle oranges before she goes.'

We were left standing alone alongside the Christmas tree.
There was a short silence. For all that the room was crowded,
we might have been the only people left on the planet.

'I'm about ready to leave,' he said. 'Can I give you a lift?'

We both knew that he lived in the opposite direction to me.

'I . . . I . . .' I stumbled over the words. 'I came in my own
car. I'm parked just outside.'

Another silence.

'You could . . . if you would like . . . I don't know – maybe
come to my . . . have some coffee . . .' I had become a burbling,
useless creature.

By contrast he seemed absolutely calm. 'Let's get our coats,'
he suggested.

There was a huge coat cupboard built in under the stairs.
As we were trying to find our coats he drew me gently aside
to allow someone to pass. The effect of his hand on my bare
arm was like an electric shock. As he helped me into my
jacket, I was aware of the infinitesimally brief caress of his
fingertips against my neck.

'We ought to say thank you to the Woods,' I said, looking
back into the scrum of people.

'Send them a card,' he said, taking my arm and guiding me
out of the front door. 'My car's here.' He pointed towards the
shadows alongside the garage.

It did not seem to matter that I had declined a lift. He
propelled me gently towards his car and held the passenger
door open for me to get inside. Then he walked round and
climbed into the driver's seat. Once he had closed his door,
we flung ourselves at each other. After several minutes we
managed to disengage long enough for Rob to drive the short
distance to his cottage and once there we spent several hours
engaged in frantic lovemaking. Later we admitted mutual
amazement at the intensity of our feelings. At the time we
said very little.

I knew that this was terribly dangerous. I believed that I
had reconciled myself to a single life, but I had miscalculated

the true potency of love and sex; the desire that had so easily overpowered me. I couldn't resist the temptation for more. When Rob turned up on Valentine's Day, bearing roses and champagne, I said 'Yes' without hesitation. I knew it was madness but I couldn't help it. I had fallen into a raging torrent and been swept too far from the bank to climb back to safety.

SEVEN

Rob's stir-fry majored on prawns and water chestnuts in a spicy, chilli sauce. We ate dinner, made love and did the dishes afterwards. In these simple, everyday activities lies true happiness. It is too easy to overrate the spectacular in favour of the comfortably mundane. As we told each other about our respective days, I managed to forget *Disappeared!*, but I remembered it as I drove home through the darkness, the wind still gusting audibly outside. It made our evening seem doubly precious and I tried to blot out the inner voice which warned me that there might not be many more evenings like that.

The timer had activated the sitting-room lights, but in spite of their cheerful glow and the warmth of the central heating, I shivered as I stepped inside and shut the front door behind me, wishing now that I had stayed at Rob's after all. We seldom stayed over unplanned on work nights. The pleasure was outweighed by the hassle of the following morning. I hated putting on yesterday's knickers for the drive home, feeling that half the bloody village had spotted you and knew precisely *why* you were driving back to your own house at seven thirty a.m.

Rob had marking to do as usual – conscientious and caring, he was a popular teacher with pupils and parents alike. Meantime, the remainder of my evening lay unconstrained before me. I had filched Rob's newspaper before leaving, and now I settled down to read it. There was more about the new royal baby . . . and the police had revealed the identity of the girl found in the lake. Her name was Kelly Jones and she came from Northampton. She had last been seen trying to hitch a lift at a service station on the M42. The police were treating it as a murder enquiry, the paper said – well, obviously. The poor girl hadn't disposed of all her clothes, then jumped into the lake herself, had she? Further down the page it explained that Kelly had been running away from home. It made a sort of bond between us – not that I had ever seriously considered running away from my parents' home. In those days I was too much of a frightened little mouse to have contemplated any such thing, but later I had become a kind of runaway, and although I never hitched lifts, I had taken chances and perhaps been lucky – unlike Kelly.

Until the day I married Alan, I had continued to live at my parents' house in Orchard Lane, meeting their midnight curfew and taking my turn with the dishes. Although it was six full years since I had last set eyes on it, I could still picture the house clearly: detached and double fronted, the garden imprisoned behind shoulder-high privet hedges which grew along the front, and by the tall conifers which had been planted at the sides to preserve my father's obsessive privacy. On sunny days my mother and her friends occasionally took afternoon tea out there, sitting self-consciously upright in deck chairs arranged around the concrete sundial which stood in the centre of the lawn. In cooler weather guests were taken into the sitting room, where they sat around the living flame gas fire, its polished surround topped with a tidy arrangement of knick-knacks – the only objects which could ever have been said to be left lying about. Obsessively tidy, my mother had been a great believer in putting things away and the house in Orchard Lane had offered her tremendous scope for this – indeed, it might have been designed with the specific provision for putting things away uppermost in the architect's mind. Capacious cupboards had been incorporated into every room, and as if this were not enough, my parents had installed various tallboys, sideboards and hefty suites of bedroom furniture, which since no one ever came to stay, also became repositories for my mother's putting away.

To me had fallen the task of sorting everything out before the men from the auction house came to cart away the furniture. It was a task of weeks rather than days – something to be fitted between work and everyday life, punctuated by visits to the nursing home to see my mother, who was all the time unaware that her home of more than three decades was being dismantled piece by piece. Alan was seldom available to help, so I spent doleful hours sorting through drawers full of old-fashioned cutlery and kitchen utensils, baking trays rusted by neglect and strange little caches of safety pins, jam jar lids and sachets of sugar – whether warning signs of my mother's impending confusion or the carefulness of a make-do-and-mend generation, I could never be sure.

I found the key to my father's desk hidden among the shelves of outdated textbooks in his study. The desk in question was one of those old fashioned, roll-top affairs, which had stood in the corner nearest the French windows for as long as I could remember. After my father's death, I'd helped my mother sift the contents of the pigeonholes, but the drawers had remained obstinately locked. She had assured me that they contained nothing of importance and claimed the key had been lost for years, which surprised me, because my father – ever the headmaster – had habitually despised the loser of any article.

Somewhat intrigued, I experienced a childish guilty thrill when I turned the key and opened the top drawer, but my excitement was short-lived. The drawer contained an ancient bottle of ink and a large supply of unused blotting paper. My father had entertained a puritanical disapproval of the ballpoint, but surely he had not taken matters so far as to covertly stockpile his own writing necessities? The middle drawer proved an equally poor show – more stationery supplies – but in the bottom drawer I found a package of letters – not more than twenty of them, addressed to my father with just his name on each envelope, which meant that they must have been delivered by hand. In that moment I could almost hear my mother's voice: 'We didn't bring you up to be the sort of person who reads other people's letters.'

Ignoring the voice and pulling out the contents of the first envelope, I scanned the top sheet. It was a love letter. I could barely believe it. My father, a man I had always thought cold and unsentimental, kept romantic letters from his courtship with my mother in the drawer of his desk.

Fascinated, I carried the whole bundle out on to the semi-circular steps beneath the French windows, where I seated myself on the top step and read the first letter. It was fairly torrid stuff. Who would have imagined such goings-on nearly thirty years ago, with the permissive society not even a twinkle in Harold Macmillan's eye? There was something faintly unbelievable about it all. My parents – Ted and Marjorie: they were not even romantic names.

Then I reached the bottom of the second page and the shock made me go cold. The letter was signed *Your loving Jean.*

I turned back to the beginning of the letter to check the date. Another shock. The letters had been written when I was a baby in arms. The realization that my father had been carrying on a passionate clandestine affair filled me with amazement, disbelief and ultimately sadness.

Almost greedily, I read each letter in turn. The story was easy to piece together. Jean taught at the same school as my father. They left letters for one another in the staff pigeonholes. They met secretly when pretending to be elsewhere. As I read my way steadily through the bundle, I wondered when this impulsive, passionate man had turned into the person I had known? The letters spanned six months of his life. The final one was dated June, 1956.

> *My dearest Ted,*
>
> *I dare not tell you how I feel as I write to you for the last time. I shall not keep our rendezvous on Thursday because if I see you alone, face-to-face, I know my heart will break. I have decided to accept the post in South Africa and I sail in a fortnight. You spoke of a choice. I cannot ask you to make a choice which will sacrifice your career, your wife and your daughter.*
>
> *Marjorie has made it clear that she will not divorce you, if you give me up.*
>
> *She had you first, my darling, for we met too late. We have had so little time, but I will always love you, always be yours.*
>
> *Jean*

Memories of my parents flooded back to me. The way their eyes never met; they never touched. The clipped little speech my father made at their silver wedding, describing my mother as his 'companion and helpmate through the years'.

The little brass key had unlocked more than just a desk drawer, for I believe it was the discovery of these letters which finally brought home to me how lives can be wasted. I had never thought of my parents as particularly happy people, but the discovery of the letters forced me to acknowledge the stark unhappiness of their lives: my father forever wishing himself having some other life with some other person, and my mother all the time aware of this. I never knew Jean, but the discovery of her letters crystallised the realization that I in turn was proceeding mechanically through a similar kind of life – a life bereft of real purpose, devoid of joy.

I could not discuss these feelings with Alan. It would have been quite useless to attempt it. He had a way of smiling patiently while I talked, waiting for me to run out of breath or ideas before carefully dissecting everything I had said in a precise logical sequence, breaking it down, line by line, word by word, until it dissolved beneath his sensible, reasoned logic. His voice all the time quiet, measured, almost hypnotic. He would demonstrate beyond any doubt that we were happily married, had everything our hearts desired, could not possibly yearn for any other kind of life.

Any suggestion that I might have contemplated a life beyond the cocoon of his protective attentions would certainly have provoked Alan's amusement. 'Oh, Jenny,' he would have said, his very tone diminishing me to the status of an eternal child as he embarked on a recitation of my latest mishaps, before moving on to query how someone who could not overcome her completely irrational fear of our own cellar proposed to face the far grimmer realities of the outside world – alone.

The letters from Jean had a cathartic effect. While I outwardly continued as normal, going to my job each day, cooking Alan's dinner and sharing his bed each night, working my way through the clearance and disposal of the house in Orchard Lane, I also conceived a plan and set about its execution. I began by extracting modest sums of cash from the salary paid into our shared bank account. Initially I hid this money in the drawer of my father's desk and, when that was no longer an option, I took my stash of notes home and stuffed it into the back of the drawer where we kept such rarely used items as dominoes and playing cards. I embarked on a lone shopping trip to purchase some new clothes, jeans, sweaters, shirts and trainers, placing them, unworn, among my existing wardrobe where they hung unnoticed. At the beginning it was like a kind of game – a private make-believe game from which, as no one else knew about it, I could withdraw at any time. I examined maps and timetables, like some dreamer who peruses glossy brochures and plans holidays to far-flung destinations, never actually expecting to go. It was a pleasurable distraction – something to take my mind off the awfulness of visiting my mother in the nursing home, a secret diversion which helped me through the shock of her death, the funeral, the paperwork, the miserable aftermath of it all.

It was soon after the funeral that I bought a rucksack and an anorak. These were more difficult to conceal and eventually I decided to put them inside one of our big suitcases, which were kept in the smallest spare bedroom. If Alan had come across these articles they would have been impossible to explain, but we had no need of the big suitcases that spring so my acquisitions lay undisturbed. Finally I rang a bed and breakfast on the south coast and made a reservation in a false name. Even then there was nothing to say that I had to carry the thing through.

EIGHT

On Tuesday it was my turn to make dinner. Not that we took it strictly in turn, or even had a regular routine about where and when we spent time together. Our relationship was still that young. I was not expecting Rob until about seven p.m., so there was plenty of time to make a casserole. Once it was in the oven I sat at the table and tried to clear my head. Was the deception of getting married in Susan McCarthy's name really any greater than my previous deceptions had been? Was I maybe even beating myself up unduly over Rob? To all intents and purposes there was no deception at all. He wanted to marry a woman called Susan, with whom he had fallen head over heels in love, and I was undoubtedly that woman. Lots of people must have little things in their past lives that they never disclosed to their spouses. Little things? Who was I trying to kid?

Thoughts of past lives brought to mind the exercise book in the kitchen dresser, whose presence had been nagging at me for some time. It might so easily and innocently be found: Rob spent such a lot of time at the cottage now. On a sudden impulse I crossed the kitchen and extracted the book from the drawer. Throwing it away felt horribly like cutting down the safety net, yet keeping it posed an even greater risk. I stood, hesitating, with the slim volume in my hand. It was all in there – my new life. Silly, silly, I must not endow the book with a special status that it didn't really have. It was only a cheap little exercise book of the kind sold in newsagents, and I knew the contents by heart.

Just putting it into the dustbin didn't seem right somehow. Or entirely safe. I reached for a box of matches and went into the yard. It was dry and still this evening, with only the occasional bleating of sheep to disturb the general quiet. Darkness had swallowed up the surrounding landscape, but the small cobbled yard at the rear of the cottage was partially illuminated by the light from the kitchen window. My shadow stretched across this pale rectangle, huge and distorted, cut off at the shoulders where the light stopped abruptly before it reached the grass: a weird, headless monster crouching over its prey, jerking suddenly at the sound of each match rasping across the side of the box. The first couple of matches blew out, but the third one lasted long enough to ignite the uppermost corner of the flimsy book cover, which was made from paper barely thicker than the pages inside. It smouldered weakly for a moment or two, but I barely had time to straighten up before the flame died away. Using my body as a shield I lit a fourth match, and this time I suspended the exercise book by its covers, holding them between my finger and thumb so that the pages fell in an arc. The flame caught hold at the bottom and climbed up the ladder made by the pages. When the heat reached my hand I dropped the book on to the yard and at this the brighter flames withered, but the edges of the pages continued to glow, blackening towards the spine until the process faltered to a halt, leaving a mass of frilly, ash-edged ridges still secured by a pair of blackened staples. Although the little book was not totally destroyed, its contents had been obliterated forever.

'Isn't it a bit early for bonfire night?' The voice and simultaneous scrunch of a boot made me scream. Rob was letting himself in at the back gate.

'What are you doing?' I was almost shouting. 'You frightened the life out of me. How long have you been there?'

'I only just got here.'

'I didn't hear the car.' I started stamping on the charred remnants, my shadow jerking about the yard like a demented clog dancer.

'I walked.'

'Walked?'

'Yes. I fancied a walk. I realized that if I went over High Plantation I could loop around Castle Rigg and take the footpath that comes out at the top of the lane. What *are* you doing?'

'Nothing,' I said. 'Nothing at all. Come inside.' I took his arm and all but dragged him into the kitchen.

He stood on the step to take off his boots and padded across the floor in hiking socks, which made his feet look twice their normal size. 'Something smells good.'

'It's chicken casserole,' I said, latching on to a possible diversion. 'I hope you're hungry, because I've done loads of potatoes for mash.'

There was no way I was going to get off the hook that easily.

'So are you going to tell me?' he asked in a playful tone.

'Tell you what?'

'What the sacrificial fire was all about.'

'Oh . . . that . . .'

'Letters from an old flame? A bit of witchcraft – burning my toenail clippings to retain your hold over me?'

'If you must know, it was some silly poetry I wrote years ago. Schoolgirl stuff – really embarrassing.' I knew it sounded lame. 'Anyway, if you're going to ask me about old flames, don't forget I could start asking you the same questions.'

Rob burst out laughing. 'I've lived in the dale for the last five years. You don't need to ask me. Any one of your staff would love to give you the complete lowdown – if they haven't already.'

'Of course not,' I said. 'Although I don't doubt that they'd love to tittle-tattle.' I seized on this as my cue to introduce the latest gossip-mongering from the Terrible Ts. '. . . The way they talk about Charles this and Di that – honestly, you'd think Maureen spent half her evenings having tête-à-têtes with the princess round at Kensington Palace.'

Rob did not refer to the bonfire again until I drove him home. 'Goodnight, my little pyromaniac,' he said. He had already kissed me and was getting out of the car, so it was too dark for me to see his face. It was probably just a casual quip, but it flagged up a warning that he was still curious and unwilling to let the subject drop.

We had developed a tacit understanding that we were not ready to move in together yet. This certainly wasn't based on false Puritanism, but rather a desire to start out together in shared mutual territory, rather than under a roof which had initially belonged to one but not the other. For me this was

yet another reminder of how different it had all been last time.
I could remember my mother plainly. 'What a lucky girl you
are, Jennifer, to be going into a ready-made home. So many
young couples have to scrimp and save to get a roof over their
heads, but you will go straight into that lovely house . . .'

At first I too had imagined myself fortunate. Alan's tall
Victorian house, with its original stained-glass lights in the
bay window, the restored mosaic tiles in the hall: who wouldn't
have fallen in love with it? Alan's collection of antique furniture, his books, his carefully chosen ceramics: didn't these
all mark him out as someone different, someone who had
personality and taste, someone who stood apart from the
common herd?

Visitors were always invited to admire any new acquisitions
– particularly the gallery of old photographs which, as their
numbers increased, progressed slowly up the stairs. He picked
them up in flea markets, dog-eared and unframed, and restored
them to their former glory. Initially this was something I had
enjoyed too. I even made up names for them: the handsome
young soldier with sword and moustache was George Frederick,
while the wedding couple next to him were Humphrey and
Charlotte. I used to speculate on how they went on to have
seven children and lived happily ever after. That was how it
had been at the beginning, but later on the pictures all started
to assume a haunting, melancholy presence. Perhaps in the
end there were just too many of them – too many unsmiling
strangers watching us from the walls of our hall. The little
girls, all carefully posed with folded hands, their beautifully
brushed hair secured in oversized ribbons, whose sad eyes
seemed to follow me upstairs. I suppose it was just another
symptom of my own general melancholia, but gradually I
became convinced that they had all died miserably and young.

Although I lived in Alan's house for almost eight years, and
he punctiliously transferred the title into our joint names
and spoke of it as 'ours', I never really felt that it was. I
raised the question of moving once, but Alan was adamantly
against it, insisting that any ideas I had about selling up were
solely connected with what he termed 'your nerves'.

Some people might have said the house was haunted, but I

had accepted that the 'ghosts' were figments of my overwrought imagination, not least because Alan was never troubled by them. Not that there were ever any visible manifestations. It was auditory phenomena that troubled me. Spending the night there alone became such a big deal that Alan encouraged me to go and stay with my parents whenever he had to be away. In those days any unexplained tick in the central heating was enough to make me jumpy.

One evening I remember in particular: it was the second winter after we were married and Alan was due home not much later than ten, so instead of retreating to stay with my mother, I was awaiting his return in the sitting room, filling in the time by listening to a discussion on the radio, when I thought I heard something beneath my feet. A sound too faint to be identified, followed by a subdued thud as if something had been knocked over. I instinctively looked down, but of course there was nothing to see except the carpet and the floorboards. I considered turning off the radio so that I could hear better, but then I dithered, because if there was someone down there, the sound of the radio might be useful in masking a call to the police. I stood up and took a step towards the phone, then hesitated. Was that another noise, or was I only imagining it?

It was theoretically possible to enter the cellar from the garden because there were some padlocked wooden doors below the front window which opened on to a chute originally intended for deliveries of coal, and at some point a previous occupant had fixed a stepladder there to facilitate entry or egress. Anyone messing with the padlock would be out of sight of the sitting-room window and well screened from the street by the laurel hedge which separated our plot from the pavement. I began to sidle towards the telephone, but then I stopped again. I had been wrong before and did not want to make a fool of myself.

I stood listening for what seemed like several minutes until I was startled by the sound of the front door opening. I gave a little shriek, which brought Alan into the sitting room at once. When I explained the source of my anxiety I caught his fleeting smile before he pretended to take me seriously. Did I want him to go and check? He was already on his way to get the big torch. (There was but a single bulb in the cellar, and it did not penetrate the furthest recesses, where wine had once been stored.)

He paused at the cellar door to say, 'You know, I ought to make you come down with me, to satisfy you once and for all that there's nothing there.' The words were not spoken unkindly, but their threat menaced me. I had always entertained a quite ridiculous dread of the cellar. For a moment I imagined him taking me by the arm and forcing me to go down with him, but of course he attempted nothing of the kind.

Alan was meticulous in his investigations, clumping down the wooden staircase and shining his torch into every nook and cranny, before going back out into the cold to check that the external hatch was still secured by its trusty padlock.

During the few minutes it took him to accomplish all this, I dithered in the hall, presumably ready to make a bolt for it in the event that the Cellar Monster pursued my husband up the stairs. 'I was going to ring the police,' I told him, shame-faced, when he returned from the garden and secured the latch on the front door.

'I'm so glad you didn't.' What did those words convey to me? Relief that I had not wasted their time, his time, my own time? Made an even bigger fool of myself than usual? The noises had seemed real to me and yet I knew that they could not have been.

Alan had been endlessly patient about 'your noises' as he referred to them – cutting the creeper away from our bedroom window because when the wind blew it made me think of fingers scratching at the glass. Then there had been the night when I thought I heard a cat mewing. 'It might be trapped in the cellar,' I said, although there was not the slightest logic in this, for how would a cat have got down there in the first place? And although he himself confessed to hearing nothing, Alan had interrupted his reading to go downstairs and check. Of course there had not been a cat and, after Alan's investigations, I was forced to admit that the mysterious noises had completely ceased.

One way and another I came to loathe that house and every-thing in it, but I never suggested moving again because the problem clearly lay not in the house but in my head. Alan was always right. That was why I could not argue with him. He was too calm, too logical, too reasonable – and I had been wrong too often. Besides which, I knew that Alan loved the house and I felt that he should not be deprived of it due to my pathetic, inadequate neediness and foolish anxieties, which must have been a tedious cross for him to bear. Only very occasionally did I ever entertain the thought that if he had been tolerant of my various weaknesses, conversely I had been a relatively useful cook and housekeeper, who had always gone along with what he wanted in bed, seldom betraying the fact that I did not enjoy those things he seemed to find the most stimulating.

My mother's death came suddenly. A stroke, a brief hospital admission and it was all over. My feelings were a confusion of grief and guilt and relief. The stress of her decline, the disposal of her home and the suddenness of her death had all taken their toll, so that by the end of it I was not really thinking straight at all. In spite of the rucksack, new clothes and secret stash of bank notes, I did not really have a proper plan. When the morning I had scheduled for departure finally arrived, I hung around until Alan set off for work, then changed into my new clothes, feeling like a child engaged in a game of dressing up. The whole enterprise had an air of make-believe about it, even as I slipped away from the house, choosing a moment when the road outside appeared deserted then heading with heart-pounding haste for the station. I had no idea what I would do after the one night I had booked in Brighton.

For the first few weeks I moved from one place to another, never staying more than a couple of nights, pretending for the benefit of seaside landladies that I was visiting friends or en route to elsewhere. It was very early in the season and everywhere seemed bleakly deserted and windswept.

Convinced that I would be recognized and accosted, 'Elizabeth Wilson' (as I had decided to call myself, for no better reason than that it was the first name which came into my head) had her hair cut in two successive towns. I had the first hairdresser take off several inches, and that night I dyed it in the hotel basin. I had settled my bill on arrival, explaining that I had to make an early start, and I slipped away the next morning before anyone was around to observe that the departing guest looked very different to the one who had arrived. A day or two later I dropped into another salon and traded in almost half my newly darkened locks for a much shorter style, reasoning that a transformation in three stages would be less easily linked up by anyone on my trail. Even if the first hairdresser reported shortening the hair of a woman resembling Jennifer Reynolds, I hoped that by the time I reached hairdresser number two I would look different enough for her not to connect me with the missing woman at all.

During these adventures in the hair salons of Brighton and Eastbourne, I cursed the stylists' innocent attempts at conversation and lived in constant fear of being recognized. I almost made a run for it when a perfectly harmless old lady stopped me on the sea front to ask for directions. It did not take me long to realize that staying alone in bed and breakfasts, then wandering aimlessly through half-deserted holiday towns all day was a sure-fire way of attracting suspicion. What I needed was a way of blending into the scenery; preferably a scheme which provided me with a little money for the immediate necessities and enough time to work out what to do next.

By the time these ideas were taking shape I had fetched up on the Isle of Wight and, thinking that the catering trade was a likely source of casual employment, I followed up an advertisement in the local paper for a waitress at the Seaspray. As it turned out, they were short-staffed and wanted someone who could start at once, so awkward questions scarcely arose. I called myself Louise Mason and gave them my own National Insurance number with a couple of digits changed. I knew this wouldn't suffice for long, but I figured it would provide me with initial cover while I tried to think of something better.

I paid upfront to rent a beach hut for the season, pretending to be a summer visitor who was renting a cottage nearby. The hut was equipped with plastic chairs and a table, a rail which I could use as hanging space and a pair of folding sun-loungers – one of which, with my sleeping bag unrolled upon it, became my bed at night. The toilet block at the end of the line of huts was fortuitously possessed of a shower, presumably installed so that people could remove the sand and salt after bathing. The toilets were kept scrupulously clean by an elderly man in green overalls who walked with a limp. He arrived twice daily, as regular as clockwork, always carefully blocking the entrance with his little yellow and red warning notice, whistling to himself as he went about his task. He never suspected the silent gratitude flowing in his direction from the most regular member of his clientele.

Overnight camping in the huts was strictly prohibited, but the blonde beach bums who had a summer job looking after the concession were always gone long before dusk had fallen. I stopped up some gaps at the front of the hut, through which the telltale glimmer of my camping lantern might have given the game away, and generally settled down to sleep early, so as to have no difficulty rising in time for the morning breakfast shift.

The loneliness did not bother me. The truth was that I was used to living alone and actual, bodily loneliness can be easier than other sorts of loneliness. It had been different for Alan. In his eyes the symbolic acceptance of a ring meant that I had become part of him, much in the way that his treasured collection of pocket watches was a part of him, though I probably ranked a little higher up the scale of things even if I was not specifically mentioned in the meticulous list of possessions updated annually for his home contents policy. It had been a misunderstanding on a monumental scale. Alan, who thought he knew me thoroughly and understood me perfectly, while all the time I had been a different person – an independent person who Alan would not really have liked or wanted to be married to, except of course that Alan would never have accepted that this different person existed at all.

I was careful never to be seen entering or emerging from the beach hut dressed as a waitress. I left for work in my holidaymaker's garb of jeans or shorts, depending on the weather, with my black skirt, white blouse and pinny neatly folded in my shoulder bag. I changed into them in another block of toilets near the cliff top, reversing the procedure on the way back to the hut. I paid to have my waitressing gear cleaned and pressed – an extravagance on my wages, but justified by the results.

Without much planning I had managed to find an ideal cover. The hotel guests were transient, staying at most a fortnight. Most of them never even asked my name, content to call me 'the waitress', or more affectionately, 'our waitress'. My colleagues were focused on serving up thirty-eight breakfasts or dinners, with little time to engage in idle chit-chat, and my weekly pay packet was put into my hand on Fridays, so that the bluff of my fictitious address was never called.

I knew it couldn't last. The summer season would end, the beach hut lodging would become impractical and sooner or later enquiries regarding my National Insurance number would rear their ugly head; so as mid-September approached, I handed in my notice and headed north, where I found work waitressing or cleaning, staying in bedsits, sometimes as Louise Mason, sometimes as Jane Smith, occasionally as Elizabeth Wilson, barely scraping a living, always moving on before fake details became a serious issue.

Most of my accommodation had a much poorer outlook than the beach hut, but shabby surroundings failed to depress me when set against the novelty of freedom. I found shops where second-hand paperbacks could be exchanged for a small fee. I bought cheap vegetables from market stalls and concocted wonderful curries at a cost of pennies. I visited galleries and libraries and museums and gardens and sought out all manner of free entertainment as diligently as I had once helped Alan search out those sepia photographs to adorn our walls, but I was always conscious that one day I might turn in for work and find a policeman waiting there. I knew that I was a missing person and concern had been expressed for my safety. I came from Nicholsfield, after all, where any woman who did not come home when expected was deemed to be a possible victim of the local 'serial killer'.

I sometimes thought about telephoning Alan or the police to let them know that I was safe, but I always decided against. Phone calls were traceable. I had been living under a false name, giving out false particulars to all and sundry – I was in too deep before I knew it. What would happen to me when the authorities caught up? Then there was Alan. Alan was clever and persistent and, given the slightest inkling that he could track me down, I knew he would not rest until he had done so. I could picture him arriving in my damp bedsit, not troubling to disguise his amazement and distaste. I could hear his voice, so calm, so reasonable, even when edged with self-righteous hurt and anger, remonstrating with me for my foolishness.

'Look what you've sunk to,' he would say. 'Goodness knows where you would have ended up if I hadn't found you in time.' He would be collecting up my things even as he spoke – very neat, very efficient.

And I would have been unable to stand up to him, unable to explain that I was happier, that the last thing I wanted to do was return to his house and resume my part as his wife. My protests would have faltered to a standstill – frozen on my lips by his uncompromising certainty. He would talk and talk until I was drowning beneath the torrent of words, sucked into the whirlpool of his logic, ready to question my own sanity.

I could even picture our homecoming, after the long, silent drive down the motorway. Him rubbing his hand across my shorn hair and saying, 'Never mind, it will soon grow again.' Then sending me upstairs to have a hot bath, while he laid out one of my 'best' nightgowns – one of the white Victorian-style ones – and prepared a tray of supper for me, to be taken sitting up in our marital bed, with its cast-iron bars at head and foot, like the bars at a prisoner's cell window.

'Divorce?' I could imagine the expression on his face. Had this latest escapade been an example of how I thought I could manage on my own? Running away and living in . . . a beach hut? Perhaps a chat with our GP would help? Maybe a prescription for my nerves – or even some kind of psychiatric referral – just to help me over the upset of my mother's death? Argument would have been useless – Alan always knew what was best. Anyone would see that my defection had been nothing more than a cry for help.

I would have forfeited my job, of course, and my unusual form of giving notice would hardly have endeared me to other prospective employers. Alan would probably have decided that the responsibilities of a normal working life put too great a strain on me and that in future it would be better if I didn't go out to work. Instead I would be allowed to sit at home, taking care of his other possessions, merging into them until any thought of escape was completely impossible.

NINE

The threat of *Disappeared!* hung over my week, colouring my every waking thought. I had always taken it for granted that after my initial disappearance any fuss would die down. The passage of time had made me feel safer; it had never occurred to me that my vanishing act would be thrust centre stage again after so many years. I had also banked on the fact that the Jennifer Reynolds case would never have generated much interest in the Dales, and been long forgotten by the time I arrived in Lasthwaite. But what would happen when reminders were thrust right under their noses? I was an incomer from the Midlands – I had that telltale accent. I had allowed my hair to revert back to Jennifer Reynolds' blonde mouse, though the length and cut were completely different and I had eschewed that Prissy Missy style of clothes for something more confident and modern. A glance in the mirror confirmed just how different I looked these days, but was it different enough? By the time I drove into work on Thursday morning I was feeling absurdly furtive. It was foolish, of course, because I had nothing to fear until the programme was actually transmitted. For everyone else it was just a normal morning: post to be opened, calls to answer, patients' names coming over the tannoy: 'Mrs Wilkins to Doctor Woods, please.' But I was on edge and avoided my colleagues as much as possible, even taking my coffee alone in my office rather than joining the doctors in their sitting room as I usually did for mid-morning break.

At about eleven thirty Dr Mac popped his head round my door. 'About that television thing, Susan,' he said.

I felt myself go rigid. 'Which . . . what do you mean?' I asked, praying that the colour wasn't really rising in my face, in direct ratio to the icy funicular which was rushing up my spine.

'Those people who're suggesting we have a television set

in the waiting room.' Dr Mac smiled. 'Not like you to forget anything. That's more in my line, eh?'

'Oh, yes, the set to go in Reception.' I recovered quickly. The practice had been approached with an offer of a television for patients to watch while they waited for their turn with the doctors. Given that Dr Woods's surgery always ran at least half an hour late, it was inevitable that people got bored, with only a few out-of-date magazines and a tank of tropical fish to look at.

'I've got no strong feelings either way myself and as it's been offered as a gift in memory of a patient, I think it needs some serious thought. Could you put together all the pros and cons for the next team meeting?'

'Yes,' I said. 'Of course.'

'Good, good. I'll leave it with you.' He hesitated at the door. 'Are you all right, Susan? You don't look your usual self.' Those wise blue eyes were appraising me. Dr Mac might occasionally be forgetful, but he had a good GP's sixth sense when it came to face-to-face consultations.

'I'm fine,' I said, rather too quickly. 'A little bit of a headache, that's all.'

'Well, well,' he said. 'Better take care of yourself. We all rely on you to keep things running around here, you know.'

'Don't worry,' I said. 'I'm perfectly all right, really.'

As he closed the door behind him I felt a trickle of sweat run down my spine. I've got to pull myself together, I thought.

The suspense was dreadful. No matter how hard I tried to keep my mind on my work, my eyes were drawn continually to the wall clock. I stood with a foot poised on either side of a gulf of contradiction. On the one hand, I did not want nine thirty to arrive, and yet equally I wanted to get it over and done with. By four o'clock I could stand it no longer. Unable to concentrate, I tidied my desk and buzzed Reception, where the internal line was answered by Helen.

'I'm afraid I have rather a bad headache, so I'm going off early,' I said. 'If anyone wants me it will have to wait until the morning.'

'OK, Susan.' I could hear the surprise in her voice. 'I'll let everyone know you've gone.'

'Thank you.' I replaced the handset without giving her time to ask any questions. I knew that everyone would be surprised, because I was never ill and never went home early. Oh, well, hopefully all the more reason for them to accept a sudden illness as genuine.

I had not been back at Heb's Cottage for more than fifteen minutes when Rob rang.

'Sue? I just tried the health centre and they said you'd gone home. What's up – shall I come over?'

'No – yes – it's nothing really. I've just knocked off early with a headache.'

'Poor you. I'll come straight across.'

'No,' I said quickly. 'You've got loads of work to do – you told me last night. And anyway, I shall be much better on my own. I'm going to take some paracetamol and try to sleep it off.'

'Are you sure? What about something to eat?'

'I'm not hungry. I can always get something later, when I'm feeling a bit better. Please don't worry about me – I'll be fine.'

'You're absolutely sure that you don't want me to come over?'

'Positive. I'll be better on my own. Honestly.'

'Well, give me a ring later on if you feel up to it, to let me know you're OK. I won't ring you, in case you're asleep.'

'Thanks.' Pre-occupied as I was, his voice was still the sweetest nectar. 'I'll ring you later if I'm not asleep.'

'Take care of yourself.'

'I will.'

'Love you.'

'Love you too.'

I rang off. I do love him, I thought. If I didn't there would be so much less to lose.

The hands on the kitchen clock had not quite reached four thirty. Five hours to kill before the programme came on. Five whole hours. It was nowhere near dark, but I drew all the curtains and even pulled down the kitchen blind, which I hardly ever did because the kitchen window wasn't overlooked from anywhere. I undressed and had a bath, pouring in some scented oil in a doomed attempt to relax. It occurred to me that if Rob suddenly took it into his head to call in, I might look more convincingly off colour if I was undressed for bed, so after my bath I rambled round the cottage in my dressing gown.

It had been no more than the truth when I told Rob I wasn't hungry, but I occupied a few minutes by heating up a tin of soup, which I ate at the table in the kitchen, my eyes straying continually towards the clock. I made the washing up of saucepan, dish and spoon last as long as I could, then watched the six o'clock news. Unable to concentrate on a book, I tried to watch the TV, but if someone had come into the cottage that evening and asked me what any of the programmes were about I could not have told them.

By nine p.m. I was hardly able to sit still while the regular presenters worked their way steadily through the national news, the local news, the sport, the weather forecast and finally the trailer for a forthcoming costume epic. Then it began. A brief burst of unsettling music, followed by Martin Bullock saying 'Welcome to *Disappeared!*' which even in that hideous moment struck me as an odd sort of introduction – as if *Disappeared!* was a definite location in which you could find yourself. He was standing in a studio in front of a huge montage of photographs, all of which, so he said, were the faces of people who had vanished without trace. Then he gave some statistics, how many people went missing every day and how many never turned up again. 'Tonight,' he continued, 'we're going to look at the stories of three women who've vanished. Three very different women, but all of them having one thing in common: each of them was reported missing on the day she disappeared and each of them remains missing to this day.'

The picture of Martin Bullock faded and the scene changed to a terrace in a northern town, inhabited by people in sixties-style clothes. With the aid of actors and a voiceover, the last known hour of Deirdre Lazenby was reconstructed.

Deirdre was twenty-two and due to be married. She had come home from work as usual and begun to get ready for a night out when she realized that she had no un-laddered nylons to wear. She turned first to her younger brother and sister, but they both refused to run an errand for her, so Deirdre had set out to buy some stockings herself, heading for a local shop, which was only a couple of streets away. After leaving the house she'd spoken briefly to a neighbour and then to an acquaintance from work. None of this would have been at all memorable or remarkable if she had either arrived at the shop or returned home . . . but, of course, she hadn't.

The police were called and they organized a search – not very competently, according to Martin Bullock, whose anti-police agenda was already emerging loud and clear. To complete the item, Deirdre's younger sister, a tearful woman to whom the years had not been kind, appealed for anyone who could throw light on what had happened to come forward.

Shirley Wallingforth was next. A divorcee with three young children, she had arranged a babysitter for the evening in order to meet some girlfriends at a local pub. The babysitter had arrived at six thirty, enabling Shirley to set out in good time for her rendezvous, and several passing motorists had come forward to confirm that they had seen her waiting at the bus stop. The girlfriends had sportingly reassembled, complete with a table full of bottles and glasses, and sporting an abundance of eyeliner, presumably in faithful replication of the night in question. These friends had a drink waiting on the table for Shirley, but at the end of the evening it was still untouched. Throughout the scene in the pub, the camera constantly returned to linger on the glass sitting on the table – an ordinary pub glass transformed into a potent symbol of Shirley's absence.

Finally the spotlight turned on Jennifer Reynolds. The opening shot was the exterior of Alan's house. An involuntary shudder ran through me – the shock, I suppose, of seeing it on TV. I sat on the sofa, clutching my knees against my chest, almost forgetting to breathe.

'Jennifer Reynolds disappeared from this house in Nicholsfield in 1983. Jennifer loved the house. She and her husband Alan devoted much of their spare time to restoring it.' This was news to me. 'Jennifer and Alan had been married for eight years.' The shot changed to a wedding photograph. 'They were very happy together and there was no reason for her to leave.'

Then came the actress. I had to grudgingly admit that it was quite a good likeness. The rest of the reconstruction was somehow rather pointless, showing the actress – who kept flicking her long blonde hair about in an affected way which I very much hoped I never had – firstly chatting to an old lady – 'Jennifer got on well with all her neighbours', then pushing a trolley round a supermarket, 'Jennifer had lived in Nicholsfield all her life', and finally chatting with colleagues 'at the local medical centre, where she worked'. Pinpricks of horror raced up and down my arms and legs at this particular revelation. The practice manager link was definitely one I could do without.

Then an actress playing a receptionist was shown explaining to an actor, presumably playing a doctor, that Jennifer had unexpectedly not come into work, and nor had she rung in sick.

'When Jennifer's husband, Alan, left the house that morning,' Martin Bullock's voice intoned while the actress-receptionist affected to look puzzled by this unaccustomed set of circumstances, 'Jennifer was getting ready for work as usual, but for some reason Jennifer never reached work that day. A neighbour noticed her car still parked outside the house in the middle of the morning.' The shot returned to the front of the house. 'The car was still there when Alan Reynolds returned home that evening. There was no sign of his wife; no sign of a break-in or a struggle. Her car keys, purse and credit cards were all in her handbag on the hall table, where they had been that morning when Alan left the house.'

The screen now filled with a picture of me. I clutched my knees still harder and felt a choking sensation rise in my throat. Surely I must look different now? Hair cut short, different clothes . . . and much older, too . . . that photograph must have been taken nearly ten years ago . . . but it was still me . . .

After what seemed like an interminably long time, but was in reality only seconds, the image of me was replaced by Martin Bullock, who for some unfathomable reason was now striding along some cliff tops, talking direct to camera. He emphasised the impossibility of people simply losing their

memory and wandering away, pointed out how difficult it
would be to construct a new life without assistance and
reminded viewers that none of these women were likely to
have done anything of the kind. Then he began to talk about
serial killers.

From my point of view, this was a line second best to
abduction by aliens. The thrust of Mr Bullock's argument
seemed to be that the police didn't want to try too hard to
discover the collective fates of these missing women because
it was bad for crime figures. In its way this line of thinking
seemed almost as unlikely as alien abduction to me, but at
least, I thought, while Mr Bullock was pontificating on police
ineptitude, the nation was not getting another chance to commit
my face to memory.

The film returned to Deirdre Lazenby's sister. 'I shall never
be at peace wi'meself until I know what happened to her.'

There was a still photograph of Shirley Wallingforth's children,
followed by a still of Alan at some sort of press conference, over
which Martin Bullock's voice intoned piously: 'For the relatives,
the uncertainty goes on.'

Then the credits rolled.

I unclenched myself from where I was perched on the sofa.
A drink. A drink would help. There was a bottle of Vermouth
in the cupboard and I poured a dollop into a tumbler and
added some ice, trying not to notice that my hands were
shaking. I badly wanted to ring Rob. I longed for the comfort
of his voice, but I didn't trust myself. Not yet. Relax. Calm
down. The programme had not been so very terrible. Only
two actual pictures of me. One in my wedding dress, looking
about twelve years old, the big frock and showy veil far more
noticeable than their wearer; the other a slightly more recent
picture, but still complete with long hair and wearing a fussy,
high-necked blouse. Of course, there was the dreadful clue
of both women working as health centre managers, but then
hundreds of people did – mostly female, lots of them blonde
and in their mid-thirties. Good grief – I downed another gulp
of Vermouth – coincidences happen.

As I nursed my drink and reflected on the programme, I
recalled that Alan had not appeared, nor apparently allowed

any filming inside the house. That was good. It would have been extraordinarily painful to see him taking part in an appeal. Alan would not have cried, but hearing his voice would have stirred my deep-seated guilt. From the footage they had included it was apparent that Alan had taken part in some sort of appeal in the early days after I first took off, but it looked as though he had chosen not to be involved in the making of this new programme.

Alan's absence from *Disappeared!* suggested that he no longer cared to participate in attempts to solve the mystery, and I took some small degree of encouragement from this, allowing myself to think that he had moved on, just as I had. Perhaps he had already found a new companion: someone much more suitable for him than I had ever been. I very much liked this new slant on things. As the alcohol warmed me, inducing a pleasant sense of impending intoxication thanks to my near-empty stomach, I began to play with the thought of a new woman in Alan's life. The newcomer would be petite, with long hair; the kind of girl who never got nervous and dropped the china, or became side-tracked by a book so that she omitted to water the geraniums or wind the clocks when she had earlier undertaken to do so. She would be transported by all that business in the bedroom.

If there was such a person living with Alan, then she must have been almost as annoyed as I was by the intrusion of Martin Bullock and his team, raking up the whole dreadful fandango about Alan's long-lost wife and thereby potentially upsetting the apple cart. Then I was struck by a new idea. If Alan had found someone else, he might be quite pleased to divorce me. He could even have taken steps to do so by now. Wasn't it possible to have someone declared officially dead after a certain number of years? Instead of being dead Susan McCarthy, I might be dead Jennifer Reynolds. Shirley Wallingworth and Deirdre Lazenby were very probably dead too. All of us dead together. The thought made me feel light-headed, poised on a tightrope between laughter and tears.

I gulped the last of my drink and poured another, unusually aware of the isolation of the cottage, the encircling darkness beyond the sitting-room curtains. The temptation to call Rob was still strong. I imagined him putting his arms around me, so loving, so reassuring. Saying that he had seen the programme and it did not matter. Saying that whatever happened, he would still love me.

In reality, I knew that as he had a lot of work to catch up on, there was every chance that he would not have watched the programme – but what if I told him the truth anyway? I went through it all again in my head, but it was useless. It's too late, I told myself. If only I'd told him sooner . . . But how? The opportunity had never arisen. How would it? Confiding that you are living under an assumed identity isn't the sort of thing which tends to crop up naturally in the course of conversation. So the deception continues, grows ever more complicated, until telling is impossible.

Suppose, just suppose, Rob had seen the programme . . .

He probably hadn't.

What if he had?

If he had recognized me, what would he do? Ring me? Wait for me to ring him? Ring the police?

What would happen if not Rob but someone else had spotted me? What about my colleagues at Belsay House, or one of the regular patients, or someone who knew me from the village stores, or maybe Rob's mother? The woman with the remarkable memory for faces – how had Miss Marple spent her evening down in Sidmouth? Presumably any third parties – Rob's mother included – would go straight to the police. How long would it take them to investigate? How long would I have to wait before the phone rang or a knock came at my door?

There is a limit to the amount of time you can sustain yourself at red alert. When midnight had arrived and there was still no knock at the door, no telephone call, I doused the lights and went to bed. To my surprise, I fell immediately into a deep sleep, which held me fast until the morning.

TEN

Martin Bullock had said that it was very difficult for anyone to simply vanish, but in some ways he was wrong. Back in the mid-eighties, so long as you had some money, it was always possible to get a room somewhere, even if it was in the seedier part of town. A woman applying for low-paid work attracted few suspicions and awkward questions could be deflected with simple answers. I learned to apply for work with small organizations that had no time for form filling and did not bother to take up references. The nation had yet to be gripped by a collective obsession for examining everyone's photographic credentials (coupled by the ubiquitous utility bill), but even so I knew that my various National Insurance numbers would ultimately be queried because they didn't match up with central records. That didn't matter so long as I kept moving on, shedding one identity in favour of another, but it was a precarious existence. The biggest difficulty was in doing without a bank account. Banks turned out to be very fussy about whose money they were willing to handle. There were certain things which one needed in order to open a bank account even then, things which came under the term 'ID'. ID – the magic key without which some spheres of life were perpetually closed, and obtaining any sort of ID seemed invariably conditional on already having some other form of ID.

I had a vague notion that fake identities could be bought, but this avenue was not an easy one to progress along. Purveyors of fake IDs don't advertise their services in *Yellow Pages* and, even supposing I managed to find someone who sold fake IDs, I had no idea how much such a thing might cost. I could vaguely remember a high-profile case of someone who had organized a fake ID for themselves by taking on the identity of someone who was dead, but I was not entirely sure how that would work. In my professional experience, people who were dead had death certificates – all their records said 'DEAD' in big letters. Surely anyone trying to resurrect a dead person would quickly attract the wrong sort of attention?

What I needed was to be able to assume an identity which was still, at least technically, alive and ongoing. To pick up as it were, where someone else had left off. I thought about this idea a lot, without ever seeing how to achieve it, but in the end my salvation came about through a conversation overheard while I was laying tables in the Heather Bank Hotel in Keswick.

It had been a quiet day and by two o'clock in the afternoon there was only one table still occupied, where two ladies were lingering over their coffee. They had talked loudly and continuously throughout their lunch, as women of a certain age and type often do. Such conversations were normally of no interest whatever to me, but on this occasion a few chance words made me prick up my ears. One lady was full of the news that the daughter of a mutual friend was going to be married abroad – not in one of those ceremonies arranged on a beach in the Caribbean, but in France – for the very good reason that she was going to marry a Frenchman, whom the loud-voiced diner referred to as 'her foreign chap'.

And suddenly I remembered Susan McCarthy. Poor Susan, who had never got as far as marrying her foreign chap and had died abroad. Susan had been buried with her fiancé in France, which almost certainly meant that there was no death certificate for her in England. In this lay possibilities for me, and I thought them through carefully.

My path had crossed with Susan McCarthy's three times. Firstly, we had been at the same secondary school, although Susan was two years younger than I. A few years after school, we had bumped into each other at a wedding. Alan and I had been invited because he was an old friend of the groom. The bride transpired to be Susan McCarthy's cousin. She had come home from university for the weekend in order to attend the celebrations and we chatted to one another for a few minutes, as one does on bumping into any slight acquaintance in such circumstances. Susan was bright and bubbly,

very full of life. I suppose I was quiet by comparison, and
hovering in Alan's shadow as usual.

It was not very long after this that another strange quirk
of fate threw us together, because when Susan graduated she
took a job with a medical research agency. It was a temporary
post, on a short-term contract – the sort of job graduates take
while they look for something more to their liking. There
was nothing technical involved – just extracting information
from records – and the agency placed her at the practice in
Nicholsfield where I was manager. The real Susan wasn't
particularly interested in medical research, so it was a wonder
she got the job at all. Her degree was in French and business
studies and her long-term plan was to work in France. She
had already done a year there as part of her degree, but the
real driving factor was that she had a boyfriend over there,
and the other staff guessed that things were pretty serious
when he arranged for a massive bouquet to arrive on her
birthday. Susan's birthday happened to be Halloween –
another stroke of good fortune, as it made a conveniently
easy date for me to remember later.

Her assignment with the practice ended at the same time
as her contract with the research agency. She went straight
over to France in order to spend some time with her
boyfriend, and word filtered back that they were going to
be married. One of the medical secretaries lived near Susan's
parents and she heard it from them. The news that Susan
had been killed in a road accident reached us a few weeks
later, via the same channel.

At first the idea of using Susan's name repelled me. It
seemed disrespectful – macabre, even – but against this I could
see that it also represented a heaven-sent opportunity. Chance
had given me vital information about Susan, and being able
to work out her precise date of birth made it easy to apply for
her birth certificate. Circumstances had also put me in possession of other vital knowledge, such as exactly when and where
Susan had last paid tax and National Insurance, and the name
and address of her last employer.

Having obtained Susan's birth certificate and rented an
address in her name, I set about reconstructing Susan McCarthy

in my own image. I re-sat my driving test as Susan McCarthy and passed first time, for the second time. Armed with a driving licence and birth certificate, it was now possible for me to open a legitimate bank account. Step by step I became Susan McCarthy. Eventually I embarked on the boldest part of the plan yet: concocting an artificial work history for Susan, for which I appropriated qualifications and a work record which closely paralleled my own. I wrote off for jobs as Susan McCarthy, stating that I had been living abroad. I asked the authorities to re-issue my 'lost' National Insurance number, claiming that I had forgotten it during my sojourn in France. I broke back in by taking a temporary post, covering for a practice manager who was ill. To these employers I offered my own qualifications: 'I'm sorry, the certificates are packed up in storage, I'm between houses . . .' And two not very recent references: 'My partner and I have been living abroad for four years, so I haven't got anything more up to date, I'm afraid . . .' They needed someone at short notice and I was available. The medical profession can be scarily lax about taking up references.

When subsequently applying for permanent posts, I now had an up-to-date reference which I bolstered with a fake, reasoning that only my most recent reference would be followed up. By the time Susan McCarthy reached Lasthwaite, the awkward partner and their life abroad – about which I could never have discoursed very confidently – were long discarded.

By Lasthwaite, the person of Susan McCarthy had been developed to the point where she had a car, bank and building society accounts – every vestige of a legitimate person. Never mind that Susan's relatives and friends were only names written in an exercise book in her kitchen dresser. It was as real as it needed to be for other people and, like a favourite novel, it had become almost real for me. I had reached a point where it would be difficult for any mere acquaintance to expose my deception, but I never deluded myself – I was confident that the authorities could uncover the truth about 'Susan McCarthy' within days, perhaps even hours.

When I woke on Friday morning, my panic returned with

a vengeance. It was almost impossible to believe that all my colleagues would have missed the transmission of *Disappeared!*. I was tempted to ring in sick, but I knew that would not do. The way to allay any suspicions was to carry on as normal, though as I got ready for work, I tried to focus on possible contingency plans. It came to me then that I should have thought about this sort of thing before – had some sort of escape route in place – but I had grown overconfident, imagining that each layer of fresh deception had erected another barrier between me and discovery. Each year that passed had made me feel more secure, more committed to my life as Susan McCarthy – less easily uprooted or transformed – so there were no funds stashed in the dresser to be grabbed for a speedy getaway, no scenario concocted for the day when I had to scarper in a hurry. I put my building society and cheque books into my handbag, with some half-formed notion that I might have to go on the run without being able to get back to the cottage, but then I took them out again, because surely the first thing the authorities would do if I was rumbled would be to freeze my assets?

If there were any suspicions, would I get wind of them in time? Have a chance to slip away? Or would the police just arrive and arrest me? I was still totally preoccupied with these anxieties when I walked into Reception and was confronted by the unexpected sight of a group of female colleagues, all clustered around the main desk. Every head swivelled as I entered and I stopped dead on the threshold. A palpable sense of shock hung in the air. The Tragedy Queen was crying, the Trollop looked wide-eyed and pale, Helen, the duty receptionist, wore a sanctimonious expression of distaste (though this in itself was not unusual), while the Trainspotter looked agitated.

Oh my God, I thought. They know. They're standing here, talking about me, wondering what's going to happen, and I've walked straight in on them.

I took a couple of hesitant steps forward, not even bothering to ask the hackneyed, is-there-anything-the-matter question, because there so obviously was. Instead, I said: 'What's wrong?' The words emerged as a croak.

'It was on the news this morning,' Helen said. 'They've found the body of a young girl. It'll be Julie Peacock.'

The Tragedy Queen burst into noisy sobs and the Trollop put her arm around her sobbing colleague's shoulder. 'Maureen knew her,' she said, presumably by way of offering an explanation for my benefit. (In fact, it later transpired that Maureen did not know Julie Peacock any better than the rest of the staff, but Maureen would not have been Maureen if she had not eked the last drop of drama from the situation.)

I recognized the name immediately. The Peacock family lived on the outskirts of Dentwhistle, the next hamlet along the valley, and I knew most of them by sight, as one did know families who were regulars at the surgery. Julie's father had a bad back; her older sister had a fractious baby and a toddler with a permanently runny nose. Julie herself was a plump fifteen-year-old; the sort of girl who sometimes accompanied her sister to the baby clinic, just for something to do.

News of the girl's failure to return home from school the previous evening had circulated swiftly through the village, but I was too far off the local radar to have received a phone call or a knock at the door, and sufficiently preoccupied with problems of my own that I had missed the item on the local radio that morning. As I stood in Reception, half-a-dozen voices competed to bring me up to speed. It appeared that the alarm had been raised late the previous afternoon. Even before the police arrived in any numbers, local volunteers had undertaken a search of sorts, and the intention had been to mount a more thorough operation in the morning, but this had been pre-empted when a man cycling to work along a local footpath at first light noticed a woman's shoe lying half under the bushes. He immediately alerted the police, and an investigation of the nearby undergrowth had revealed a body, concealed not far from where the path joined the main road. The item on the radio had been nothing like so comprehensive, but the local grapevine was buzzing with supplementary information and there seemed no doubt as to the victim's identity.

'It's terrible,' said the Trainspotter. 'Nothing like this has ever happened in the dale before.'

It was a sentiment that I would hear repeatedly throughout

that day and in the days that followed. Life's normal allotment of tragedies: death in car accidents, death in faraway wars – these events had visited Lasthwaite as they did elsewhere, but violent, bloody murder was an unwelcome stranger, never before entertained.

For the staff of a medical practice, death is something of an occupational hazard. When it was an unexpected death, or worse a child, or a stillbirth, the day would be tinged with sadness, particularly if a favourite patient was involved, but Julie Peacock's death provoked something different. Fear and shock and curiosity blended into a highly charged mix which stalked the building, preying on nerves and emotions like a virus. In this atmosphere, anything unusual in my own demeanour was liable to be ascribed to the general sense of trauma which pervaded the entire community. Shocked as I was by the girl's murder, it took no more than minutes for me to appreciate a possible knock-on effect, for surely even if anyone in Lasthwaite had watched the programme about three non-local women, who had all gone missing years ago, any interest this might normally have provoked was going to be submerged beneath the news of something happening here and now, much closer to home. I had been unexpectedly reprieved.

All the same, I was nervous and watchful as I followed my usual routines. I had a bad moment early on, encountering the Trollop in the ladies' loo. I entered to find her pursing freshly glossed lips in the mirror, but she turned on catching sight of my reflection and said, 'Susan, I wanted to ask you about last night's duty book.' The release of the breath I had held between the words *last night's* and *duty book* was audible, but she was still distracted by her own appearance – now fiddling with an eyelash – and appeared not to notice, continuing without waiting for a reply: 'It was Doctor Milly's turn on duty' (the staff had already adopted an unauthorized abbreviation for the trainee), 'and he didn't leave it on the shelf for me to type up – nor the tape neither. When I asked him about it, he said he couldn't remember where he'd left it, then he rushed off to go on a call with Doctor Woods. I can't type the out-of-hours visits on to the computer without the book and the tape,' she added unnecessarily, as if I didn't know the system.

'Well, don't worry too much,' I said. 'I expect it will turn up before the end of the day.'

I made a mental note to ask Terry Millington about it myself when I saw him at morning coffee in the doctors' sitting room, but this came to nothing as he was still out on a maternity case with Dr Woods, and I was forced to resort to leaving a message in his pigeonhole instead. The out-of-hours duty book had occasionally been mislaid before (usually by Dr Woods) so I was not unduly concerned. It was just another snagged nail in the routine of the surgery – one among many that day.

For afternoon break I joined the staff in the much larger common room as usual, where I found them speculating freely on the fate of Julie Peacock and comparing notes on how they would be getting home.

'I shall be keeping my doors locked,' declared the Tragedy Queen. 'I shan't rest until Frank's home – luckily he's usually back just after me.' She glanced pointedly in my direction.

Everyone was aware that of them all, I was the only one who lived alone.

'Will you be all right, Susan?' asked one of the district nurses.

'I'll be fine.'

'I don't know how you can sleep at nights,' declared the Tragedy Queen. 'I couldn't live up there, all on my own.'

'I'm sure it's nobody local,' said Jayne, one of the health visitors. 'Whoever did it will be miles away by now.'

'Don't you be so sure.' It was the Trollop now. 'The police must think it's someone local. They're going to do house-to-house. It said so on the radio at lunchtime.'

'That doesn't mean it *is* someone local.'

'Well, I bet it is. There's some very funny people live round here.'

I intervened to remind everyone of the forthcoming team meeting, thereby pre-empting a general trespass into entirely unprofessional speculations upon the murderer's identity, based on insider knowledge of confidential psychiatric reports which were sitting in various patients' files. 'I want to run through the new protocol on test results again,' I said. 'We're getting it right most of the time but there are still one or two glitches. And we need to have views on the proposal to install a television in Reception,' I went on. 'Can I suggest that if anyone feels they are likely to be affected, they have a word with me? Then I can set out the main points so that we have a framework for the discussion when we actually get round to talking about it.'

More than one face registered disappointment at my attempt to divert us back to the workday norm. The television had been a major topic of conversation up until now, as any little excitement or proposal of change was wont to be, but minor changes in the workplace paled into insignificance with the possibility that the dale might get its moment on *Crimewatch.*

The Tragedy Queen, never happier than when worrying needlessly, brought some papers into my office at around four that afternoon. This gave her the opportunity to linger and say, 'You will be careful, won't you, Susan? We're all worried about you, living up there on your own.'

I took this latter remark to indicate that since the conclusion of afternoon break, my possible fate at the hands of a crazed killer had been the subject of horrified speculations in Medical Records.

'Thank you, Maureen,' I said as patiently as I could. 'But I'm used to living on my own. It really doesn't worry me.'

'I know.' Maureen looked as if she thought this eccentricity on my part was half the cause of the trouble. 'The thing is that you mustn't get too complacent. Keep your doors locked and don't open them until you've seen who's there.'

'Thank you, Maureen,' I said, a shade more firmly. 'I'll bear that in mind.' I opened one of my desk drawers and pretended to be searching for something.

Maureen evidently wanted to linger, but as I did not look up or say anything further, she could find no excuse for prolonging her visit. It was probably just as well – the more she twittered, the greater the temptation to lay out the facts, to point out that statistically the chances of being murdered in one's own home were millions to one against. For hundreds of years, I reflected, women living in the country had never locked their doors. Now even in places like Lasthwaite they did. Yet until yesterday, no woman in Lasthwaite had suffered a violent death at the hand of another. It was not reality but fear which made women lock their doors when darkness fell, I told myself.

I wondered idly what Maureen's reaction would have been if I had said, 'I used to be like you. When my husband went away on business, I used to go and stay with my mother, so that I wouldn't have to spend the night alone in our house. I even used to be scared to go down into the cellar. Yes, really. I was frightened to enter a room, because that's all a cellar is – just a room in my own home. But I'm not afraid any more. I've slept in seedy digs and even in a beach hut. These fears of yours are childish fears, no more substantial than the bogeyman behind the wardrobe and the monsters you used to think were under the bed. Realize it, Maureen. Shrug them off and be free.'

ELEVEN

The highly charged atmosphere sapped my energy so that by the end of the day I felt physically and emotionally exhausted, but like a marathon runner breasting the tape, when I finally opened the car door and tossed my handbag on to the passenger seat I experienced a moment of elation. I had made it. No one had seen the programme – or if they had, no one had guessed. There had been no long looks or leading questions. The programme about those long-ago disappearances had not merited a second thought thanks to events much closer to home. My relief was instantly followed by a wave of self-loathing. What kind of odious person had I become that I could find anything to be thankful for in the death of a young girl? I felt an irrational sense of guilt, as though I had somehow contrived Julie Peacock's murder myself in order to provide a distraction for everyone on the day following *Disappeared!*.

I engaged first gear with rather more force than was necessary and pulled out of the staff car park. It occurred to me then that no one had bothered to ask how I was feeling after yesterday's spurious headache. Even Rob had not rung, which was unlike him – especially as he had seemed so anxious about me the night before.

As I rounded the bend below Rosecroft I had to brake to avoid Bob Fox, who was standing in the road, flagging me down. He had evidently been lying in wait for me and this in concert with his urgent signals that I should stop coupled alarm to my uncertainty. It was all very well dismissing gossip about the peculiarities of the Fox family, but a local girl had been murdered and somebody must have done it. As I slowed down I could see Bob beckoning urgently in the direction of the house, and sure enough his brother Jim emerged from the yard gate and came hurrying to join him. As the Fiesta came to a halt I wound my window down, holding the car on the clutch, aware that I was gripping the steering wheel with an unnecessary degree of force.

Both men were dressed in their usual working attire – wellington boots, coats held together with string tied about the waist, and caps shiny with age – which they wore summer and winter alike.

'Have 'e the number?' Bob enquired of Jim, as Jim began to fumble about, first in his outer and then his inner pockets.

'Is everything all right?' I asked, feeling that some encouragement toward an explanation was needed.

'Eh, lass, don't say you 'aven't 'eard?' said Bob before turning back to Jim to chivvy him some more.

''Course she'll 'ave 'eard,' retorted Jim gruffly. 'There's nobbut deaf Joe as won't 'ave 'eard.' He finally located what he was looking for and withdrew from his pocket a crumpled piece of what had once been a brown envelope. With rare directness he handed me the paper and said gravely, 'Yon's our number. For t'phone. If you so much as hear owt amiss, you ring yon number and we'll be up to yours faster than you can say what's to do.'

'Thank you,' I said gravely. 'Thank you very much.'

There was something both comical and touching in the thought of Jim and Bob charging up the lane to my rescue.

''Aven't to worry if it's a false alarm,' Bob said, as if to reassure Jim.

'Aye. We'll come up for a look and if it's a false alarm, well, no more need's be said,' Jim nodded at Bob. 'Better to be safe than sorry.'

'Thank you,' I said again. 'I'll keep your number next to the phone, just in case – though I'm sure I shan't need to use it.'

'Next t'phone, aye.' Bob nodded back at Jim.

'It's a bad business,' said Jim solemnly. 'A reet bad business.'

'Lass 'as nowt to fear,' said Bob. 'Anybody prowling round ere'll likely finish wi'a backside full o' lead.'

'Aye, we've old gun at ready for 'un.' This thought seemed to lighten Jim's mood considerably, for he smiled as he waved me on my way.

I experienced more than a twinge of shame as I continued up the lane. That's what this sort of thing does to people, I thought. It brings out the best in people like Jim and Bob, and apparently the worst in horrible, paranoid people like me.

As I got out of the car I could hear another vehicle approaching up the lane and, glancing back, I saw that it was Rob. Even through the windscreen, I could see that he looked tired and drawn. As he emerged from the car the weight of the day hung on him like a damp greatcoat.

We embraced briefly.

'I'm sorry I didn't ring, Sue. Are you all right?'

'Perfectly,' I said, disengaging myself long enough to get out my key and open the front door. '*You* don't look too good.'

'It's been an awful day,' he said.

'Drink?' I suggested.

'Please.'

I was trying to read his face. Was it the Julie Peacock tragedy that had overwhelmed him, or was it something else? 'I heard the news as soon as I got into work this morning,' I said, pouring generous slugs of Vermouth on to ice cubes. I had made quite a dent in the Vermouth the night before and we had only bought it the previous weekend. I shoved the bottle back out of sight as quickly as possible and hoped that he wouldn't have noticed. 'I suppose she went to the comp?' I asked.

'Yes. It's been awful. Kids upset – some in tears. Staff breaking down. The police in and out all day, reporters hanging round the gates. An absolute nightmare.'

I handed him a drink while squeezing his shoulder with my spare hand. Julie Peacock. He was only upset about Julie Peacock. He hadn't seen it. No one had. 'Let's sit down,' I said. 'I won't start the dinner just yet.'

Like everyone else, Rob seemed unable to talk or think of anything but the murder. He too was thrown off balance by the shockwaves of something so terrible happening in our little corner of the world.

I told him about my meeting with Jim and Bob.

'It's a good idea to keep their number handy,' he declared with surprising vehemence. 'As they say, they can get up here in minutes – they're a lot closer than I am – and it would take the police twenty minutes or more to get out here if you dialled 999.'

'But I don't think there's any real likelihood of me needing to ring them, or the police,' I said, feeling brave and logical in the well-lit comfort of the sitting room. 'I don't suppose the man who did it is a local at all. And if it is someone Julie knew, then it was probably an isolated thing – you know, a quarrel that went wrong or something, in which case it won't happen again. There's absolutely no reason to believe we've got a killer stalking up and down the valley, looking for his next victim.'

Rob turned to look at me, his brow furrowed with worry. 'Don't be complacent, darling, please,' he said. 'You're too precious to lose.'

A warm feeling surged through me. I reached over to squeeze his hand.

'Poor old Jim and Bob,' I said. 'I don't think they can believe something like this has happened. This is the sort of thing they hear about happening to other people, not something that happens here, on their own doorstep, where they've lived all their lives.'

'I can hardly believe it myself,' Rob said. 'All day I've been thinking that I was in the middle of some horrible nightmare. I taught the kid last year, although I didn't get to know her very well – and to be honest, I didn't particularly take to her, which almost makes it worse. I suppose I'm no different to Jim and Bob – I just can't believe it could happen here. I've never known anyone who ended up murdered before.'

'I did once,' I said. 'Not very well. She was a girl who used to go to Aunt Millicent for piano lessons.'

'Who was Aunt Millicent?'

I tried not to register the horror I felt. I had spoken so casually, so completely without forethought.

'Who was Aunt Millicent?' he repeated.

'She wasn't a real aunt,' I blurted out. I was reacting like someone who has been accused of something, speaking far too defensively. I attempted a lighter tone. 'She was a sort of family friend and I just called her Auntie. I went to her for piano lessons too, but I was never very good. I gave up playing ages ago.'

'You never mentioned this before.'

'Why should I have done?' I tried to sound casual. Cast around desperately for a way of diverting him on to some other topic, but nothing sprang immediately to mind.

'No reason,' he said. 'So who was she, then?'

'Aunt Millicent?'

'No, the girl you knew through having piano lessons with Aunt Millicent.'

I was conscious of my heartbeat growing louder and faster, like the approach of a faraway cavalry troop. It would be dangerous to invent things, because I was completely unprepared. There had been no time to construct something plausible and commit it to the exercise book in case I needed it again in future. Then I remembered that I hadn't got the exercise book any more and this only increased the sense of being up there alone on the high wire with the safety net gone. The remnants of ice cubes clinked softly in my glass. I didn't want to look down in case I found that my hand was shaking. I would just have to stick as near to the truth as I dared and try not to trip myself up.

'It wasn't while I was having piano lessons,' I said, trying to sound natural and comfortable, rather than cagey and careful. 'It was years afterwards, when I was grown up. Millicent was an old friend of my mother's, and I only bumped into this girl because I called in at Millicent's to drop something off for Mum – some magazines or a knitting pattern, or something like that. I was going into the house as this girl was coming out at the end of her lesson. Then of course when it happened – when she was killed, Millicent was very upset and she reminded me that I had actually met the girl. Although, of course, I'd hardly met her really, just – you know – passed her in the hallway.'

'What was her name?'

'Who?'

'The girl.' His voice was non-committal, but I knew instinctively that for some reason the question was important to him.

'It was Antonia,' I said. 'I'm afraid I don't remember her

second name. But she was fifteen, like this other girl – I do remember that.' I endeavoured to adopt a tone which suggested that I was trying to be helpful. 'They never caught the man who did it.'

'Antonia,' he said thoughtfully. 'Not the sort of name you would easily forget.'

'Which is probably why I haven't.'

'What year was this?'

'Oh, good grief, Rob – I really don't remember.'

'Well, roughly. You must remember roughly.'

What does it matter? I wanted to shout. How can it possibly matter? Aloud I said, 'About 1981 or '82, I suppose. I can't remember exactly. It was before my mother died.'

'Are you still in touch with this Auntie Millicent?'

'No,' I said. 'I lost touch with her after Mum died . . . of course, the contact had always been through Mum . . . and I expect she's dead herself by now. She was quite a bit older than Mum, I think.'

He was looking at me oddly, almost as if he was trying to read my mind. He turned away abruptly and began to stare at the dark reproduction of the sitting room which was reflected in the window panes where I hadn't bothered to draw the curtains. Suddenly I was so afraid – so immensely afraid. I clutched his hand and raised it to my lips. His skin was warm and smooth. 'Don't let's talk about people dying any more,' I pleaded. 'Let's try to talk about something happy.'

He turned back and took me in his arms. 'Let's go to bed.'

There was no work to get up for the next day. No need for Rob to return home. I lay awake that night, long after he was sleeping. I knew that I had slipped up badly. I'd relaxed and let down my guard. In the end Julie Peacock had not proved such a useful distraction, because if we hadn't been talking about her, I thought, the subject of murdered schoolgirls would never have entered my head. Now I had foolishly referred to Aunt Millicent and Antonia Bridgeman in front of Rob, and the uneasy memory of the expression on his face kept coming back to me. He had not looked suspicious exactly, but somehow there had been more than mere ordinary curiosity writ there. Then again what could I expect? I had represented myself as the only child of only children, so it was small wonder that the casual production of an aunt had set him back.

For of course, Millicent was my aunt – my mother's sister. She had given piano lessons too, that much was true enough. 'Poor Millicent,' as my mother sometimes referred to her, Millicent being the only one of my mother's sisters who had been burdened with the tiresome necessity of earning a living.

Far from being an only child, my mother had been the youngest of three girls, whose stories of growing up between the wars, of tennis parties, dances, and tea carried out into the garden by a uniformed maid were cloaked in wistful grandeur. The eldest sister, Felicity, had married a clergyman and moved with him to the north of England, where they had three children, all so much older than me that I never felt they counted as proper cousins, in spite of my being called upon to serve as one of the gaggle of bridesmaids at each of their weddings. Aunt Millicent, the middle sister, never had children. Her husband, Uncle George, had been badly shot up in the Second World War and couldn't work so money was tight, and Aunt Millicent augmented his pension by giving music lessons at the upright piano in her front room.

I had thought to leave all of my past life behind, but it was always there, lurking beneath the surface like a sleeping volcano, the danger of an unexpected eruption ever present. As I snuggled closer to Rob's sleeping body, enjoying the steady rhythm of his breathing, I had an awful premonition that I had not heard the last of Antonia and Aunt Millicent. It was another time bomb ticking away – another lighted fuse to worry about.

TWELVE

Next morning I woke to the sound of drizzle whispering against the window panes, and when I peeked between the curtains the cloud was so low that I couldn't see beyond the dry-stone wall on the opposite side of the lane. Rob was still asleep, so I slipped into my dressing gown, collected my clothes and tiptoed downstairs to the bathroom: a modern addition to a building whose original structure had not allowed for indoor plumbing.

I had showered and dressed, and was sipping a mug of tea at the kitchen table when the doorbell rang. I saw the police car through the front window as soon as I entered the sitting room and came to an abrupt halt alongside the sofa. Someone had seen the programme after all. I thought of the back door, but it led into an enclosed yard whose only gate led back out into the lane. I doubted if I could climb the wall at the back of the yard, and if I did I would be seen from the lane as soon as I attempted to cross the open fields. Maybe if I lay low and didn't answer the door they would go away. Then I heard a movement above my head. Rob must have heard the doorbell too, and was heading down to answer the door . . .

I forced my legs to propel me across the room and knelt cautiously on the window seat, which brought the two police officers – a man and a woman – into my line of sight. They were standing at the front door, patiently awaiting a response to their summons. I shrank back into the room, praying that they hadn't seen me. Then I remembered that someone had said there would be house-to-house enquiries about Julie Peacock.

I took a deep breath to compose myself, stepped into the small square hall at the bottom of the stairs and opened the front door just as the policeman was reaching for the doorknocker to reinforce his original summons. When the female officer launched into a preamble about the murder enquiry I almost sank against the doorframe in relief. There was no porch to provide shelter and I could see that the paper on their clipboard was going to get wet, so I invited them to step inside. They didn't need a second prompt. In spite of travelling around by car they looked cold and their dark uniforms were already beaded with tiny raindrops, turning them into pale renditions of a Pearly King and Queen. When I offered to make them a cup of coffee, they accepted gratefully. They both looked very young, I thought, the chap even more so than the WPC.

I was about to go into the kitchen when Rob appeared, wearing just his jeans. The WPC allowed her appraisal of his torso to go on just a little too long as he said, 'I saw the police car out of the window. Is there anything wrong?'

'It's just routine enquiries, sir, about the Julie Peacock murder.'

Rob took over the coffee making operation while I, as the householder, explained who we both were, gave them the address where Rob normally resided and went through the preliminaries of having known Julie very slightly, which was probably the response they were getting in varying degrees, from every household in the area. How far did routine enquiries go? I wondered. How likely were they to check on the identities of the people they were calling on?

By the time Rob rejoined us with four mugs of coffee on a tray, the questions had become more specific. Would I mind saying where I had been on Thursday, at around the time the girl left school? I told them about leaving work early and driving home. Since my route had not taken me anywhere near the vicinity of Julie Peacock's last known movements and I had not left the house again that evening, nor seen anything or anyone unusual, I had nothing much to tell them. It was easy, I thought, just like sitting a very simple test at school. I tried to relax. There was no reason why the police would not take me at face value. Then I looked across at Rob and realized that something was troubling him. He was leaning forward in his chair, frowning, waiting for the spotlight to turn on him. I couldn't understand it. He was normally so laidback.

When the WPC asked him about Julie Peacock, he at once

admitted to having taught her, though not during the current school year. Asked when he had last seen her, he seemed uncharacteristically irritable, saying that he couldn't possibly remember. 'I see hundreds of kids around the school every working day of the week and I quite often bump into the ones who live locally outside school as well. How can I possibly say whether I saw the girl last week or the week before?'

It may have been his tone, or perhaps they did not like receiving such a vague response, but for whatever reason I could tell this was not going down very well. I tried to see what the WPC was writing, but the angle of her clipboard made it impossible, and then she caught me looking, which was awkward. I tried to engage her with a smile, but it didn't work.

Now they wanted to know what Rob had been doing between four p.m. and six p.m. on Thursday afternoon. He began by explaining how he had tidied up in his classroom as usual, before ringing first the medical centre and then my cottage just before he left the school. As I had been feeling unwell and didn't want him to come round, he had driven straight home and not left the house again until next morning.

'You say you drove straight home, sir?'

Rob, tight-lipped, nodded an affirmative.

'Which way did you go?' asked the young policeman. There was a spark of interest in his voice. He must have worked out that in order to get home, Rob would have driven along the same route the school bus had taken, must have passed the place where Julie got off it that afternoon to walk up the lane towards her parents' house. A spot only yards from the place where she had been murdered and dumped on the nearby bridle path.

'My usual way.' Rob was well aware that his audience had made the connection. 'Along the main road, turning off at The Horseshoes pub, down Mill Lane. Then Higher Bank Road, Upper Lasthwaite Lane, then there's that little three-way turn off – my place is down the middle one.'

'Did you see the school bus?' asked the WPC. 'Overtake it, perhaps?'

'No, I didn't.'

'Did you see Julie Peacock at all?'

'No,' Rob said sharply. 'Don't you think I'd have told you if I had?'

Please, I thought, please don't use that tone. However daft the question, don't whatever you do say anything to antagonise them or make them more suspicious.

The WPC tried again. 'Can you be exactly sure of the time you set off from the school, Mr Dugdale? You may be a very important witness.'

Rob spoke very slowly and carefully, like a bad actor delivering well-rehearsed lines. 'I can't be sure of the exact time because I didn't look at my watch. Last lesson had finished. I'd collected up my books and papers and sorted out a few things in my classroom. Then I went down into the bottom corridor. There's a payphone there, which I used to make my phone calls. First I tried the medical centre, but when I found out that Sue wasn't at work, I tried the number here and spoke with her for a few minutes. After that I went straight home. I didn't see the school bus. I didn't see Julie Peacock. I didn't see anything out of the ordinary at all – and I didn't notice what time it was when I got home.'

'Did anyone see you leave the school, sir?' The young policeman took a turn. 'Anyone who might be able to help us with the timing? A colleague say, or a cleaner, or the caretaker.'

Rob thought for a moment before saying, 'There may have been someone. I don't specifically remember there being anyone about, but it's a big building. I suppose someone might have been looking out of a window or something. There were still a few cars in the car park when I left.'

'Now when you reached the point where Julie Peacock got off the bus – you know where that is?'

Rob nodded.

'Was there anyone there at all?'

'No one.'

'You do know, sir, that Julie's body was found only a few yards away from where she got off the bus?'

I wanted to go to Rob and put my hand in his, but I stayed where I was. He finished his coffee and put his mug down on the edge of the hearth with elaborate care, as though positioning it in one precise location was immensely important. Lives might have depended upon it. Then he placed his hands palms down on the arms of the chair, fingers spread out. It was a peculiar posture, uncomfortable and unnatural. He had gone very pale, like someone about to be sick.

'I know,' he said. 'I saw it on TV last night and I recognized the place. I mean, obviously I recognized it, because I drive past it every day. I do realize that on Thursday I must have driven past not long after it happened. I know that's where Julie used to get off, because once or twice I've actually caught the bus up there and overtaken it while it was standing there. Another kid, Luke Robinson, used to get off at that stop as well, but he left school at the end of last year.'

'When was the last time you saw Julie getting off the bus there, Mr Dugdale?' The WPC's head was bent, ready to note down the reply. I couldn't see her face and her voice was carefully neutral.

'I honestly don't know. A week or so? Probably longer . . . I mean, it's not the sort of thing you make a note of. Certainly not on the day she was killed. I really want you to catch the person who did this,' he added, the words tumbling out abruptly. 'I want you to catch this person and I wish I could help you, but I can't. I didn't see anything at all.'

That was pretty much the end of it really, but as soon as they had gone, Rob said, 'I'm going to be a suspect. You realize that?'

'Not really.' I gave him a hug.

'Of course really. I knew the girl. I was virtually on the spot when she was killed . . .'

'That's rubbish. Come on,' I said, falsely cheerful. 'Have your shower and I'll do a cooked breakfast. I've got bacon and some mushrooms if you fancy them.'

The fried breakfast was a mistake. We sat toying with food we did not really want, mushrooms cooling, eggs congealing, little puddles of grease appearing beneath the sausages.

I tried to find other things to talk about, but Rob kept coming back to the murder enquiry. 'If I'm under suspicion, they'll suspend me from school.'

'Of course they won't,' I said briskly. 'They can't suspend you just like that, without any grounds.'

'Being a suspect in a murder enquiry. I bet the governors will think that's grounds enough. When a young girl's involved it's dead easy to suspend a teacher, to ruin his career.'

'You're not a suspect,' I said. 'Or at least, no more than anyone else. Think about it logically. Everyone in Lasthwaite knows Julie Peacock by sight. Half the men in the dale won't have an alibi for the time she went missing. Lots of people drive home that way: it's the main road in, for goodness' sake. I bet you're not the only teacher from the comp who was driving that way after school on Thursday afternoon. They can't suspend every teacher who drove home alone that afternoon – they'll have no staff left.'

He considered this. 'Quite a few people do go that way,' he said. 'The trouble is I happened to be there at the right time. Think of it. She must have been lying there . . . maybe she was still alive when I drove past. If only I had seen something. If only—'

'Stop it,' I said, laying down my knife and fork with a clatter. 'It's too horrible to think about.'

'But you do see,' he said, his eyes searching my face for clues, 'that I am on the spot. That perhaps no one else will admit to being there . . . which leaves . . .'

'No,' I said unnecessarily loudly. 'It doesn't signify anything. There's no evidence to involve you at all. You're just a witness. Just someone who can help them by saying that when you passed the place where she got off the bus there was nobody there. If they can find out what time you drove past, it will help them prove what time it happened.'

'But . . .' he began.

'Rob, please – I don't want to talk about it any more.'

For a moment I thought he was going to carry on regardless, but he swallowed back whatever he had been about to say and shook his head.

We gave up on the rest of the breakfast. He helped me clear away and wash up, and later we drove into Richmond, where he bought himself a new sweater and we had lunch in our favourite tea shop. We did not talk about Julie Peacock any more, but the subject hovered silently in the background.

'Don't think about it,' I had said. But how was one not to

think about it? Murders you just heard about on the news could haunt your thoughts for weeks. The slightest personal connection with a case made it a hundred times worse. Rob's discomfort at his proximity to the murder scene gave me a strong sense of déjà vu. I could still remember the eerie sensation of my second-hand connection to Antonia Bridgeman's murder. My involvement then had been tenuous, if slightly more substantial than I had indicated to Rob.

I had indeed met Antonia Bridgeman only once and it really had come about much as I had told him, while I was running an errand for my mother. Alan and I had called at Aunt Millicent's to drop something off, arriving just as the girl was putting on her coat at the end of her music lesson. The weather was foul that day and as we were going Antonia's way, we had given her a lift home. The journey only took a matter of three or four minutes by car, so there hadn't been much time for a conversation. I think I asked her what grade she was up to, and possibly where she went to school. All totally inconsequential; I don't suppose I would have remembered anything about it at all, except for the fact that three weeks later to the very day, Antonia was murdered.

On the day she died Antonia had attended her music lesson then set off home as usual. She was fifteen and a responsible sort of girl, with her own latch key. On that particular day it happened that her parents were both out when she should have returned home, so she was not immediately missed. When her mother did arrive home, she was surprised to find the house in darkness and no indication of her daughter's whereabouts. She gave it half an hour and when there was still no sign of Antonia, she tried phoning a couple of the girl's friends, thinking that Antonia might have called in to see one of them instead of coming straight home. Drawing a blank with them, she tried the piano teacher's house next, but as chance would have it, Aunt Millicent was round at my parents' house, where I too happened to be that evening because Alan was away at a big sale in Cheshire.

Our first intimation that something was wrong came when Uncle George phoned and asked to speak to my aunt – a singular occurrence which at once alarmed Millicent, who thought that he must have been taken ill. She almost fell out of her chair in her haste to get to the phone, but after a couple of minutes she came back into the room and told us that Antonia's mother had rung Uncle George to establish that Antonia had been for her lesson and set off for home at the usual time. Mrs Bridgeman was beside herself, Millicent reported, before declaring that under the circumstances she had better return immediately, to sit with Uncle George in case the police came.

My mother and I had tried to persuade her that this was most unlikely, but she would not be swayed, so in the end I had driven her home, staying for a cup of tea with her and Uncle George before returning to my parents' house for the night. In the event Millicent was correct. The police turned up to question them later in the evening, and poor Millicent became officially the last known person to see the girl alive.

Antonia's body was found about a week later, in a wood a few miles outside town. The police said she must have been taken there by car. There were very few clues. Antonia's parents always insisted that their daughter would never have got into a stranger's car. I remember thinking that she had got into ours willingly enough – though of course that was hardly the same thing.

There had been a lot about the case in the press, both locally and nationally. Some of the papers made a big thing about there being a serial killer in the area, but the local police played that one down. It was after Antonia Bridgeman's murder that one national Sunday paper ran a piece about the number of young women who had gone missing in the Nicholsfield area. Like the Bermuda Triangle, the Nicholsfield area seemed to have very nebulous boundaries. The paper printed a whole page of photos, most of them not proven murder victims at all, just women who had gone missing at one time or another, some of them with little or no apparent connection to Nicholsfield.

None of this proved anything, but there were a lot of people who were prepared to believe that there was a serial killer operating around Nicholsfield. My mother certainly did and I, who was prey to every kind of hysterical fear in those days, went along with it wholeheartedly, always arranging to stay at Mum and Dad's whenever Alan spent a night away on business.

At least there was no question of Julie Peacock's death being part of a pattern. No one had ever been murdered in Lasthwaite before – and it was a long way from Nicholsfield, even by journalistic stretches of the imagination.

THIRTEEN

D
on't think about it, I had said.

Impossible, of course.

The dale was suddenly full of police cars and journalists. Rubber-neckers too. People started to place flowers at the roadside. Complete strangers arrived by car to leave their tributes, some bringing teddy bears and similar girlish mementoes, which quickly became bedraggled and tatty in the rain, then dirtied by the passing traffic. I found this very odd and not in the least comforting or dignified. It did not provoke thoughts of appropriate solemnity, suggesting at best a bunch of pagans leaving their offerings at the site of a virgin sacrifice, or at worst a mawkish public afflicted by ghoulish curiosity and looking for an excuse to get in on the act.

For the first few days the murder was headline news. There was film footage on the local and national bulletins showing the school bus as it paused alongside the hedgerow, already bedecked with its strange assortment of tawdry soft toys and wilting flowers. A television reporter interviewed some passers-by in the village who said how dreadful it was, and how much Julie had been loved by everyone who knew her.

Then Julie's parents were put through the ordeal of a press conference. Her mother broke down and had to be escorted out, her personal tragedy played out under the relentless gaze of the cameras. Though I scarcely knew the Peacocks, the sight of her mother's grief brought tears to my own eyes. Murder casts a long shadow. In a week or two, the media would forget all about Julie Peacock, but while the rest of the world carried on with its affairs, life for her family would never be the same again. Murderers destroyed not one life but many, I thought.

Tentacles of suspicion encircled the village. Even today a rural community is small and enclosed, with inhabitants quick to point the finger. In Lasthwaite there seemed to be no shortage of suspects: people suddenly remembered rumours they had heard about Julie Peacock's father, who was said to have an uncertain temper. Then there was poor old Jim and Bob – the last survivors of a farming dynasty who had been thought 'tuppence short of a shilling' for generations. Mrs Metcalf's handicapped son came under a certain amount of suspicion, as did Luke Robinson, the boy who had previously caught the bus at the same stop as Julie, and was alleged to have been seen waiting for her there on various afternoons in the recent past.

Dr Millington, the newest arrival in our community, was also known to have been visited by detectives. He had been out and about on call that evening, and though the missing duty book had been recovered, his slapdash notes and the accompanying, indistinct Dictaphone tape did very little to establish a coherent alibi. Not that the police seriously suspected him. It was pre-Shipman and medics were still on a similar footing to the angels.

As for Rob, he had been right to assume that he too would be a suspect. In the days immediately following the murder, the police questioned him twice more. Not surprisingly, he was unsettled by this attention. His initial shock turned to frustration, beneath which I sensed a whole spectrum of emotions.

'Everything has changed,' he said one evening.

'Not for us,' I said.

'Yes – for us. Nothing is the same. After last Thursday you start to doubt everything.'

'You mustn't let it get to you,' I said.

'Last week I thought I had everything in the world I wanted. You were the final piece which . . . which completed my jigsaw.'

'So that's how you see me? Small and flat with a few nobbly bits?'

He grinned. 'I'm a geographer, not a poet. OK – you're the stamp that completes my collection—'

'Metaphors are getting even worse,' I said. 'Anyway, I'm still here. You're still here . . .'

'But it doesn't feel as though you're . . . well . . . safe any more.'

'Darling, I am perfectly safe. You're starting to sound like Maureen at work.'

'I just want you to know that I love you,' he said unexpectedly. 'I'll fight for you if necessary.'

He was looking out of the window when he spoke, as if in expectation of an invading horde. I had a sudden vision of him wrestling a wild-eyed assailant to the ground, moments before Jim and Bob panted up with their shotgun.

'Of course,' he turned to me with a grim smile, 'it might be a case of you fighting for me – starting when you have to come and bail me out. Do they grant bail in murder cases?'

'You won't be arrested. You're innocent.'

'Perhaps they'll ask me to do a DNA test or something like that,' he said.

'Well that would be all right,' I said. 'In fact, it would be a good thing. It would rule you out.'

'I don't know. You hear about these cases where the police plant evidence and fit people up.'

'Not really,' I said. 'They want to find the person who actually did it. What would be the point of framing you?'

'Crime statistics. It's another solved case, isn't it?'

'Don't be silly,' I said, but my tone carried no conviction.

I wondered if the police really were in the business of massaging the statistics. That was what Martin Bullock had been hinting at in his *Disappeared!* programme, and what at least one journalist had accused the authorities of, all those years ago when Antonia Bridgeman was murdered; now here was Rob, usually the most sensible of citizens, banging the same drum.

'You don't think it's me, do you?'

The question startled me. 'Of course not,' I exclaimed. 'Why on earth should I think it was you?'

'You might.' He paused, took a breath. 'Since the night Julie Peacock died you've been different.'

I didn't let him get any further. 'I'm not different. I'm the same. Exactly the same as I was before.' Before what? Aren't we all a little bit different every day? Isn't it true that our cells keep on breaking down and being replaced by new ones, so that after a certain number of years every bit has been regenerated. After seven years – or was it ten – you had become a completely new person.

'I might be suspended from school,' he said abruptly.

'Of course you won't be.' We've had this conversation before, I thought. We're going round in circles.

'The Head had me in today. She'd had a call from a parent. Someone who'd heard about what happened at my last school – goodness knows how.'

I had been fiddling with something in my bag, but I looked up at this, straight into his eyes.

'There was this other girl, you see. At my last school. The police will find out about the other girl too. It will be on my record.'

FOURTEEN

I had never been given to praying, but that night I prayed fervently that the police would solve the Julie Peacock case quickly: not just to get a dangerous individual locked up, nor to satisfy the bereaved family; not even just for Rob's sake, but for the good of the community at large. It was not the nervousness of the women (although requests for tranquillizers and sleeping pills at the practice were up). No, it was the parasitic suspicion implanted in people's minds, feeding and growing, singling people out – a virus which had the potential to poison us all, causing permanent long-term damage. The valley was positively rippling with rumours. People knew to whose doors the police had returned after the initial house-to-house enquiries had finished. There could be few secrets in a little community like ours.

People would start speculating, putting two and two together. Rob was a popular teacher but he was still an incomer and now someone had found out about an earlier investigation at his previous school. 'I should have told you about it before,' he said, though I saw no reason why he should. It was just a trivial episode from his past, explanations for which would never have arisen if it had not been for Julie Peacock.

It was a simple enough story: a teller of tall tales called Mandy Rudge had hinted to her school friends that she was having some sort of relationship with Mr Dugdale. She had shown them a cheap bottle of perfume which she claimed he had given to her. One of her friends had promptly spilled the beans to her mother, who had not hesitated to inform the school. Rob had been suspended with immediate effect while the allegations were investigated.

Though Mandy Rudge admitted that the whole story had been concocted to impress the other girls, and Rob was exonerated as entirely blameless, he decided it was best to move to another school, in another area, where gossip and speculation about his sudden mid-term 'leave' could not touch him. Even so, the story had caught up with him. You can sink the past with lead weights tied to each corner, but it still bobs back to the surface at the least opportune moment. It was not that the Head at the comp did not know about this episode – as Rob had said, it was on his record, rather she had called him in to tip him off that a local parent had somehow found out about it . . . and if one parent knew, that could lead to rumours circulating which 'might put the school in a difficult position'. A sabbatical of some kind might become necessary . . .

'The school,' Rob had repeated with a hollow laugh as he'd related the conversation to me. 'Let's not worry about the police's no-smoke-without-fire attitude to anyone who has ever been accused of anything, or the torch-lit vigilante procession heading down the road to drag me out of my place and string me up from the nearest tree.'

'People round here aren't like that,' I had said, but I knew it wasn't true. People were like that everywhere.

To be unjustly suspected is a horrible burden. With every day that passed, more and more people would be wondering, speculating about the killer in their midst. I knew all this because I had been through it all before. Girls had been disappearing in the Nicholsfield area over a period of almost a quarter of a century (although the fact that I was one of the most notable among them gave me more reason than most to think that talk of a serial killer might be a shade over dramatic). Statistically Nicholsfield might not have had any more women disappearing than other places of comparable size in middle England, but ever since the Marie Glover business a young woman disappearing in Nicholsfield tended to make the news.

Marie Glover vanished when I was ten years old. By the time Marie's name hit the headlines, she and her family were living on a new estate on the outskirts of town, but before that the Glovers had lived near the school where my father taught and Marie had been a pupil there. Although she was only fourteen Marie had a job, working for an hour every day after school at her uncle's shop. After work she always cycled home; a short journey, part of which took her along a country lane.

It was conjectured that when she reached the lane that afternoon she must have realized that she had a puncture and got off her bike to have a look.

By pure chance a police car was travelling down the lane about twenty minutes after Marie finished work at the shop, and the officers noticed her abandoned bicycle with its flat tyre propped against the hedge, but of Marie there was no sign.

The girl was reported missing and a huge search was mounted. My father was among the volunteers. Marie's body was found dumped four or five miles out of town.

For seemingly months, pictures of Marie were on show outside police stations and in post office windows. A mobile incident room was set up. A policewoman came into school to warn us children about taking lifts from strangers. Rumours ran around the playground about strange men following people home, sometimes in blue cars, sometimes in red; but gradually the excitement died down. Every so often something would happen to recall the story into the local news, but eventually the little grey caravan which had been the hub of the investigation closed down.

Interest in the fate of Marie Glover revived a couple of years later when another Nicholsfield girl went missing. She hailed from the council estate near the gas works and the general consensus was that she had run off to London, but with no positive sightings of her, alive or dead, rumours of a connection between the two persisted.

I was thirteen when Sally Walsh vanished. Sally was only three or four years older than me, and she too had been a pupil at that same primary school. I remember remarking on this to my father one evening while we were sitting at the dinner table, but he had not appeared at all interested, not even pausing in the act of forking a piece of fishcake into his mouth.

'She was, wasn't she?' I persisted until, having swallowed his fishcake and followed it with a sip of tea, he eventually said in a disinterested, non-committal way: 'It's entirely possible. Hundreds of children have passed through the school, Jennifer. I cannot possibly recall every name.'

'Get on with your tea, Jennifer,' my mother said. 'Before it goes cold.'

My mother would never come right out and remonstrate with me for introducing such an alarming subject as murder to the tea table, but she would certainly have done her best to divert the discussion elsewhere at the first possible opportunity, working on her usual premise that unpleasantness, if ignored, would go away.

Unlike my mother, I couldn't banish things from my mind so easily. I spent a good deal of time after that pondering uncomfortable possibilities. If anyone were going to accept a lift from a trusted person already known to them, wouldn't their old headmaster present an ideal candidate?

Marie Glover had been abducted at around a quarter to five in the afternoon – a time when a lot of men were still at work. Unemployment was less common then and my father's working day finished long before most men's did. He had a motor car, when so many people were still restricted to buses and trains. He had a blameless character and would never be suspected. He had known two of the missing girls. More crucially, they had known him and would hardly have refused his offer of a lift.

I didn't know what to do. Ought I go to the police? Perhaps find some way to tip them off anonymously? For several weeks, I was in a state of feverish inner turmoil. I had no special friend in whom to confide my suspicions. No one with whom I could talk things through.

In the event nothing more was heard of Sally Walsh either. She slid out of the local papers and into Martin Bullock's legions of missing persons.

Three months after Alan and I got married, another young woman was murdered. She was not actually from Nicholsfield, but from Banbury, which was a good forty miles away. It had been almost ten years since the Marie Glover murder and there was probably no connection. Just the same, I felt a familiar prickle of unease when I realized, on piecing things together, that my father had not been at home on the evening when the girl died.

My father was not at all the sort of person to attract anyone's suspicions. The traditional perception of a man who stalks and kills little girls or young women is not a married man with a respectable career and a nice house in the suburbs. In plays and films such men are inevitably slightly sinister characters who usually live somewhere seedy. Everyone from playwrights to 'criminal profilers' underscored the theory that the type of men who raped and murdered young women were misfits and loners – those were the kind of men at whom the finger of suspicion inevitably pointed. Yet I wondered . . . how about successful killers, the ones who never got caught? Perhaps like the weather forecast, these perceptions were generally right, but sometimes dangerously and spectacularly wrong. Suppose the killer was actually a pillar of the community, quietly watching from the sidelines while everyone else dashed about in search of dangerous loners?

'Loner' was not an expression people would readily have applied to my father. He would certainly not have used the word himself, in all likelihood dismissing it as modern slang. Yet in many ways my father had been a loner. It was true that the church had been packed to capacity at his funeral. There were ex-colleagues, numerous acquaintances from the circle of people with whom, for the sake of his wife's social pretensions, he occasionally joined for dinner dances, cheese and wine or charity luncheons. His wife's family and an assortment of neighbours from Orchard Lane had turned out in force, but not one person attended whom my father would have named as a close personal friend.

There was, of course, nothing sinister or suspicious in this. Many men must live lives devoid of real friendships. It is possible that other people imagined us a close family, hidden away by the hedges and conifer trees, sufficient unto ourselves. They had no way of knowing that behind the evergreens each of us lived in their own separate invisible boxes, never quite reaching out to touch one another.

Some children manage to get close to their parents by sharing in their enthusiasms, but in this I faced a particular difficulty, because the fact was that my father had no interests. His dismissal of popular music in favour of the classics never led him to attend concerts or purchase recordings. It was perhaps not so much that he liked this music himself, but rather that he felt it was the kind of music a headmaster ought to promote.

Similarly, though he counselled me against reading what he chose to dismiss as 'trash', his gold-embossed copies of Dickens, Austen and Hardy lay untouched on the shelves, save for the attentions of my mother's feather duster. He pruned and weeded and marched solemnly to and fro behind the lawnmower, but his interest in the garden extended only to the achievement of tidiness and symmetry. Not for him the heady joys of cultivation: so far as I could discern, the fragrances and colours of the seasons left him unmoved.

Neatness and order were the watchwords of my father's life. The daily ritual of shoe cleaning, the weekly polishing of the car. Perhaps the influence of his time in the army was strong. Certainly this careful turnout of himself and everything associated with him (even the brushes and jar of hair cream on his chest of drawers stood symmetrical and to attention, awaiting an inspection which never came) engaged a great deal of his time.

There were also the periods spent in his study. I would sit on the semi-circular steps leading into the garden, engrossed in Noel Streatfield or Arthur Ransome while my father remained behind the closed French doors, engaged in I knew not what, seemingly oblivious to the sunshine. Coupled with his being neither a drinker nor a smoker, my father's lack of hobbies made him a very difficult person when it came to buying presents, so I was relieved when one Christmas he expressed the desire for a paperweight to adorn his desk. One of the antique shops near The Market Square had a display of paperweights in the window and I went inside to have a closer look. The man in the shop was informative and charming, playfully insisting that he would only let me buy the paperweight of my choice if I accepted an invitation to join him for dinner.

I was thrilled and flattered. An invitation to dinner from a man I judged to be at least seven or eight years older than me symbolized the equivalent of an entrée to the jet-set. Thus it was that I encountered Alan and was, from the very first moment, completely in awe of him. By the time I met him he was not only conducting a thriving business through his shop but also taking commissions to furnish rooms, or even whole

houses, seeking out ornamental lamps and fire irons for people
too rich, busy or lazy to source these things for themselves.

He already had a house of his own: a detached Victorian
villa which he took me to see at an early stage in our relationship. A virgin still, I'd half hoped this excursion would be the
front for an opportunity to hop me on to his brass bedstead,
but he had restricted himself to no more than an arm around
my shoulders, his purpose genuinely that I might admire his
Victorian watercolours and a fire screen, hand-embroidered
with pansies.

That someone with acknowledged expertise in any field
could find something to admire in a person so ordinary and
dull as myself seemed well-nigh incredible. Alan had a car
and paid for things by credit card, which represented the height
of sophistication in the mid-nineteen seventies. He treated me
with deferential care and in the beginning I was flattered by
it. It is impossible to say precisely when I began to feel suffocated by it. Initially I saw only the charms and none of the
constraints. All this went down incredibly well with my parents.
In particular with my mother, who said Alan was 'such a
gentleman' and predicted that 'he will take good care of
Jennifer' as though it was tacitly understood that I could never
be expected to take care of myself. When my boyfriend of a
few months produced an engagement ring (genuine Victorian
setting, of course) both my parents appeared to be delighted.

It seemed to me then that I must love Alan. He was clever
and interesting and successful. I am ashamed to say that I was
absurdly proud to be the prospective mistress of the period
home he had lovingly created. I didn't realize that he was
constructing another invisible box for me. It was kindly done.
Whereas my father's unfulfilled academic expectations had
weighed heavily upon me, Alan's loving care held fewer
obvious challenges. He never minded that I couldn't grasp the
principals of dating chairs, nor remember the simplest of
hallmarks. 'That's my department,' he would say. 'You be
yourself.'

Except, of course, that wasn't what he meant at all. He
wanted me to be the self that he thought I was. He wanted
the rather vulnerable, dependant girl, the gauche, not quite

grown-up Jenny – naïve and innocent. At work I obtained practice manager's certification and swept my efficient broom into every corner of the medical centre, but at home I could never be trusted to make a major decision for myself. Alan's love was stifling. His concern and watchfulness made me nervous. I became like a fly, trapped in the spider's silken threads, but while I thrashed, silent and helpless, Alan always remained calm, always knew what was best. Some couples have an enormous age difference and it matters not a jot, but our eight years was a gulf – an ever-widening chasm. Alan's maturity versus my regression into childhood.

Escape seemed the only answer and running away the only means of escape, but this constituted an admission which at first I could barely make to myself. It meant that I did not love Alan after all. Had it all been an innocent mistake, or did it mean that for me it had always been a sham? Accustomed to accepting blame, I concluded that it must have been the latter. It was unforgivable and I knew that I would have to carry the guilt forever.

FIFTEEN

On the night of Julie Peacock's funeral I lay awake, watching the passage of clouds across the moon through the slit where the curtains did not meet, trying to stave off my instinctive, restless movements so as not to disturb Rob, whose steady breathing sounded beside me as regular as the ticking of Aunt Millicent's metronome.

The entire village had turned out to pay their respects to the dead girl and her family, many packing into the church and others lining the main street and either side of the Green as the coffin went by. I had joined the rest of the staff in standing out on the pavement at the front of the health centre, our normal work briefly suspended. In the afternoon the event had inevitably been the subject of discussion in the common room. The Tragedy Queen (who had naturally taken time off to attend the service itself) thoroughly approved of the sermon and hymn selection, while noting regretfully that things were not what they used to be, when every curtain along the route would have been drawn, all shops and businesses closed and shuttered for the duration.

The Trollop disagreed, dismissing the closing of curtains as old fashioned and mawkish. 'People have different ways of showing solidarity nowadays. You should have seen the number who turned out last night to help with the food for the funeral buffet in the church hall. Me and our Ellen must have cut five loaves of ham sandwiches – they'll all go, mind. That Dentwhistle lot can down a plate of sausage rolls before you can blink.'

The Tragedy Queen looked a bit ruffled at this, perhaps sensing some implied criticism in her own lack of participation in the catering, but the Trollop had already segued into slightly different subject matter, saying, 'Pat Metcalf was buttering next to me – you know, Doctor Milly is lodging with her – and she said she reckons his girlfriend has thrown him over. She only found out by accident 'cause she asked him, casual like, when she was serving his breakfast the other day, if the girl was coming up again soon, as she hadn't seen anything of her since that first time, and Doctor Milly said something like, "Oh, you won't be seeing anything of her again, I'm afraid", and Pat said he looked right down in the mouth about it.'

'Your life's not your own when you lodge at Pat Metcalf's,' reproved Helen, the receptionist. 'She told me that the police had been back to question him about the murder again – honestly! As if a nice young doctor would be mixed up in something like that.'

I found myself wondering how much they talked about Rob and myself when I was not around. Over the last few days Rob had repeatedly speculated that other people apart from the police might suspect him, and though I tried to reassure him, I sensed that there was something more behind his words, something he could not bring himself to articulate: that perhaps it was not the doubts and suspicions of our neighbours he feared, but someone much closer. I was acutely aware of my failure to support and reassure him as I should have done. Yet when I tried to find words which underlined the bond between us, I was constantly brought up short by my own duplicity. Every profession of confidence sounded hollow to me, because I knew that underneath my assurances of mutual trust there lay a rippling pool of deceit.

These uncomfortable thoughts always came into their own on sleepless nights, lying awake with a door at the back of my mind ajar and dark thoughts slipping one by one into the open, like wisps of smoke stealing out of a burning building, precursors of worse to come. At three in the morning it wasn't difficult to believe that I was to blame for everything. Close contact with me seemed to bring people nothing but unhappiness.

To make matters worse, it seemed lately that every line of conversation led inexorably to a sign marked red for danger. Subjects which began innocently could unexpectedly lead into a minefield. The forthcoming school concert was a case in

point, causing Rob to ask me, apropos of nothing in particular:
'You didn't ever play in your school orchestra, did you?'

He was sprawled comfortably in the armchair nearest the
window, his long legs almost reaching the fireplace, stretching
and flexing his arms, almost as if to emphasise the casual
nature of the query, but I felt myself stiffen – I was afraid I
knew what direction we were about to go in.

'Not me. I'm not a bit musical.'

'You had piano lessons from your auntie.'

I tried not to be fazed. 'Only when I was little. I don't think
I really wanted to learn. I'd probably never have gone if the
piano teacher hadn't been a friend of my mum's.' Hoping to
divert him, I asked, 'Did you ever play anything?'

'No, I wasn't interested.' He grinned. 'I wanted to be a
scientist, so I used to get those junior chemistry sets for
Christmas. Little test tubes and crystals that turned purple
when you warmed them up.'

'So what went wrong, Professor Beaker?'

'Oh, it was totally different at school. No purple crystals at
all. Loads of theorems and equations and stuff. I might have
been better off learning the piano, but then, my mum never
had a friend who was a music teacher.'

I just smiled at him.

'Sue,' he said suddenly. 'You do trust me, don't you?'

'Of course I do.' I was across the room in a moment, kneeling
in front of him, holding him tightly. 'I love you,' I said, the
words muffled by being spoken into his chest. 'You have no
idea how much I love you.'

We held each other close, but the moment was tempered
by a nagging sense that something trembled in the air above
us. A question unasked and unanswered.

Now, as I lay beside him in the early hours, I replayed the
conversation over and over in my head until it became stale
and sour: his questioning of my trust and my inability to
convince him of it. Was it just my imagination, or was there
a Grand Canyon of doubt opening up between us? Well, it
was me who must bear the responsibility for that. I was the
one holding something back, the one teetering on the high
wire, one false step away from falling into Niagara.

Disappeared! had made me paranoid. Lately I had developed a theory that while local people probably accepted me at face value because they thought they 'knew' I was Susan and therefore could not be Jennifer, strangers represented a different kind of danger, because to them I did not have a firmly defined identity and therefore could be anyone at all. I had all but shielded my face when a man came to read the gas meter. And when no immediate danger presented itself, I managed to conjure one up, imagining a situation in which one of my aunt Felicity's grown-up children, last heard of living in Yorkshire, decided to bring their teenage children out for a walk in the Dales. Suppose they came through the village and recognized me? I might once have reassured myself that that our previous encounters had been so infrequent as to render mutual recognition most unlikely, but with my anxiety levels at high alert, my long-lost Yorkshire cousins were just one more item on a growing list of dangerous possibilities.

After a night of insomnia I spent most of Saturday feeling like a zombie, but a solid night's rest put me right and when I rose the next day it was to a familiar lazy Sunday morning: the coffee pot, the toast, newspapers spread across the sitting room, jeans and bare feet, a happy disarray. Daylight, normality, routine. Rob seemed relaxed, his usual self, and my improved mood matched itself to his. Outside it was a typical Dales day, rain whispering against the window panes, everything beyond the glass blurred and uncertain. They had never filmed *All Creatures Great and Small* on days like this.

Rob was sitting in his favourite chair in front of the window and I was in the act of collecting up our plates, being careful not to tip any toast crumbs on to the floor. I had got as far as the kitchen doorway when he spoke unexpectedly.

'Jennifer.'

I swung round involuntarily. He was smiling, a funny, triumphant kind of smile. I stood absolutely still, conscious of the colour draining from my face. My fingers were pinching the plates so hard that they might have left a permanent imprint.

'Jennifer,' he repeated. 'I knew it would come to me.'

'What? What are you talking about?' I could barely force the words out.

'Jennifer Dunwood. A girl who used to be at the comp a few years ago. Her brother was the speedway rider. We were trying to remember her name in the staffroom on Friday afternoon, and none of us could.'

I continued to stare at him.

'Sorry, love,' he said. 'Did I startle you? You know how it is when you can't for the life of you remember something, then it comes into your head out of the blue, just when you're thinking about something completely different.'

'Yes,' I said weakly.

I retreated into the kitchen as quickly as my trembling legs would take me. My hands were shaking as I put the plates down on the draining board. I took several deep breaths, running some water into the sink to buy time. It had been a horrible shock. The automatic reaction of years which had surfaced right on cue. Somehow I had to go back into the sitting room and pretend that nothing had happened, which it hadn't – not for him. I had to keep on reminding myself of that. It had been a horrible jolt, but he hadn't noticed. Well, hardly noticed. He hadn't followed me out into the kitchen, so he couldn't have realized how upset I was.

Then I heard him going into the bathroom. I went back into the sitting room and took *The Sunday Times Magazine* into the window seat, ready to be suitably immersed in something when he returned. Minutes passed. Out of curiosity, I glanced across at the page he had been reading, which was folded open on the arm of his chair. I could read the headline without moving: Clairvoyant Gives Police New Lead in Jennifer Reynolds Case.

There was a muffled sound of plumbing in action, followed by the bathroom door opening. I sprang back behind my magazine.

'Tell you what,' said Rob from the doorway, 'I'll wash these bits and pieces up and we'll go down to the pub for our lunch. You haven't got anything special in, have you?'

'No – lovely – great . . . I'll get some shoes on.'

From the kitchen came the sound of water splashing into

the sink and a burst of pop music as he turned on the radio. Aretha Franklin. Why that particular song, at that particular instant? Of course those weren't really the words, but it always sounded as though she was singing, 'Who's fooling who?'

SIXTEEN

If Rob noticed that I was quieter than usual over lunch, he gave no sign. We had both ordered the traditional Sunday roast, but while Rob tucked in with gusto, I regretted my folly the moment I saw the size of the portions. There seemed to be a lot of strangers eating in the pub that day, and I wondered if the macabre attraction of driving past the murder site was bumping up the number of visitors.

I had managed to slip into a corner seat at a table where I could be inconspicuous, penned in on two sides by walls and on the third by a high-backed settle, which hid me from the adjacent diners. At the table immediately behind us, a newly arrived group were discussing their order. Though invisible, their voices carried. 'So you're the sausage.' It was a woman's voice, overloud, perhaps to compensate for the deafness of a companion. She had the kind of flat northern accent and elongated vowels which are a gift to comedians. 'Aileen is the cottage pie? No – wait . . . Oh, sorry – Aileen is a steak and mushroom pie, you're a sausage and I'm a jacket potato.'

Rob caught my eye, conveying in a look the vision of a jacket potato, complete with handbag and plastic mac.

'Stop it,' I hissed, half convulsed. 'Behave, or when you grow up you'll turn into a sausage too.'

'I'd rather be a steak,' he said. 'Mean and lean and medium rare.'

I glanced down at my plate, where the gravy was beginning to congeal. 'To the French we're all *les rosbifs*,' I said.

'Didn't you say that you've never been to France?' he asked. 'Why don't we go this summer? We could drive over and tour around Normandy.'

'Mmm,' I said, feeling my new-found relaxation ebbing away. 'Sounds lovely.'

'You don't sound very enthusiastic. Had you got something else in mind?'

'No, nothing at all.' The unexpected mention of driving in France had thrown me completely off balance, conjuring an instant vision of the open-topped car and the doomed lovers, bringing a flapping mass of black crow worries straight back into my head.

'It was just a thought,' he said. 'It would be nice to get away this summer, but maybe we'd do better to hold out for a last-minute bargain instead. Josie at school got a package to Crete last year, absolutely knock-down price, and when they got there it was a villa with a private pool. They had a great time. Walked the Samaria Gorge, went to Knossos . . .'

I nodded while trying to think of something to say which didn't include the words 'don't have a passport'.

'Trouble is,' he continued, 'I suppose you could just as easily end up on top of the local disco.'

'Probably better not to risk it,' I said. How did passport records work? Did they keep a list of distinguishing features, such as *mole on left cheek*?

'You're not in a very optimistic mood. Where's your sense of adventure – your gambler's streak?'

'It would be just my luck to end up on top of the local disco.'

'So what would your dream destination be?' he asked.

'I'm not sure.' Photographs. They must keep your last photograph. By no stretch of the imagination could I ever pass as the original Susan McCarthy.

'Go on. Everyone has somewhere. Suppose money was no object: where would you really like to go?'

I forked in another lump of cold roast potato, playing for time while I pretended to consider this. A sudden panicky thought advanced from the back of my mind. Suppose Rob had a nest egg and having ascertained my dream destination, secretly bought the tickets and presented me with them as a wonderful surprise? I had never thought about getting a passport. Passports usually lasted for ten years. Would hers even have expired yet? I attempted some frantic mental calculations.

'Come on,' he coaxed, cutting in on my thoughts and making me lose count. 'There must be somewhere you've always wanted to go.'

'Australia,' I said. It came to me in a flash that being the other side of the world, Australia would be the most logistically difficult, to say nothing of expensive, surprises to spring.

His smile broadened. 'That's amazing. I've always wanted to go to Australia. You knew, didn't you? That's why you said it.'

'No, honestly.' I affected to be as immensely pleased as he was over this newly discovered mutual interest in all things Antipodean. 'I had no idea you wanted to go. You've never mentioned it before.' And if you had, I certainly wouldn't have done.

'What do you want to see most?'

Now I was in trouble. Fancy even trying to bluff to a geography teacher. What had I been thinking?

'Everything,' I said, airily. 'All the usual tourist stuff, of course: Ayers Rock, the Opera House . . . kangaroos . . .' I gestured vaguely, as if to encompass such a breadth of common ground that there was no need to enunciate it.

'Do you think we might be able to afford it,' he asked, 'when we pool our resources?' He looked so keen. His face always lit up when an idea grabbed him. It made him look younger, and as vulnerable to disappointment as a kid about to learn that his birthday treat has been cancelled.

'We could get rid of all our duplicate saucepans and toasters and stuff like that at a car boot sale,' I said, faking enthusiasm. 'That ought to raise a bit of extra cash.'

'If only our numbers would come up on the pools,' he said. 'I could whisk you away tomorrow.'

'But there's about twenty of you in the syndicate.' I tried not to sound too pleased about it.

'It would have to be a very big win.'

'Very big.'

'If only I'd been a stockbroker instead of a teacher.'

'But you can't add up.'

'Probably not such a handicap in these days of calculators,' he said.

'And anyway, you'd hate being a stockbroker. You like being a teacher.'

'Not on a Sunday afternoon, when I've still got books to

mark and lessons to prepare and I'd much rather take you back to bed – which, sadly, does remind me . . .'

'I know.' I smiled. 'Come on, we'd better make a move. I can't eat any more of this and anyway, it's gone cold.'

I didn't trust myself to so much as glance in the direction of the newspapers until Rob had collected his things and gone home. Jennifer Dunwood – an ex-pupil? It was plausible. Everyone has those lapses of memory when they simply can't remember a name, followed by the triumphant recall of the missing information often hours or even days later – inspiration provided by some unrelated reminder.

Or had it been a test? Had he called out the name Jennifer to see how I would react? To see whether I would automatically answer to this unexpected, yet compelling appellation? I kept remembering the expression on his face when I spun round. Delight that his ruse had worked? Or merely pleased that he had solved a niggling query? The newspaper headline could easily have provided the prompt – the name Jennifer leaping up at him from the page, giving his memory the jog it needed to remember the name of the speedway rider's sister.

Had Rob seen that wretched programme on the television? I had assumed not, but I didn't dare ask him, because if I did he would be sure to ask why I was interested, and there was no point drawing his attention to it unnecessarily. Until recently he had never shown any sign of being suspicious. The doppelgänger episode at his mother's had gone completely unremarked. The business about the music lessons had been unfortunate, but I was pretty confident his interest in that topic had waned. It was one of our jokes that he couldn't add up. How many clues did it take to arrive at an equation where Susan equals Jennifer?

Once he had gone home I was finally able to investigate the headline which had been fizzing in the back of my mind for the previous two hours. The item disturbed me profoundly. The accompanying photograph was a rather grainy reproduction of the same old wedding picture. The text made a reasonable stab at relating the known facts about my disappearance, although it got my age wrong and erroneously stated that Alan worked in a museum. There was nothing much there which could obviously be linked to me, but coming hard on the heels of *Disappeared!* it provided another unwelcome bit of publicity for what had, until now, been a largely forgotten case – and as I read on, I realized that I had Martin Bullock and his team to thank because, immediately after watching the programme, a 'well-known West Country Psychic' claimed to have been on the receiving end of some sort of vision concerning Jennifer Reynolds's whereabouts and had contacted the police to tell them all about it. The police would only say, rather cagily, that the clairvoyant had been in touch with them. 'Any new information we receive will be followed up,' a police spokesperson was quoted as saying.

The clairvoyant, one Stan Butters of Glastonbury, had given a long interview to the newspaper, explaining that he had a record of helping the police, particularly in the matter of locating missing bodies. According to Mr Butters, he had seen my body taken from the boot of a car and dumped in a lake, and he thought that if he were allowed to hold an item which had once belonged to me – something of a 'personal nature' – he would be able to pinpoint the precise stretch of water on a map, enabling the police to go off and search in exactly the right spot.

'Dream on, Stan,' I said, aloud, but I shuddered in spite of myself.

I went to bed early again that night and soon fell into a deep sleep, but the clairvoyant's pronouncements must have stayed with me, for I had a strange, vivid dream. I was swimming beneath the surface of a dark green pool and everywhere I looked there were girls' faces staring back at me: Marie Glover, pale and smiling, just like the picture outside the police station; Antonia Bridgeman with her music still clutched in one hand; and other girls, girls in Victorian frocks with enormous hair ribbons, girls who had stepped out of their frames on the walls of the staircase and come to bathe in the depths of this huge viridescent pond, all of them circling, closing in on me.

Frightened now, I tried to swim away. The surface shimmered above me. Sun and air. I forged upwards, but my hair had grown long again, the way it used to be, and it was spreading out in the water, becoming entangled with the long hair streaming out from all the other girls who crowded around me, like pale strands of water weed, skeins and skeins of it, knotting with mine, trapping me and holding me down. My breath was running out. I was suffocating, drowning down there in the shadowy depths.

I awoke with a little cry. It echoed around the silent bedroom, before vanishing into the dark. The sky was overcast and there was no moon.

SEVENTEEN

Monday brought a deviation from the usual routine. Moira, one of our longest-serving receptionists, was celebrating her sixtieth birthday, so as well as the usual cards and cakes there was a small retirement presentation after work. The entire staff packed into the common room for a short speech from Dr McLeary, followed by Dr Woods flamboyantly popping some bottles of indifferent sparkling wine. Afterwards there was a meal at The Bull, where two big tables had been laid for us, complete with party poppers and unseasonal Christmas crackers, which created some forced laughter amid jokes about the imminent appearance of Father Christmas.

My role within the practice compelled me to participate in events such as these, but I didn't really enjoy them, because they always reminded me that my sense of belonging was a chimera. All the other women had long-standing connections with the dale: ties of blood, marriage or a shared schooling. No name thrown up in conversation was liable to be unfamiliar to any of them. They were not unkind or obvious about it, but it was there all the same, so I was glad when Terry Millington, fellow incomer and usurper of the practice newbie role, took the seat opposite mine. However, as the meal progressed I realized that he was talking relatively little and drinking rather a lot. I found myself hoping that he wasn't on the rota to pick up out of hours calls that night.

On occasions such as these we all did our best not to talk shop, but with the biggest item of local gossip firmly off the table (murder and birthdays don't mix), the conversation at our end of the table had begun to flag by the time we were eating our desserts.

Suddenly, as if gripped by a bright idea, the Trollop turned to me and said: 'I were reading about that practice manager who disappeared in the Midlands, Susan, and I wondered if you ever came across her, you know, at a meeting or a conference or owt?'

I momentarily considered pretending not to know who she was talking about, and decided against. 'Not knowingly,' I said. 'I mean, she might have been to some of the big area meetings. I was at a practice in Coventry at one time and Nicholsfield – that's where she used to live, isn't it? – is only about thirty miles away.'

'She's one of those people with a very ordinary sort of face,' the Trollop mused. 'Not especially memorable.'

I toyed with the last spoonful of my sticky toffee pudding, before realizing that shoving it into my mouth would provide a perfect excuse not to reply.

'Did you see that programme about it the other night?' asked the Trainspotter. 'I recognized that actress in the reconstruction. She's been in *Coronation Street . . .* and *Casualty.*'

I masticated steadily as the pudding turned to pap in my mouth. This was it. The conversation I had always dreaded, happening right here, right now. The excessive sweetness of the pudding began to tickle the back of my throat. In a minute I was going to have a coughing fit and spray a mush of semi-digested sticky toffee slush all over the table.

'I didn't watch all of it,' the Trollop said. 'It was on the same night that Julie . . .' she glanced down the table, but Moira and everyone else at that end were completely immersed in some other topic, '. . . you know . . . our Keith had been out searching, and I went into the kitchen to get him some supper when he came back in.'

I managed to swallow the sweet, pulpy stuff remnants without incident and took a gulp of water.

'I think she's been on *Emmerdale* as well,' the Trainspotter continued to muse. 'Tell you what, Susan, you look a bit like her.'

I attempted nonchalance. 'Like who?' Was it a trap? Were the two of them testing me out? I didn't think they were subtle enough to have bided their time then concocted a two-pronged attack like this, but who knew what they got up to in Medical Records when they were supposed to be working?

'That actress who's been in *Emmerdale.*'

'And *Coronation Street* . . . and *Casualty,*' Dr Millington put in. His tone was mischievous and he was trying to catch my eye, share in a joke, but who was the butt of it?

'Only in certain ways, of course.' The Trainspotter had caught his expression too and appeared to be ruffled. Maureen was in awe of all the doctors and hated the idea that one of them might be laughing at her, particularly for some reason she could not understand.

'You get these likenesses, don't you?' the Trollop put in. 'Our Joe's boy was the spit of David Essex at one time – you know, when he was younger – but he grew out of it. Doesn't look a bit like him now.'

'Everybody's supposed to have a double,' the Trainspotter remarked. 'Though I must say, I pity mine, whoever she is. Is coffee included in the price, do you remember? Mind, I don't want coffee, I want a cup of tea.'

'I'd rather have tea an all,' agreed the Trollop.

'I'll go up to the bar, shall I, and see about it?' The Trainspotter pushed her chair back and heaved herself to her feet.

And that's it, I thought. Bomb defused. Panic over. Maureen doesn't think I look like Jennifer Reynolds, she thinks the actress playing Jennifer Reynolds looks a bit like me. Of course they don't think I'm Jennifer Reynolds, because that would be ridiculous, far-fetched, extreme. Someone who's mentioned in a TV documentary doesn't turn up on your doorstep in Lasthwaite any more than your numbers come up on the pools or Michael Caine drops into the pub for a pie and a pint. These things happen to other people. You don't seriously expect them to happen to you. You don't seriously remark on a likeness because you think your colleague is a mystery woman, leading a double life. You dismiss it as a coincidence, because coincidences – unlike Michael Caine dropping in to the local pub – happen all the time.

'They won't find that missing practice manager anyway,' Helen, sitting on the other side of me and previously silent, cut in on my thoughts, 'because she'll be long dead by now. That's what the chappy was saying in the papers.'

'Aye,' said the Trollop. 'There's always some poor lass copping it somewhere.'

The group fell silent, no doubt remembering one poor lass in particular.

'So . . . how many wants coffee and how many tea?' asked Maureen.

After that the conversation turned to more cheerful matters: forthcoming holidays and how long each of them had to go before retirement. Any mention at all of the dreaded TV programme and my resemblance to the actress in the reconstruction, and therefore by definition to the missing woman herself, ought to have shaken me, but I left the pub feeling elated. I had done it. I had changed my appearance just enough. No one suspected. I was safe. As I drove home I experienced a lightness of heart which I hadn't known in weeks.

I drove past Rosecroft, where a light was showing behind a grubby downstairs window pane, pulled up outside Heb's Cottage and let myself in. Not knowing how long Moira's 'do' would go on for, I hadn't arranged to see Rob that evening, and it struck me that it would be very nice to have a long, lazy bath, complete with fancy oils and scented candles, and maybe a glass of wine while I lay soaking. Indulgence won out. I paused to go through the mail before heading upstairs to undress, and one bath later I was back upstairs and had just finished drying my hair when the doorbell rang. The sound of his car must have been drowned out by the hairdryer, but I knew it would be Rob, come to surprise me, so I barely secured my dressing gown before I ran downstairs and flung open the door.

Surprise crackled through me like an electric shock.

Terry Millington leered at me from the doorstep. 'Evening,' he said. 'Can I come in?'

He stepped forward decisively as he spoke and I automatically stepped back to make way for him, one hand on the door and the other dragging my dressing gown further together, conscious of my near nakedness and his unexpected proximity.

He strode confidently into the sitting room then turned to face me, his back to the fireplace. 'Well, well,' he said. 'It's very quiet up here, isn't it?'

Even from a few feet away, I could smell the drink on his

breath. There had been a couple of previous occasions when he had appeared for morning surgery looking suspiciously the worse for wear – something which I assumed the doctors would have flagged up – but if any of them had had a word with him about his alcohol consumption there was no sign that it had taken effect.

'I . . . look . . . it's not a very good time. What do you want?'

He gave me a silly, sideways look as he said, 'Funny place for a woman to live. You must get lonely up here, all on your own.'

Oh my God, what was this? Was he coming on to me? Surely not. I was at least ten years his age. He must have known that I had a regular boyfriend – or did he? How well attuned was he to the local grapevine? He had a room at Pat Metcalf's, but how much notice would he have taken of her running commentary on local affairs? I adjusted my dressing gown so that it was no more revealing than my normal working attire, but I still felt very exposed. He carried on standing there, grinning stupidly at me, clearly poised on that level of intoxicated recklessness that can lead almost anywhere. There had to be a way of defusing the situation without embarrassment. My job, my precious security – I couldn't afford to slap him down and thereby make an enemy of him. Even half-baked GP trainees could be surprisingly dangerous. How could I, in any case? He hadn't really said anything to be slapped down about.

'If there's something you want to discuss,' I said, 'then we can do it in the office, tomorrow.'

His face took on a mischievous expression. 'What I've got in mind isn't suitable for a discussion in the office.'

He's really, really drunk, I thought. His voice had become a drawl, with a hint of an accent that I couldn't quite place – something he'd managed to lose at uni, I supposed, suppressing it so as not to betray common origins.

'Nice little dinner we all had this evening,' he said, his eyes never leaving my face. 'All very friendly. Not so friendly now. No offer of a drink.'

'I told you, it's not a good time.'

'Nice little chat. Film . . . TV programmes . . . actresses . . . actresses who look like you.'

He could not fail to take in my sharp intake of breath.

'Went back to my digs, after the pub. Not much else to do round here, is there? I was on duty the night they showed that programme. Taped it, though. Hadn't got round to watching, but I fast forwarded to the bit with the actress . . . the one who looks like you.'

He left the words hanging in the air, but when I said nothing, he continued: 'Wonder what you'd be willing to do to stop too many people making that connection?'

I gripped the lapels of my dressing gown together. I couldn't decide what he meant, what he might be threatening. A particularly awful scenario began to suggest itself, in which I could imagine myself having to explain how it was that he came to be inside my home in the first place; defend myself against the accusation that I had encouraged him, led him on. Except that I knew there couldn't be any defending myself, any complaint or accusation. Susan McCarthy could not take a colleague to court, because Susan McCarthy was dead. He could do with me whatever he chose and I could not risk saying a word. Did he know that? Had he really discovered my secret and decided to take advantage of it? Or could I talk him out of it? Persuade him that he was mistaken? I had mentally configured many scenarios in which someone recognized or challenged me, but none of them had ever panned out quite like this. I glanced down at my feet and wondered if I was going to be sick.

The doorbell sounded so loudly in the confined space of my tiny hall that I gave a little scream. Terry Millington appeared equally startled. I spun round and opened the door.

It was Jim Fox, his purplish-red complexion awash with worry beneath his shiny cap. 'Beg pardon, but Bob was going down t'lane in t'Land Rover and saw yon car parked outside yours. Didn't recognize un and thought t'were a bit funny like. Took a bit of a liberty, comin' up to see as all's well.'

'Oh, thank you, Jim.' I felt like throwing my arms around his neck. 'Will you come in? It's Doctor Millington's car. He called in unexpectedly . . . to ask me if I've got a spare set of keys for the surgery.'

Clearly taken aback by my attire, Jim looked even more
embarrassed than usual. 'Aye,' he said, backing away from
the door. 'Doctor Millington's car. I know it now. Bob
should've recognized it an all. Very sorry . . .'

'No, no. You did the right thing. Thank you – thank you
very much.' I stepped back invitingly, willing him to enter.
'Please, come in.'

But Jim was already turning away. ·

'Thank you,' I called helplessly after his retreating form
and received a raised arm in return as he headed back down
the lane. I stood on the step, trying to come up with a plausible
reason for calling Jim back, or even running after him, but
what could I say? My colleague has menaced me by mentioning
my resemblance to a television actress and asking if he could
stay for a drink?'

I reluctantly closed the door and turned back to face the
sitting room, where my visitor was still standing with his back
to the fireplace, smiling at me; a knowing smile, like a captor
who enjoys a joke at the hapless prisoner's expense before
tying him on the rack.

'Of course,' I said, taking care to retain as much distance
between us as possible when I re-entered the sitting room,
'Jim and Bob are the eyes and ears of the world. I expect the
fact that your car was seen parked outside my cottage will be
all over the pub by ten o'clock this evening.'

I looked him in the eye, hoping the import of my words
had sunk in. He was a young doctor hoping to go into general
practice, for goodness' sake. He couldn't afford to have
rumours of impropriety circulating around the district.

'Jim or Bob always come up to have a last look round at
night, too,' I lied. 'I didn't ask them to but since Julie Peacock
was killed they've started checking up on me. It's very sweet
of them.'

Among the banshee panics screaming through my mind was
the thought that Dr Millington had been the on-call doctor on
the evening Julie died, and that he had no alibi, but he didn't
react when I mentioned her name, just continued to regard me
speculatively before saying, 'Plenty of time for a drink before
then.'

I didn't know what to do. One part of me just wanted him to go away, but I knew that locking the door on him solved nothing. Had he worked it out? Or maybe it was just a fishing expedition? How was I to know? What on earth was I going to do?

'A nice little drink and a chat . . . about actresses.'

He made as if to take a seat, but missed his footing and had to grab the back of the chair for support before pulling himself upright. He was further gone than I thought.

'You've had quite enough to drink.' I recognized that sharp, reproving voice. I had never realized before that I could sound just like my mother. 'I suggest you drive home very carefully. If you leave now, we can both try to forget this ever happened.'

A look of uncertainty crossed his face for the first time, encouraging me to push my possible advantage. 'If you leave now, we'll consider this episode closed. The doctors are already concerned about your drinking. You can't afford to have them know you've been turning up drunk on my doorstep, making all kinds of weird suggestions. Doctor Mac may come across as a soft touch but he's a stickler when it comes to the reputation of the practice.' I was getting into my stride now, sounding more and more confident. 'Quite frankly, I don't want the hassle of reporting this, but nor do I want it going all round the practice that you've been up here after work, so if I hear another word about any of it I'll be making a formal report.'

He opened his mouth to speak, but I had the bit firmly between my teeth. 'It isn't the first time you've been drunk when you were supposed to be on duty. The night Julie Peacock was murdered, for one. That's why the duty book couldn't be found, and then turned up in a mess. And why the tape was incomprehensible.'

'That's crap . . .' he began.

'The evidence is right there in the book. Writing all over the place – you can't read a word of it' – just like most doctors, I thought – 'and no proper times entered in the arrival column. It's lucky for you there were no real emergencies that night, but sooner or later you're going to pick the wrong night to go AWOL in the pub, and then the shit will really hit the fan.'

And it isn't just the pub, I thought. He's a lot drunker now than he was when we left The Bull. He must drink alone in his digs too.

He wiped the back of his hand across his mouth. The effect of the alcohol was kicking in hard and he was looking a lot less confident in the face of my offensive. I opened the front door and held it for him. 'Goodnight, Terry.' It was a masterful impression of a confident woman, in control of the situation.

He regarded me doubtfully then lurched across the room towards the open door. I sidestepped neatly to make way for him.

'For goodness' sake, drive carefully on the way home.' My voice was kinder now. 'The police have stepped up patrols round here, since . . . since it happened. You can't afford to lose your licence.'

'You . . .' he began, but I cut across him with a firmly repeated, 'Good night.'

'Take care,' I called again, after his retreating form. Then I closed the door and leant against it, but only for a moment. I took the stairs two at a time and once in the bedroom dragged my suitcase from the top of the wardrobe on to the bed.

EIGHTEEN

R un, I had to run. Before he had time to phone someone, alert someone, spill the beans. I undid the outer straps, unzipped the case and opened it wide. Then I stopped. What should I take? How much could I fit into the case? How much into the car? As if from another world I heard his car revving and then shunting to and fro beneath my window as he turned it preparatory to renegotiating the narrow lane. He was so drunk he might well write himself off on the way home. That was a terrible thought. I had not wished for that – not really.

But he was very drunk. Drunk enough not to remember in the morning? That was, as he had succinctly put it himself, 'crap'. It was very rare that people genuinely suffered complete amnesia after drinking. Particularly if they were habitual drinkers.

Why are you still standing here? Pack up, get out, don't stand here thinking about it when every minute brings the hounds a bit closer at your heels.

What about Rob?

In the past I had always thought to run. That had been my default plan, although I had never needed to put it into operation. But in the past there had been no Rob. Tears sprang into my eyes at the thought of leaving him. It would be as if he were dead – a sudden bereavement. I flopped down beside the suitcase, reaching for a tissue from the bedside box to scrub my eyes.

Damn Terry Millington, damn him, damn him. But did he actually know? Or did he only suspect? And when he sobered up, would he doubt the reality of his suspicions? Think, think calmly. And where are you going to run to? There's no place prepared and the hunt would be on. Running away would only confirm Terry Millington's suspicions and ensure that he reported me – fresh publicity had given a new impetus to the case. It would be as bad as when I originally left Alan. And it was harder now – there were more CCTV cameras, more identity checks. I would have to abandon the car and my bank accounts – anything traceable to Susan McCarthy. I would have to start all over again. And maybe all for nothing.

There's no time for this, I argued with myself. You have to go – now. Every minute you waste here . . .

But even if he goes straight back to Mrs Metcalf's house and rings the police, they're hardly going to take much notice of a drunk. They won't do anything until tomorrow morning at the earliest. Who starts checking up on identity theft at this time of night? Stop panicking and start thinking clearly. That's the way forward.

I forced myself to go back to the conversation in the pub. The Trollop and the Trainspotter had evidently watched at least part of *Disappeared!* but they had seemingly both dismissed any resemblance as coincidental – after all, the BBC had located an actress who looked a bit like Jennifer Reynolds, so why was it difficult to believe that there might not equally be some superficial resemblance between the actress and me? They were used to me being Susan. Terry Millington, on the other hand, had fewer fixed perceptions. He had only known any of us for a matter of weeks and that might have made him more open to the idea that I *could* be someone else. Their discussion had probably made him curious to watch the programme, not because he suspected that I was the missing woman, but because he was intrigued to see just how much I looked like the actress. Only then, when he watched the programme, he must have realized what that resemblance really meant.

He had the programme on tape. That meant he could rewind and watch it again and again, comparing my face to . . . my face. Go now, pleaded that voice in my head again. You have to go now.

But he couldn't be sure. I did some mental rewinding of my own. I had given nothing away. In fact I had behaved pretty much as an innocent person – a genuine Susan McCarthy – might have done. I had ignored his references to actresses, as if they meant nothing to me and I didn't even know what he was talking about.

I had a lot to lose, but so did he. Complaints about drunk-enness on duty might see his placement curtailed altogether. It would be a black mark on his record. Would unmasking Susan McCarthy be worth it? Why should it matter to him what I called myself? Of course, if I did complain about him, he might do it out of revenge . . . Had he thought I was striking a bargain with him: silence for silence? Or merely expressing the genuine sentiments of a practice manager startled by the arrival of a drunken medic on her doorstep talking nonsense?

And how sure was he anyway? In the cold light of day, he might conclude that he was mistaken. I did not see how he could check up on me without embarrassing himself if he turned out to be wrong. Wrongful accusations against a colleague were liable to couple 'drink problem' with 'unhinged'. I closed the suitcase lid and refastened the zip in slow motion.

This is madness, yelled that voice in my head. Pure and utter madness.

I would have to watch him very closely. There was always the chance that he would start a rumour, setting other people on the trail. I wasn't worried about the practice staff, because gossip seldom crossed the great medical-clerical divide, and I was prepared to gamble that Terry Millington wouldn't say anything to the other doctors, just in case he was wrong. But what about the evenings spent in the pub? Was he a chatty drunk, or did he just have a couple of pints before retreating home with his stash from the booze aisle? How about Pat Metcalf? If he so much as let slip a hint to her it would be all over the valley by nightfall.

You're gambling on a drunk? exclaimed my wiser twin, but I ignored her. I crawled under the duvet, still in my dressing gown, with all the lights left on downstairs, trying to convince myself that I could weather the storm. I have to get a good night's sleep, I told myself, because tomorrow, whatever happens, I have to act normally.

NINETEEN

'Acting normally' ought to have become second nature to me by then, but even so I was on tenterhooks the next day, dreading my first encounter with Dr Milly, freezing at every tap on the office door, but our paths didn't cross until mid-morning, when I met him emerging from the doctors' sitting room. Determined to give nothing away, I looked him in the eye and smiled. 'Good morning, Doctor Millington. Are you feeling better?'

'Fit as a king, Susan – and yourself?'

I ignored what I fancied was a glimmer of amusement, replying, 'Very well, thank you. You evidently got home safely.'

'I did. You were quite right to send me packing. I'd enjoyed a few too many and I had no business turning up like that.'

'Quite,' I said firmly. 'Well, least said, soonest mended.'

'Mum's the word.' He grinned and tapped the side of his nose – that most theatrical of conspiracy gestures – then walked away towards the consulting rooms.

I tried not to take undue notice of him during the next few days, because I did not want him to think that I was worried. Susan McCarthy had nothing to worry about, because the whole idea of her being a missing person masquerading as someone else was so ridiculous as to be beneath her notice. But it was hard, so hard to focus on ordinary workaday realities when a part of me just longed to take Terry Millington aside and ask him to level with me. 'Was the resemblance just some daft idea you entertained while drunk, or do you seriously suspect something? Do you *know*?'

The episode had unsettled me so much that Rob picked up on it, asking more than once whether I would prefer not to spend the night on my own. Knowing nothing of the Dr Millington problem, he put my jumpiness down to the fact that there was still a murderer loose in the neighbourhood, which to be honest was also an issue, because my earlier confidence had been undermined by a series of restless nights, when every creaking board brought alternate images of a visit from the local killer, or a half-drunk doctor with a policeman in tow.

Ordinarily I would have welcomed the comfort of Rob's presence in my bed, but ever since the *Disappeared!* programme I'd been caught on the horns of a dilemma. Being with Rob was becoming like a game of roulette, in which the fun and excitement was constantly overshadowed by an ever-present threat of the ball falling into a slot labelled Found Out. Who knew when something else about Jennifer Reynolds might be lurking within the pages of a newspaper, or would pop up on the TV screen? My former identity had come to haunt me in much the same way as had a jack-in-the-box which someone had given me as a child – a garish creature, whose sudden appearance and rictus grin had always made me cry. In any other household the wretched thing might have been discarded or given away, but my mother was a keeper par excellence and the jack-in-the-box – which had a dodgy catch, liable to be set off by any unexpected movement – dogged me for years as it was put away in one place after another, ever ready to leap out when I was least expecting it, the clown-face grinning hideously and the box emitting a sinister gurgle of laughter which faded to a horrid, wheezing moan.

Fortunately nothing more appeared in the papers or on TV about Jennifer Reynolds and, more importantly, Rob made no further mentions of Jennifer – Dunwood or any other. The topic of foreign travels was similarly forgotten as he became increasingly preoccupied with the school's forthcoming geography field trip, for which he carried the lion's share of responsibility. 'I don't see how they could go ahead with the field trip if I'm suspended,' he said.

I had given up my remonstrations to the effect that he would not be suspended, so I merely said, 'Jolly good reason not to suspend you, then.'

The week of the field trip is indelibly etched on my memory. After work on Monday we ate supper at my cottage, then walked hand in hand up the lane and along the bridleway to the crest of the hill, not returning home until the evening star winked brightly above the trees of the rookery. Later we made love with exquisite tenderness and he stayed the night, because it was our last opportunity for the best part of two weeks. (The field trip did not leave until Wednesday morning, but Rob, ever conscientious, said he still had a lot of things to do, so we had agreed that meeting on the eve of departure was impractical.) He was going to be away for almost a fortnight because the school sent two groups of pupils to the field centre, one straight after the other, and Rob stayed the whole time, taking first one group and then the next through the same course.

I awoke in his arms that Tuesday morning and lay for some time watching the pale light creep across the room. In spite of his impending absence, I felt safe and happy. The warm curve of his body next to mine exuded love and security. He was sleeping calmly and easily beside me and I sensed that with the field trip to focus on, much of the tension and anxiety about the Julie Peacock affair had lifted from him.

It was less than three weeks since Julie had been murdered, but her death had already been forgotten by the national media and was slipping out of the local papers too. Even among residents of the dale, it was no longer invariably the principal topic of conversation. The police had been from door to door, potential witnesses had been questioned and a fingertip search made at the murder site, but if there had been any significant discoveries they were not communicated to the public at large. The fires of village speculation had begun to smoulder, though there were still people ready to reignite them with an injection of local fuel. From the snippets I gleaned in the common room and elsewhere, Rob appeared to rate well down the list of suspects still under consideration by the amateur sleuths who gathered in the Post Office, or the bar of The Black Bull. There was speculation that young Luke Robinson had been sweet on the girl, but he was generally thought a nice, quiet lad who earned an immediate gold star with most habitués of The Bull as he planned to follow his father into farming, when so many of the youngsters were turning away from the traditional ways. There had been a certain amount of head shaking among some of the older residents over Julie's father, who was said to have 'an evil temper on him' when he had a bit too much to drink. Then there were the various inhabitants of the dale generally thought to be 'short in the upper storey'. With half-a-dozen or more locals who had credentials such as these, no one was putting money on it being that nice Mr Dugdale who taught at the comp.

I kept a discreet eye on Terry Millington, still wondering how much he knew or had guessed, but he had done nothing further to increase my concerns. With the duty book now being kept in exemplary fashion, fewer administrative cock-ups and no repetition of his unsolicited home visit, I hoped that he had taken my warning to heart and was focused on getting his act together rather than contemplating facial similarities between members of staff and actresses in TV documentaries.

It's going to be OK, I thought. Everything is getting back to normal. Everything is going to be all right. Our plans haven't been diverted or derailed. Rob and I will be together forever. Together . . . forever . . . I shaped the words silently and they filled me with light-hearted joy.

It came to me as I lay there that there was a very simple way to solve all the problems posed by the wedding. I would suggest a special licence. We could slip away, just the two of us, and come back married. No fuss, no expense, totally romantic. I knew in my heart that Rob would love the idea (even if his mother did not). This was obviously not the time to mention it – not in the rushed goodbyes of a working day, with his mind already focused on the field trip – but it was something to have up my sleeve for when he came home. I exhaled a great sigh of satisfaction. He stirred alongside me and when I turned to look into those deep brown eyes, I saw that he was smiling.

When Rob had gone I decided to walk into work for a change, reasoning that the exercise would do me good. There was a cool breeze, but the sky was blue and sunbeams danced ahead of me along the lane. There was smoke issuing from the chimney at Rosecroft, where I knew Jim and Bob would be taking a late breakfast after already putting in a couple of hours work. The smell of wood smoke followed me along the lane. A comfortable smell, instantly evocative of all that was

good about life in Lasthwaite. We never had a real fire when
I was a child. My mother had said it made dust.

At Belsay House the sun reflected off the window panes
and the lion's head doorknocker positively glowed. I made a
mental note to praise Linda, the cleaner. Everything seemed
calm and cheerful that morning. No crisis loomed; no shortage
of appointment slots or missing files. There were no messages
awaiting me from complaining patients, no awkward meetings
looming. It was turning out to be one of those truly good days
on which anyone would feel glad to be alive.

As usual, I took my coffee with the doctors when they broke
off between morning surgery consultations and home visits,
joining the rest of the staff in their much larger common room
in the afternoon. It was a gesture of friendship and solidarity
on my part as much as anything else, even if I would sometimes rather have taken my Nescafe in the privacy of my office.
By the time I got into the common room on that particular
afternoon the Trollop was in full flow – a juicy scandal about
her ex-sister-in-law and a fireman. Finding that the kettle had
just boiled, I made myself a coffee and found a chair.

A lot of the staff preferred to have tea in the afternoon and
there was a big pot stewing on the table, next to the box
containing the afternoon biscuits, a daily treat foresworn by
the perpetually dieting Trollop, but indulged in by the nurses,
who were all size twenty-two and above. No digestives today,
I noted, just wafers which left a crumbly pink dust in the
bottom of the tin, and a couple of chocolate chip cookies. I
took one of the latter, wondering idly why people brought
wafers in because they always got left to last. Digestives, fig
rolls and anything involving chocolate – those were the popular
ones.

I listened with perhaps as much as half my attention while
the Trollop approached the climax of her tale. The denouement
drew gales of laughter from the less inhibited staff, while the
lip-pursers made polite laugh-like noises. As the laughter died
away there was a brief comfortable silence while people drank
from their mugs, ate their biscuits or looked out at the sky,
which was clouding over.

The Tragedy Queen was next to speak. 'I see they've found

that woman's body. You know, the one what's been missing for ages.'

'Jennifer Reynolds,' the Trainspotter put in helpfully. 'I heard it on the news this lunchtime.'

'Eeee – never? Well, how funny with it being on the telly just the other week,' said the Trollop. 'Do you remember how we were talking about her at Moira's leaving party?'

The Tragedy Queen nodded. 'I said to Frank it'll be that psychic chap. He said he knew where to find her.'

'No,' said Jacky, a big, down-to-earth district nurse. 'It'll be new information from somebody who saw it on the telly. Something in that programme will have jogged someone's memory.'

'Guilty conscience, more like,' said Jean, the receptionist. 'Made someone think they ought to tell what they know. There's always someone knows something.'

I was in a nightmare. Breathe – try to remember to breathe.

'Have they said it's her for definite?' This from the Trollop.

'Well, they don't, do they?' said the Trainspotter. 'Not to start with. The television people seemed to think it was her. And they usually know, don't they?'

'They never give out the name to start off with,' another voice chipped in. 'They have to notify the relatives and such like first.'

Don't look at me. Please don't any of you look at me, at my guilty, Jennifer Reynolds face.

'I remember when she went missing,' said the Tragedy Queen, who in common with Stan Butters of Glastonbury, occasionally fancied herself gifted with clairvoyance. 'I remember saying then – you mark my words, her husband's done away with her.'

It was a nightmare, but I would wake up soon.

'I reckon that's why they put it back on the telly the other week – you know, to get people interested again. And now someone's given them a tip-off.'

'I bet he did do it, that husband. He looked right creepy – you can always tell.'

'Wasn't she the one who was supposed to have gone off without taking any money or clothes?'

'That's right. Left her car keys and credit cards on the kitchen table and just walked out.'

'No . . . hang on, though, didn't they think she'd been kidnapped? Weren't there some bloodstains and a broken window?'

'No-o-o. That wasn't the Jennifer Reynolds case. You're thinking of that other woman down in Dorset.'

It was just a terrible dream: any minute now I would wake up. I would be lying in my bedroom with the moonlight sliding in where the curtains don't quite meet at the top.

'Mind, I thought *her* husband had set that up . . .'

The conversation rambled off down other speculative avenues of kidnap and murder while I drank my coffee, very slowly and carefully. Say nothing. Don't get up from your chair while they're all still in here. Wait until you're certain that you can stand up without your legs giving way.

No one seemed to notice that I made no contribution to the discussion. I didn't even have to invent a headache. Back in my office, I tried to make some sense out of it all. How could my body have been discovered?

I considered the possibility that the Tragedy Queen had made a mistake over the name. Then again, several of them seemed to have heard the news item, presumably either before they set out in the morning or when they went home for lunch, and no one had corrected her about it. Probably the identity was mere speculation. Well, obviously . . . it would have to be.

I desperately wanted to talk to Rob, badly needed to see him, hear and touch him. I didn't want to be alone any more. Not ever. It had all got too complicated. Somehow I would have to tell him the truth – Rob loved me, he would know what to do. It was no use calling school because he would be in classes, so instead I rang his cottage and left a message on his answering machine.

'Hi, sweetheart – it's me.' I tried to keep my voice on an even keel. Mustn't worry him by letting him hear how upset I was. 'I know we said we wouldn't call each other tonight because you've got such a lot to do, but I want to see you so much. Please ring me when you get home.'

When I put the phone down, it rang immediately and I snatched it up, full of foolish false hope, but it was only a call from the switchboard – would I speak with a Mr Duggan from Everbright Hygiene? I said I would. Mr Duggan wanted to make an appointment to talk through the health centre's requirements. I arranged to see him the following week, managing to keep almost half my mind on the conversation I was having.

Jennifer Reynolds's body. How could they have found Jennifer Reynolds's body? It wasn't possible. It was a mistake. A horrible, terrible mistake.

TWENTY

Rob generally reached home not much later than half past four, but by the time I left work at ten past five he still hadn't called. I was tired by then and the sky had clouded over so that choosing to leave the car at home now seemed like the act of an imbecile. Denuded of sunshine, everything appeared harsh and cold, the earlier promise of spring entirely gone. Rosecroft looked particularly gloomy, with no discernible signs of life – not even the tell-tale whiff of wood smoke – and in the clump of trees at the back of the farmhouse the rooks were making a huge commotion, one of those discordant clamours of the kind employed by film makers, whenever they want to create a sinister atmosphere for a story set in the English countryside.

I was half hoping that Rob would overtake me as I walked up the lane, or maybe even be waiting at the cottage, but when I got there the place was deserted. I let myself in at the front door, collapsed on to the sofa and kicked off my outdoor shoes. The discovery of 'my' body was the final straw. Somehow, I had to find a way of telling Rob the truth. As soon as I could summon up the energy I took off my coat, picked up the phone and pressed his number, but I got the answering machine again.

'I'm just trying to get you, again,' I said lamely. 'Speak to you soon.'

I hung my coat in the lobby, put the kettle on and made a mug of coffee, all the time wondering where he could be. He was always home by now. Surely he wasn't outside, chopping wood? He wouldn't bother to get a stack of wood in before he went away – not with so many last minute things to do – and anyway, he usually heard the phone from the garden. He must have gone to the supermarket, I thought. Probably picking up something for the trip. But surely that didn't take an hour?

I took my mug of coffee into the sitting room and perched on the arm of the chair, where I could see not only the television, but also through the window to the gate, where I was hoping against hope to spot the arrival of a certain geography teacher.

The body was the fourth story on the six o'clock news. It had been found at the edge of a field on the outskirts of Nicholsfield, a few hundred yards from the road. Contrary to speculation in the health centre common room, it appeared that neither the West Country clairvoyant, nor even a tip-off from a witness with a troubled conscience had been responsible for the discovery. A local farmer had been doing some drainage work and disturbed what appeared to be a shallow grave containing human remains. The police were not confirming anything, but for some reason the press had got hold of the idea that it was Jennifer Reynolds. 'Speculation' – that was the word they used. 'There is speculation that the body may belong to Jennifer Reynolds, who has been missing from Nicholsfield for more than six years.'

It might not have been such a newsworthy story if it hadn't been for Martin Bullock's programme putting the case back into the public eye, I thought. As it was, one of the better-known reporters had been rushed to Nicholsfield to be filmed at the roadside, making statements to camera which could just as easily have been conveyed by the team in the studio. He began by explaining just where and when and how the remains had come to be discovered, adding that although the police were refusing to confirm speculation that the body had been identified as that of Jennifer Reynolds, they would say that the remains were those of a female, and appeared to have been there for some time. Reporters had also managed to winkle out the information that the police were trying to contact Alan Reynolds, who was thought to be away from home on business.

I thought of Alan, perhaps staying in a hotel somewhere, switching on his bedroom television to catch the news, or else reading about it in tomorrow's *Times.* Poor Alan. They might ask him to identify the body. Though surely there would be nothing left but bones by now? You couldn't identify bones. The television drivelled inexorably on, through the weather forecast and into the regional news. Nothing now, I noted, about Julie Peacock. This evening it was the turn of some other poor dead woman to have her fifteen minutes of fame.

All through the news, I perched on the arm of the chair, ready to flick the set off the moment Rob returned my call, but the telephone remained ominously silent. Please ring. Please, please ring. Without warning, I broke down and began to cry. Muffled sobs, followed by louder sobs graduated into an uncontrolled howling which made me feel thoroughly ashamed of myself. It took me several minutes to regain control. Eventually I dried my eyes, blew my nose and went through to the bathroom to wash my face. After that I went upstairs and changed out of my work suit and into my jeans, occasionally catching sight of my face in the mirror, reddened and blotchy, Jennifer Reynolds staring reproachfully at Susan McCarthy.

Seven o'clock came and still no call from Rob. Why didn't he call? And what was I going to say to him when he did? Seven thirty. Still no word. When he hadn't rung by eight, desperation got the better of me and I tried his number again, but I put the phone down before it had a chance to ring out. The thought of having to leave another message – my voice echoing around his empty sitting room – unnerved me.

Where on earth was he? Logic said that he must be at home because he had to get ready for the field trip. Wasn't that the whole reason for his not seeing me? I knew he would be leaving first thing in the morning and he had already warned me that the field centre was very basic: equipped with a single payphone, whose caller's every word could be overheard by anyone standing around in the communal area. This made it all the more imperative that if I was going to talk to him, it needed to be now, tonight and preferably face-to-face. Maybe I should drive over to his cottage? But what was the point of that if he wasn't there? And if for some reason he had decided to come over to my place, we could easily take alternative routes and miss one another.

Theories about his whereabouts crept unbidden into my mind. The prolonged silence could no longer be explained by a quick call at the shops en route home. School was finished by four o'clock – that was four hours ago. Suppose there had been a car accident? Always everyone's first idea. Or was there some other reason for his failure to contact me? Had he lied about getting ready for the trip? Was he actually planning to go somewhere else, do something that he didn't want me to know about? Or suppose the police had taken him in for further questioning about the Julie Peacock business? I tried to dismiss these speculations as hysterical, but I was so unnerved by the discovery of the body in Nicholsfield that I felt capable of believing almost anything.

Then I noticed that it was getting foggy outside. Sometimes fog simply rolled across the dale out of nowhere – great cart-wheels of grounded cloud, tumbling across the fields and abruptly enveloping everything – but tonight it began gradually, the visibility diminishing by degrees, dulling outlines until the furthest ridge was lost to sight, the change becoming more obvious as trees faded to mere shadows and little wisps of mist came riding past on the air. I remembered that I had left my bedroom window ajar and went upstairs to close it against the dampness in the air.

At the upstairs window I paused to look down the lane, hoping to see the blur of headlights approaching through the gloom, but there was no hint of another human being at all. The fog had transformed the garden into a swirling tapestry of uncertainty, affording no more than temporary glimpses of the dry stone wall and the dark grass. A spider's web on the outside window frame was illuminated with tiny droplets of water, a perfectly bejewelled, geometric work of art.

I hadn't bothered to turn off the television and as I stood at the window the raised voices of soap opera characters reached me through the floorboards. On the rare occasions when I saw soap operas, the characters always seemed to be quarrelling with one another. Either that or sleeping with someone else's partner. In real life there was never anything like so much quarrelling or sex. Well, not in my life anyway.

Yet tonight, the mist swirling outside the bedroom window and the raised voices coming up through the ceiling – impossible to hear what they were saying and yet knowing with certainty that they were quarrelling – brought back a memory of real life: of standing in my bedroom in the house in Orchard

Lane, looking out into the fog and being aware of raised voices below, voices emanating not from the television but from my mother and father. It was almost as though I was watching a film of my fifteen-year-old self standing at the bedroom window, watching the swirling mist play games around the rose bushes, while wondering in a disinterested sort of way what my parents might be quarrelling about.

The shouting had ended abruptly, followed by the briefest silence before the front door slammed – hard. Moments later I heard the base of the garage doors rasping as they opened outwards across the gravel – the wooden doors always swelled in the damp. Daddy must be going out in the car while Mummy sat alone downstairs, unwilling to follow him outside and pursue the argument in the garden where the neighbours might hear.

I heard the familiar sound of tyres on gravel as Daddy reversed the car down the drive, turned into the road and headed away. The car was being driven a little faster than usual; the engine revved marginally harder than it was accustomed to. For all that I recognized these signs of parental agitation, I knew that if anyone had been passing my father would have concealed his temper beneath a friendly greeting. Not by so much as an impatient tug at the gates, nor a backward glare in the direction of the front door, would he have betrayed his feelings. No tattling gossip would be able to arrive home and hazard the opinion that the Freemans had been having a bit of a barney.

After the car had gone I remained at the window watching the fog drift around the garden. I suppose a lot of daughters would have gone downstairs, maybe hugged and kissed their mother, offered some small kindness, some gesture of sympathy. We did not hug and kiss. We were not that kind of family.

The next morning they found another body. This time it was in the woods at Sampton Sandyrest, a local beauty spot. It was almost a year to the day after Sally Walsh had vanished, but it wasn't Sally Walsh, it was a different girl; a girl who had only gone missing the night before. After that I was sure I knew.

The sound of an approaching car cut across my reverie. For

a moment I thought I was imagining it – still reliving the memory of that other car in that other time, but the loom of the headlamps appeared as it approached the bend, the driver negotiating the narrow lane slowly in the difficult conditions. I raced down the stairs and threw open the door, but as the driver emerged from the murk it was not Rob, but Terry Millington. I momentarily considered shutting the door and ignoring any summons from the bell, but instead I stood waiting on the doorstep, as if turned to stone.

I couldn't make out his expression until his face came within range of the bulb in the hall. This time he wasn't drunk, just very, very angry. I belatedly attempted to slam the door, but I was too late and he barged in, his raised voice echoing up the stair well. 'Why did you do it?' he shouted.

I retreated, staring at him.

'Why?' he repeated, jabbing a finger in my direction as he followed me into the sitting room, where I stepped smartly aside, putting an armchair between us, while noting in an oddly detached way that my life had just slid from highly bizarre to scarily surreal. 'I thought we had an agreement,' he shouted. 'I've watched that fucking tape. I don't know why you changed your name and I don't honestly care. I wasn't going to tell anyone. It was just the booze talking the other night. I'm a doctor, right? I'm used to keeping secrets.' In a part of my head which wasn't wondering what the hell was going to happen next, it occurred to me that he wasn't acting much like any doctor I had ever met before. 'On my honour, I wasn't going to tell a soul, but you couldn't keep your side of the deal. Just like a fucking woman, you had to go telling tales to old McCleary, saying that I've been known to sink a few before going out on call.'

I found my voice. 'I never said anything about you to Doctor McCleary.'

Something in my tone must have carried conviction, but he evidently interpreted it as a tactical lie, saying impatiently: 'Well, to one of the others then. Woods or Hindmarsh. What does it matter? I'm on a warning, thanks to you.' His voice was still loud and angry.

I took a deep breath. 'I swear to you that I haven't mentioned anything about your drinking to anyone. Nor has anyone asked me about it. I never told anyone about your coming up here either, but I can promise you this: if you don't stop appearing on my doorstep, making wild allegations, I won't just be telling the doctors, I'll be making a complaint to the police.'

His laughter was so loud, so unexpected, that I jumped visibly. 'Wild allegations? I told you, I watched that tape. I don't get why the others don't see it. Or maybe they do, but they don't report you because they think it's none of their business.'

I took another deep breath. 'If you are talking about my supposed resemblance to that poor woman, Jennifer Reynolds . . .' There it was, I'd said the name out loud and it hadn't scorched my lips, and the sky had not fallen in, '. . . I assume you can't have heard that they've found her body, not far from where she originally went missing. It was on the news earlier today.'

That stopped him dead in his tracks. He scrutinized my face for a moment, then abruptly sank down uninvited on the sofa in an attitude of complete deflation. 'You're having me on?'

'I don't joke about things like that.'

'Oh, shit,' he said. 'Oh, shit.' He waited a moment before adding: 'I've just made everything much worse, haven't I?'

'You clearly have a problem, Terry,' I said. 'But you're a good doctor too. The patients like you. Some of them are asking to see you specifically, and believe me, that's a compliment round here, where newcomers aren't always accepted. Doctor Mac's a good man. He'll give you another chance, if you ask him.'

'So far he's just warned me to be careful, not to let it happen again.' He seemed suddenly smaller somehow, younger than his years. 'I've got to cut out the drinking, watch what I'm doing.'

'And yet here you are . . .'

'I know. But I thought . . . and if it wasn't you . . .'

'Lasthwaite's a rural community,' I said. 'There are no secrets here.' Well, OK – I'm lying. There must be secrets everywhere.

'And you're not . . .'

'No.' At least not until that woman turns out to be someone else.

'You won't say anything? About me coming up here. I'm really, really sorry . . . and you know, you do look just like that Reynolds woman.' His face was contorted into what he imagined was a winning smile.

I hesitated, pretending to consider, the way a woman who could afford to complain about being hassled might. 'This has to be the last time,' I said.

'It will be. Believe me, I'm going to straighten myself out. This has been a big wake-up call.'

I interrupted him because the deceit sickened me – my lies and his habitual drunk's self-delusion. 'Please just go. I'm expecting someone and if you're here, I'll have to explain why and I . . . I don't like lying.' Hypocrite, liar, liar, pants on fire. How is it that you aren't struck down by a bolt of lightning every time you open your mouth?

He looked at me curiously, focusing properly on my face for the first time. 'You're upset. I'm really sorry – and it's not just me, is it? I've picked a bad time . . .' He hesitated, en route to the door. 'If there's anything . . .'

I followed him, all but shooing him out. 'Goodnight, Terry,' I said firmly before I closed the door.

A bad time, I thought. You can say that again.

Rob finally rang at just after ten p.m. I had been pacing about, wondering what on earth to do, and when the call finally came through I almost knocked the telephone on to the floor in my eagerness to grab it.

'Hello, Sue? Is everything all right?' His voice was tinged with anxiety.

I didn't know where to begin. 'I just wanted to talk to you,' I said. 'I was getting worried when you didn't answer. Where have you been?'

'We had a meeting straight after school, for the pupils going on the field trip.' Even as he said it, I remembered him telling me about it. 'After the kids had gone, the staff stayed on to run through all the details again. You know what a fusser Louise Bunstead is. It was well after six by the time we got away. Then I called into Safeway, so I didn't get home until

just after seven o'clock. I never noticed the light flashing on
the machine until a couple of minutes ago. I wasn't expecting
anyone to ring so I never thought to check it.'

It all had the absolute ring of truth. His answering machine
was tucked up on a shelf above his desk. It was a silly place
to have it really – you could easily not notice the message
light flashing.

'I'm sorry,' I said. 'I'd forgotten about the meeting after
school. I was going to suggest that I come over and cook your
supper.' Face-to-face. It would be far, far better to tell him
face-to-face. 'Or I thought perhaps I could help you with your
packing,' I added rather desperately, 'but I suppose it's too
late now.' Please say it isn't. Please tell me to get in the car
and come over.

'Afraid so. I whizzed myself up an omelette as soon as I
got home. I've just got to do a final check through my kit and
then I'll be turning in. To tell the truth, I'm absolutely
knackered.'

'Poor you,' I said.

'It was sweet of you to offer,' he said. 'I'll miss you.'

'I shall miss you, too.'

'You are all right, aren't you? You sound . . . well, I don't
know, a bit strained . . .'

'I'm fine,' I lied. 'It must have been the tape distorting my
voice, although I wish you weren't going away. If I could just
see you before you go . . .'

'I'm only going to the other side of the Pennines for a
couple of weeks,' he said.

'I'll miss you,' I repeated.

'Take care of yourself while I'm away. I'll try to phone, but
it's pretty hopeless with half of 9C hanging on your every
word.'

'I love you,' I said, rather desperately.

'I love you too. Are you sure you're OK?'

'Of course I am.'

'Goodnight then, sweetheart.'

'Goodnight. Have a safe journey.'

'Goodnight.' He made a kissing noise at the other end of
the line. 'Bye for now.'

'Bye, darling.'

As the call ended I experienced a feeling of terrible emptiness. Had there been a chance there, a glimmer of a chance? *Is everything all right?* his very first question, inviting me to embark on an instant confession that my all-rightness had seldom been less in evidence and that I had earth-shaking news to impart.

I went over it in my mind. Three times during the course of the conversation he had asked and three times I had given an affirmative. For how can one begin, even begin to say that today on the news there is talk of a body and everyone says it belongs to Jennifer Reynolds, but I and perhaps only I, know that this is not so and the reason I know – are you hearing this, Rob? Can you even begin to take this in? I know this dead woman, whoever she may be, is not Jennifer Reynolds, because *I* am Jennifer Reynolds. Susan McCarthy? Oh, you may well ask. Susan McCarthy *is* dead. As dead as a Dodo. As dead as that woman whose body they have found in a ditch in Nicholsfield.

Are you still there, Rob, or have you dropped the phone? Can you believe any of this? Well, of course you can't believe it. How can you know where the lies begin and end when you're hearing these things from someone who has told you so many lies, covered up, concealed, papered over the cracks. And what can you expect except concealment? She was brought up to conceal things. Raised in a house of secrets and silences. Taught to hide feelings behind the façade of preoccupation with the ordinary.

Tears rolled down my cheeks and dripped unchecked on to my sweater. 'I'm sorry,' I said aloud. 'I'm so sorry. I never knew how to love or be loved, until I found you. I never knew how to be open enough to let someone get really close. And now it's too late. We've lost our chance.'

TWENTY-ONE

As soon as I got downstairs next morning, I switched on the breakfast news. The TV people were still talking about the body that had been found in the field and hinting that it belonged to Jennifer Reynolds. In a new development, police had gone to the home once shared by the missing woman and her currently absent husband and removed 'various items', presumably to help confirm or deny the identity of the body; though how anything they found in the house might do that was not explained. According to the presenter, the police were still trying to establish contact with Alan Reynolds, who was thought to be away on business somewhere in the North of England.

The words sent an involuntary shiver down my spine. For as long as I had known him, Alan had travelled all over the country in search of suitable pieces. He favoured auctions in the north because he said there were still bargains to be had there: you could pick up some very nice items at a third of the price you would pay for them in tourist haunts like London and Stratford. At the back of my mind, I had always known that one day I might literally bump into Alan, coming along a street in a Yorkshire town, browsing the antique shops, or on his way to an auction, in pursuit of something he needed to fulfil a commission.

A familiar feeling of guilt stalked me as I made my way to work. Poor Alan, who had already been left to deal with my original disappearance, was now about to be subjected to the distressing news that his erstwhile wife had been murdered and her body found buried in a field. And it was all my fault. This whole dreadful string of events was a direct result of my actions and mine alone. If I'd had the courage to simply state that I wanted a divorce – just dealt with my problems in a normal way – none of this would have happened. What could really have been so difficult about that? Now that the whole

business was several years behind me, even I found my actions
difficult to understand, still less justify. This whole sordid mess
was entirely of my own making.

As the day progressed I experienced a growing sense of
misery and confusion. I tried to carry on as normal because
I didn't know what else to do. I didn't want Alan to suffer
over the misidentified woman, but at the same time the revelation that she was not Jennifer Reynolds would put me right
back to square one with Dr Millington. He *said* he would
not have betrayed me, but even if he didn't, someone else
inevitably would. He was probably right about other people
guessing but deciding to do nothing about it. Not the Trollop
or the Trainspotter, but maybe someone else. It was only a
matter of time before my luck ran out. The obvious answer
was to cut and run.

But then there was Rob.

Before Rob became part of my life I had become accustomed
to living alone. In fact, I had enjoyed it, positively revelling
in the independence, but now life seemed impossibly empty
and worthless without him; even his going off for a few days
at the field centre had thrown me completely off beam. That
first evening he was away, I deliberately took time over cooking
a favourite pasta dish from scratch. I ate slowly, tidied up at
a snail's pace, finished some ironing and poked the fire so
many times that I all but put it out. When I put the cork back
into the bottle after a second glass of wine, I kidded myself
that I felt relaxed rather than sick and panicky as the nine
o'clock news approached.

It was worse than ever. The Jennifer Reynolds murder story
had moved up from fourth item to second. The body had still
not been positively identified, but now there were unconfirmed
reports that the police might be looking for other bodies at
the Reynolds' home. The reporter who had previously been
despatched to cover events from a lane alongside the field
where the body had been found was now hanging about on
the pavement, a mere ten yards or so away from the house I
had once shared with Alan, the gate of which appeared to be
manned by a uniformed policeman. I sat rooted to my chair,
too astonished to move. The coverage included an interview

with a too-eager neighbour – someone I didn't recognize, who
must have moved in after I had left. He was a thin-faced man
with a prominent Adam's apple, who told the reporter that
from his upstairs windows he had definitely seen policemen
digging in Mr Reynolds's garden.

I emitted a guffaw of semi-hysterical laughter. 'Much good
that will do them,' I said aloud to the screen. Clay soil too.
Jolly hard work for somebody to do all for nothing.

Meantime, the police confirmed that they were still trying
to establish the whereabouts of Alan Reynolds, who they
wanted to talk to urgently, in connection with his wife's disappearance. They even showed a picture of Alan. Good grief!
They were treating him like a serious suspect.

A later bulletin on another channel said pretty much the
same things, accompanied by more exterior shots of the house,
including some obviously taken from a neighbour's upstairs
window (perhaps the man with the prominent Adam's apple,
cashing in when an opportunity presented itself). There wasn't
a lot to see. The back garden was mostly obscured by the
shrubs which grew alongside the fence, but within the limited
field of vision afforded by this snooping post, it was possible
to discern a couple of men in coveralls, moving in and out of
a gap between some conifers. Again the viewers were shown
a picture of Alan and told that the police were anxious to
speak to him in connection with their enquiries.

I wondered where Alan was at that precise moment. He bought
a newspaper every day of his life. It was a ritual. He must have
read about the discovery of the body. Perhaps the significance
of it and the fact that the police would want to make contact
had not dawned on him when he read about it in the morning
edition. Well, even if he had managed to miss the items on the
radio and television news, which seemed unlikely, he would see
it all in his paper tomorrow and get in touch with the police. He
wouldn't be too pleased to hear that the local constabulary had
been messing about in his garden and I could imagine his fury
when he read about their ferreting in the house. With more than
a ghost of a smile, I pictured the baffled Plod going through
the collections of Edwardian sheet music, the piles of hand-
embroidered table linen; peering hopelessly into cupboards and

drawers full of postcard albums and old photographs with no hint of anything remotely useful to their enquiries. I could just imagine Alan arriving home. Sweeping angrily into the hall, almost without pause rearranging the sticks in the base of the hat stand before shirtily instructing some ham-fisted constable to come out of the sideboard, where the best china was kept.

That was it, of course. Alan would return home. He would confirm that the body in the field was not mine, and then, and then . . .

It did not happen like that at all.

By Thursday's lunchtime news it was obvious that the police were actively hunting for Alan. There was talk of people phoning in with possible sightings of him as far dispersed as North Wales and Southend-on-Sea. There was also definite confirmation that the police had begun digging up the garden.

'Police have refused to confirm precisely what they are looking for,' said the female reporter, talking directly into the camera which was filming her on the pavement outside Alan's house. Her serious expression belied the silliness of the comment. It was hardly as if the police went about digging up gardens on the off chance of finding a cache of Thornton's Continental chocolates or the odd long-lost garden gnome.

Worse still, on the evening bulletin the announcer stated that the police had confirmed they had reason to believe that the body found in the field earlier in the week *was* that of Jennifer Reynolds, who went missing in 1983. They were refusing to rule out the possibility that there might be other bodies in the garden.

'You've got it all wrong!' I shouted at the screen. 'Wrong, wrong, wrong.'

Fate had made a mock of my hopes that the Jennifer Reynolds case would fade back into obscurity. On the contrary, the British public were getting a good look at my old mug shots every day. No one else had mentioned my remarkable resemblance to the dead woman in my hearing, but what might they be saying when I wasn't there? Medical Records ran on gossip the way my sitting room fire ate up logs. Once it was announced that the body in the field was not mine, it could only be a matter of time . . .

I lay in bed that night, trying to make sense of it all. The glow of the bedside light softened the lines of everything in the room, creating a semblance of security and calm, but the faint sound of raindrops pattering against the windowpanes intruded like a message in Morse code, borne on the wind from some persistent, far distant operator, determined to engage my attention.

Suppose the police never did discover their mistake? The jury in the health centre common room had already pronounced Alan guilty in absentia. The journalists on the national dailies were slyly infusing their copy with the suggestion that his continued absence was indicative of guilt. An innocent man would have nothing to fear in coming forward. This was the verdict of my colleagues, the press, and presumably the public at large. Personally I was not so sure. Hadn't Rob feared the possibility of the police deliberately manufacturing evidence of his guilt in order to improve their clear-up rate? However much I reasoned that the police don't do any such thing, I wasn't one hundred per cent surprised that Alan might not care to stake his freedom on the theory. The idea of a police force committed to massaging crime statistics seemed to be all the rage – why should Alan's thinking be any different?

Even if the police always played with a straight bat, they were still capable of making mistakes. The fallibility of the British justice system had been amply demonstrated over the last few years. Television pictures of men released after years of wrongful imprisonment flitted through my mind. These released innocents always looked strained and odd, even in the midst of their joy at being set free. They always looked older than their years, with prison pallid skin and badly cut hair, and their faces confirmed what we all secretly knew in our hearts: that prison is not the sanitized giggle of a Clement and La Frenais comedy, but a nightmare hell of excrement and violence; an experience calculated to break the mind and spirit of a sensitive man within days of his incarceration.

These men who had served time for crimes they never committed, surely they were all victims of mistaken, rather than malicious investigation? Criminal justice was prone to mistakes just like any other sphere of life, and the police were obviously on the verge of making a big mistake over the identity of that poor dead girl in the field. Alan's continued absence was in itself suggestive in a highly misleading way. The complete disappearance of Jennifer Reynolds re-enforced this deceptive picture. For all I knew there might be other counterfeit evidence – something the police had found in the house, perhaps, which was open to some kind of misinterpretation. Maybe there was an old witness statement, coincidentally containing a description of a suspect which happened, by evil chance, to fit Alan. All or any of these things would increase the weight of spurious suspicion against him. If Jennifer Reynolds had never 'gone missing' there could not have been any confusing of the body in the field with hers. Alan would not have been implicated and therefore could not have been suspected of anything.

After leaving Alan I had tried to pretend to myself that my departure had not caused him any great distress, vaguely defended my behaviour as a pay-back for past unhappiness. This unhappiness might not have been entirely his fault, but a part of me tended to lay the blame at his door – thought that at the very least he ought to have been more perceptive, more flexible: most of all that he should have allowed me to be the person I really wanted to be. Six years later, confronted with the inescapable consequences of my actions, I could no longer pretend that I had not done Alan any harm. Whatever his failings as a husband might have been, I could not make-believe that he deserved the ordeal of being a wanted man; maybe the ignominy of being arrested and put on trial, ultimately even imprisoned for something he had not done – indeed, for something which no one had done – a crime not even committed, because this murder of Jennifer Reynolds was a crime which had somehow been manufactured from bits and pieces of other lives and other crimes: a crime that never was, with a mismatched body and its murderer wrongly identified.

I lay down and switched off the lamp, but the parade of wrongly convicted men seemed to stare reproachfully at me out of the darkness, while the rain whispered messages in dots and dashes that I couldn't read. After thinking in circles for hours, I reached no conclusion, except that the crux of the matter lay in somehow confirming to the authorities that Jennifer Reynolds was alive and well. Everything hinged on this. If the police were satisfied that Jennifer Reynolds had not been murdered, they would be forced to accept that the body found in the ditch belonged to someone else and set about establishing who that might be. They would realize that Alan was not a person who needed investigating – after all, he would never have been under suspicion at all if his wife hadn't disappeared. They would curtail their fruitless excavations of his garden, return his belongings and announce to the press that they had no further interest in Alan.

The most obvious means of achieving this was to simply walk into any police station and 'give myself up', but the consequences of this from my point of view were potentially devastating. It would almost certainly make the news headlines – little hope that a tip off wouldn't bring reporters running from John o' Groats to Land's End to cover such a sensational story. My new life would be publicly blown to smithereens. The doctors would very likely fire me – a perfectly legitimate move as I had obtained my post by deception, which would in turn be a massive source of embarrassment to the practice for hiring me in the first place. There might be criminal charges involved, once the appropriation of Susan McCarthy's National Insurance number was discovered.

Then there was a whole lot of other collateral damage to take into account. What would the feelings of the McCarthy family be on hearing of their daughter's callously resurrected identity? What of Rob's mother, facing the other residents in her sheltered housing complex? There would be a fearful fluttering in the dovecots when it emerged that Mrs Dugdale's son had become involved with this duplicitous woman and her double life. (You could be sure the papers would say double life – it was an eye-catching headline, if ever there was one. *Murder Victim turns up alive and well. Double life of health centre manager – turn to page 2*.)

The coward in me very much wanted to run away – back to the beach hut, where the television news could not intrude its nightly reminders of this labyrinthine knot. From nowhere I remembered Rob once saying, a propos of nothing in particular, that he was prepared to fight for me if necessary. We had something worth fighting for. Above all I had to remember that.

If only I could come up with a way of clearing Alan without actually going public. On the other hand, unless I went public Alan would probably never come out of hiding. He must be suffering from the same sort of paranoia which afflicted Rob, when he had imagined himself prime suspect in the Julie Peacock case. Alan, too, must have convinced himself that the police were out to fit him up. To make matters worse, he was probably labouring under the illusion that the body in the field really was that of his former wife, because unlike me he had no evidence to the contrary.

If I went to the police claiming to be Jennifer Reynolds, they might dismiss me as a crank. What definite proof could I offer them? The best person to identify me would be Alan, but he was on the run. Round and round in circles. A few hours of sleep interspersed with periods of fretful waking brought me no nearer to a solution – and how much time did I have? It was entirely possible that the police would succeed in their efforts to track Alan down and arrest him before Rob got back. It would only take a tip off from some over-observant hotel receptionist. Not only would that be terrible for Alan, but with every day that the uncertainty continued, my own position became increasingly insecure, because so long as the press continued to pursue the line that Alan was the Nicholsfield Serial Killer, the whole wretched affair was guaranteed to stay in headlines. Terry Millington had sussed it already and surely everyone in Lasthwaite could only keep on looking at those old photographs so many times before they realized that they were looking at old pictures of Susan McCarthy?

TWENTY-TWO

t was while I was sitting in the staff common room, eating my lunch of fruit and yoghurt and half listening to the latest gossip about the Trollop's numerous relatives that the mists of confusion lifted. The obvious solution was for me and Alan to go to the police together, and in a moment of sheer inspiration the realization that I above all people knew how to make contact with Alan crystallized. He might have gone into hiding, grown a beard, assumed another name, but there was one thing, one daily habit, I was sure he would not have abandoned. Alan bought a copy of *The Times* every day and, before he retired for the night, he would have read every word, including the business pages (which I never so much as glanced at), the puzzles (which I had never been able to complete), even the job advertisements, so that he knew – should the need ever arise to know such a thing – roughly what an up-and-coming legal executive might expect to be offered by way of a salary in the city. It was a habit which made him formidably well informed and enabled him to converse intelligently on a wide variety of topics.

Every Valentine's Day, the personal columns in *The Times* erupt into annual silliness and this always provided a rich source of amusement to Alan, who would read aloud the messages which tickled him most, speculating that 'Snugglebunnikins' and 'Lucky Ducky' were probably ultra-respectable city gents. He had also been taken with another (perhaps less likely) idea that these pet names would provide a marvellous cover for spies or criminals. People could covertly contact one another, he said, by placing what appeared to be perfectly innocent romantic messages or requests to get in touch and make up after a quarrel, but which were in reality something completely different. We had laughed over the possibilities this presented, and even gone so far as to suggest silly code names for ourselves. I was to be 'Sweetie-Pie' and he would be 'Toodle-Doo', or something of the sort – I couldn't remember exactly what.

'What are you grinning at?' asked one of the district nurses. Cocooned in thought, I had not realized I was grinning at all.

'Nothing,' I said quickly. 'It was just something a friend said to me the other day. It suddenly popped into my head. It's not worth repeating,' I continued to improvise desperately. 'It's one of those things where you had to be there.'

She seemed satisfied by this and returned her attention to the Trainspotter, who had started to say something about an ongoing storyline in *Coronation Street*. Meanwhile, I crossed the common room, dropped my yoghurt pot and apple core into the swing bin and washed my teaspoon in the sink as I considered the possibilities thrown up by this idea. Obviously any scheme would require a very careful strategy on my part. I wanted to help Alan, but not at the cost of my freedom. We would have to find a way of avoiding publicity, and it would need to be understood from the outset that once the business of the body in the ditch was sorted out I intended to disappear from his life again forever, but surely Alan would be so grateful to be freed from police suspicion that he would be willing to accede to whatever conditions I might care to impose? (Even if he was initially inclined to recall that if it hadn't been for me, he would never have been in this awkward position in the first place.)

The theory was fine, but putting it into practice was much more difficult. In no time at all I had covered two sides of paper with possible messages. I didn't want to initiate interest from every crank and lonely heart in the country, but then again I dared not be too specific, lest some highly intelligent or semi-clairvoyant *Times* reader cottoned on to what was being said. I needed something which was instantly compre-hensible to Alan but meant absolutely nothing to anyone else.

My final version was: *Sweetie-Pie alive and well. Concerned about your situation. Identify yourself via same means.* My message appeared in the Saturday edition of *The Times* and I went through agonies during the next forty-eight hours as I awaited any response. In the meantime, there was no respite

from unwelcome reminders of Alan's plight: every news bulletin
carried a reminder of the operation being conducted at his house
and the Sunday papers had a field day. With essentially no new
material, apart from the discovery of one woman's body in a
field, they filled entire pages with stories of missing women
and girls, accompanied by the old familiar pictures of Marie
Glover, Sally Walsh and all the rest, with the whole serial-killer-
in-Nicholsfield idea resurrected. All sorts of odd clues about
sightings of mystery men in cars and sinister men lurking in
country lanes, none of whom had ever been satisfactorily identified, were dredged up and recycled, with inevitably a grainy
picture of Alan and me on our wedding day on an inside page.
Meanwhile, the police were still appealing for Alan to come
forward and help them with their enquiries.

I was on the step of the village stores when they opened
for business on Monday morning, along with Mrs Lindsay-
Scott, whose clothes bore evidence of an early stint in the
stables, and Mr Henderson, dapper as usual, complete with
his terrier on a lead at his side. While he was asking her
opinion on the chances of a local runner in the Hornby Castle
Point-to-Point, I fussed Jeff, interest in the little dog providing
a convenient way of not betraying my agitation while I waited
for the door to be unfastened.

'You're an early bird this morning,' Mrs Lindsay-Scott's
voice boomed out above my head, forcing me to straighten
up and leave off stroking the dog as I vainly tried to think of
a reason for my presence. Not that wanting to buy a paper
was a hanging offence.

'I've never been to a Point-to-Point,' I said, deciding a
diversionary tactic was necessary. 'I'm not even sure that I'd
know how to put a bet on.'

'Easy, m'dear. Just choose your horse and hand over your
money – there's no mystery to it.'

'It's a grand day out.' Mr Henderson added his encouragement. 'Nowt to beat it on a nice day. Picnic chairs into the
car and away we go, eh, Jeff?'

'Do they allow dogs?' I asked.

Mrs Lindsay-Scott emitted a friendly bark of laughter. 'Dear
girl, the place is always teeming with dogs. Pongo has a

marvellous time, hoovering up discarded picnic remnants before I can stop him. He's a dreadful animal, really – no discipline, but what can you expect with Dalmations?'

We all turned at the audible sound of bolts being drawn back behind the shop door. I stood back to let the others pass, trying not to appear too eager, and managing to restrain myself from opening the paper until I made it into the security of my office. I had assumed that my message would only solicit interest from one particular individual, but I was mistaken. To my amazement Sweetie-Pie had provoked three replies in the personal columns. One was from a man called Derek, who said it was good to receive this positive news and invited me to contact him through a box number. A second correspondent, identifying him or herself only by the letter J, rejoiced in 'Sweetie-Pie's good news', exhorting me to pray to the Lord Jesus that I might be 'found indeed' – a sentiment not at all in keeping with the spirit of my intentions. The final message was the shortest: *Toodlebum requests Sweetie-Pie's intentions be stated via same channel.*

It was a curiously abrupt message. Then again why should Alan, the husband I had deserted, be anything but cool when I suddenly decided to initiate contact? Not only had I caused untold pain by walking out on him in the first place, the manner in which I had elected to do so had resulted in his present predicament; moreover, perhaps the sudden reappearance of his estranged wife, when he might reasonably have assumed her to be gone for good, suggested all sorts of unpleasant complications to him. I needed to reassure him that I posed no threat to whatever romantic or domestic arrangements he had in place now – all I wanted was to establish with the authorities that I was not the body in the field. Once things were sorted out we could both go our separate ways. No strings. No complications.

Could this be accomplished without any publicity, if Alan and I made a discreet appearance at a police station to vouch for each other? Might it still be possible to continue with my Susan McCarthy life? Surely a police force engaged in a major murder investigation wouldn't want to interest themselves in what I had been up to for the past six years?

No, that was hopelessly optimistic. They would probably throw the book at me – everything from deception to wasting police time. Was Alan's freedom that important to me? Maybe if I just lay low everything would sort itself out without my intervention. Alan was a smart cookie. Surely he could work something out for himself without Sweetie-Pie along to hold his hand?

I was still engaged in this inner debate when a tentative rap on my office door preceded the entry of the Trollop. She was carrying a set of patient's notes in her hand and something in her manner alerted me to the possibility of a problem above and beyond the normal routine.

'Susan, have you got a minute?' She spoke in the tone habitually adopted by a member of staff initiating an awkward conversation of a confidential nature – urgency coupled with a voice slightly lowered, as if there might be listeners posted outside the door.

'Of course. Is something the matter?' I could feel my heart speeding up, because lately any unexpected request for a word with me might be a precursor to a conversation about my similarities to an actress, a murder victim, or 'something a bit odd' that Dr Milly had let slip.

'It's this file. Not the file exactly . . . well, what's in it. I think . . . well, I know we can't . . . but I think we should . . .' She stumbled on, searching my face for help, but drawing a blank because I hadn't the first idea what she was getting at, or whether it had possible consequences for me. 'It's Luke Robinson's file,' she said. 'You know Luke Robinson?'

'Not really.' I forced my features into my calm management smile. It wasn't about me. It was a work thing – just a work thing.

'He's this lad. He used to go to the comp, but now he works with his dad on their farm.'

I nodded to confirm that I knew this much. He was the boy who used to get the bus at the same place as Julie Peacock.

'He's been under the Young People's Psychiatric Service for ages. I've been filing the letters. You can't help seeing what they're about.'

'Everything in a patient's file is confidential,' I interrupted gently, while thinking that there hadn't been a word of this in the village stores. The boy and his parents had evidently managed to keep the referral quiet – there were more secrets in Lasthwaite than I thought. 'Even if you happen to see something accidentally, you know you're not allowed to discuss it with anyone, or divulge it.'

'I know.'

We all knew. It was a golden rule. Patient confidentiality was paramount. Not only was this an unquestioned given, but quite a few of the staff actively liked it, because it inflated their sense of importance, made them the guardians of secrets – even if the secret was no more than a prescription for a cough linctus.

'So whatever you saw – accidentally – on Luke Robinson's file, you mustn't discuss it with anyone – including me – in or outside the building.'

It was not as if a longstanding employee like the Trollop needed any such warning, but in framing the reminder I was essentially warning her not to step any further over the line, so I was shocked when she continued inexorably: 'The letters from his psychiatrist say he has violent fantasies directed at fellow pupils. Everyone knows he was hanging around Julie Peacock.' She was meeting my eye, staring me out.

'That's between Luke Robinson and the doctors treating him,' I said firmly. Whatever I thought privately about the matter I had to tow the party line. 'I'm surprised at you—'

'Someone should tell the police,' she interrupted. Her voice had a surprisingly decided quality which brooked no argument. 'He might be dangerous, Susan. He might do it again. And what about all the decent men around here who're under suspicion?'

'It's not our decision.' It was my turn to interrupt. 'We're not responsible. We don't make the rules, but we have to keep them. Besides which, this boy might be completely innocent – have you considered that?'

'I've got a thirteen-year-old niece . . .'

'You are not allowed to reveal the contents of a patient's records. You wouldn't only lose your job you know, you could be prosecuted. You might go to prison.'

'And what if he's never arrested and he hurts someone else?' she asked. 'Would I rather have that on my conscience? I'll leave the file here so's you can read it yourself.' She dropped the file on the corner of my desk and made for the door.

'No . . . wait,' I protested, but she had already closed the door behind her.

I brought my hand down hard on the desk, the impact sending my pen skittering on to the floor. Not now, I thought. Don't try to involve me in this now when I've already got enough dilemmas to hog-tie Confucius. There was no dilemma here anyhow. We're not allowed to blow the whistle, even if psychiatric reports made it obvious that Luke Robinson was guilty of everything from sheep shagging to multiple homicide.

Yet even while knowing that she was one hundred per cent in the wrong, part of me paid the Trollop grudging admiration. She was by no means the first person in the medical world who thought that public safety ought to score higher than an individual's right to gag his doctors and associated staff. A tiny minority believed that far from keeping silent, medical professionals had a positive duty to work with the police where it might prevent other people being put at risk, particularly in an era where psychiatric patients were routinely cared for in the community and detaining anyone on a mere suspicion that they might present a danger to others was all but unheard of.

I'd never had the Trollop down as a woman of strong enough convictions to put her job on the line for a principle. Why, oh why did her conscience have to rear its head just now? It was a disciplinary matter, of course. Staff were not supposed to peruse correspondence relating to a patient unless they actively needed to. I couldn't just ignore the confession that a member of my staff had done so, or that she was now threatening to go public with the information she had gleaned.

My head was beginning to spin. At any moment I might hear that 'my' corpse had been reclaimed by its rightful owners, which would probably lead to me being unmasked as the real Jennifer Reynolds by Dr Millington. Dr Millington had been treating me with exaggerated politeness since his last visit to my cottage, but how vindictive might he feel when he discovered that all this self-abasement had been for nothing? On the other hand, if the corpse in the ditch continued to be identified with me, then I might have to unmask myself to get Alan off the hook. And as if all that wasn't enough, the staff I was supposed to be managing were either individually or collectively (for Medical Records tended to operate as a pack) on the point of plunging the practice into a massive breach of medical ethics.

My little world was falling in on itself. I can't cope with all this, I thought.

I dumped a computer print-out on top of Luke Robinson's file, trying to make-believe that out of sight genuinely equated to out of mind, and returned to the vexed question of communicating with Alan. If the initial message had been difficult to formulate, the second was even worse. There was an afternoon deadline for placing any items which were to appear the following day, so I had to work on the wording at my desk, stuffing my various attempts out of sight every time someone entered the office. After numerous false starts I came up with: *S to T. Want nothing except to get you out of present difficulties. Must avoid publicity.*

With the message phoned through I tried to catch up on my regular work. It was getting on for half past five by the time I was done for the day. Most of the staff were long gone by then. I began to tidy the top of my desk, ignoring the Luke Robinson file for as long as possible. The correct thing would be to send it back for filing. I had no business reading a patient's notes just because a member of staff had directed me to something interesting in the contents. Yet in a strange way, I felt as if the Trollop had dared me to do it. Only now did it occur to me to question why, if she intended to leak the information to the police, had she bothered to involve me at all? If she had simply photocopied the relevant pages and passed them on anonymously, the source of the leak might never have been traced. The file was accessible to anyone working in the practice if they wanted to get hold of it. It was easy enough to slip into Medical Records and pull a patient's file. For that matter the boy's psychiatrist, or more likely the medical secretary who typed up his reports, could have been responsible. So why flag up her intentions to me?

Did she want me to be complicit in order to shield her
during any ensuing investigation? Or could she be letting me
know what she planned to do in order to protect her colleagues?
If so it was a brave admission – I knew she couldn't afford
to lose the job. Apart from the occasional opening in hospitality, work was all but impossible to come by in the dale.
Maybe she was challenging me to do the deed? Well that
definitely made her Crazy Woman. Even under normal circumstances I had my career to think about. *No one* breached
medical confidentiality.

I had my coat on and a hand on the door knob when, seized
by a sudden impulse which would have done Crazy Woman
credit, I returned to my desk, sat down and opened Luke
Robinson's file. It was more bulky than was normal for a
healthy seventeen-year-old. Words and phrases jumped from
the page, turning me cold. When Linda the cleaner popped
her head in at my door, I jumped and cried out.

'Ee, sorry Susan, I didn't know you were still in here. I'll
come back.'

'No, no. It's fine, I was just going.' I scrabbled the file
closed and locked it in my desk drawer with an undue haste
which was fortunately lost on Linda, who had dragged a black
bin liner across the floor and was engaged in upending my
waste paper basket into it.

We wished each other cheery goodnights, though my mood
was anything but cheery as I climbed into the car with those
phrases still buzzing around my head . . . *obsessive behaviour
. . . violent ideation . . . paranoid delusions, particularly
regarding various school friends . . . admits he has sometimes
followed these girls without their being aware of it . . . particularly fixated on a girl he calls Julie . . .*

TWENTY-THREE

Alan's reply bounced back within twenty-four hours of mine: *S and T ONLY to meet at last port of call 6th inst. Signify agreement or not.*

What the hell was he talking about?

The sixth was only the day after tomorrow. I had to reply, but how could I agree to meet him if I didn't know where to go? I puzzled over the message all day, but I couldn't get it. 'Port of call' was one of those irritating phrases Alan had been prone to use a lot. As in, 'I think we'd better make Sainsbury's our next port of call.'

Did he mean the last place we had ever been together? Well, surely not. That had been our kitchen, breakfast time, the day I went away. With police swarming all over the house and the press there in force, he couldn't possibly be proposing that we walk into the middle of that three-ring circus?

Did he mean the last place we had specifically gone to together? A pub lunch at The Ship? Or had it been somewhere else altogether? I realized with alarm that while our last outing might have been etched forever in Alan's memory, I had no accurate recollection of it at all.

I could understand him being cagey. He probably suspected a trap of some kind, so he wanted me to come discreetly and alone, to a location encoded in a way that only I would know where to go – except that I didn't. I ripped the relevant square out of the newspaper and kept it on my desk, concealing it under Luke Robinson's file whenever anyone came into the office.

I experienced a moment of anxiety when I went into Medical Records and saw that the Trollop's desk was empty, but my tentative enquiry met with an immediate reminder from the Tragedy Queen that she was on a scheduled day off. Something to do with her mother and a hospital appointment. Well, at least while she was tied up at the Infirmary she couldn't be faxing documents through to North Yorkshire Police.

I read the little scrap of newsprint, limp and dispirited from repeated handling, over and over again. To meet on the sixth with no time specified. I tried to decipher it by considering the practicalities of this arrangement. Alan had evidently worked out that it was no use turning himself in to the police on the strength of a newspaper advertisement proclaiming his wife alive and well, since that proved nothing without the physical presence of the woman who had placed it. Obviously he had no intention of sitting all day in a pub in Nicholsfield where he might attract suspicion, or risk being recognized by somebody who would alert the police. It had to be a spot where he was not at risk of recognition: somewhere well outside his usual haunts, where a lone man could hang about all day if necessary, without attracting undue attention.

When this line of thought got me nowhere, I began to play around with the words themselves, moving letters about, discovering words such as total and local, and coming up with enigmatic messages such as 'Call at Fort Pols' – wherever that might be. Alan had always been much better than I was at anagrams and puzzles.

The deadline for Thursday's edition approached and passed, but I was still no wiser as to what on earth he meant. If you can't work it out then you can't go, whispered the voice of treachery in my head. Maybe it's a sign that you should stay here and keep your head down, wait for everything to blow over.

I took the clipping home with me and laid it on the kitchen table while I prepared, then consumed my evening meal – not that I needed a visual aid, for by now I knew the words by heart. Knew them by heart and yet couldn't work out the riddle he had set for me. I burned a little at the thought of Alan laughing at me. How could I be so dense? Solving conundrums, unravelling cryptic clues; it was another area of life in which he had been smugly superior. I felt all the old frustrations welling up. Alan had always enjoyed being smarter than I was. Well this time he might have been just too darned clever for his own good. Poor old Jenny, I thought. Never more than the foil for his ready wit, his stooge, his second in command . . . that was it! I blushed at my slowness, my stupidity. On boating holidays I had always been his second in command and we had, quite literally, called at ports – ports being Alan's nautical speak for any stopping-off place during a voyage.

Our last holiday afloat had been on the Broads, a long weekend which had begun and ended at the boatyards in Stalham. I had been an idiot, looking for something far too complex. Alan intended me to go to the boatyard at Stalham. A busy boatyard would provide good cover for our meeting. He could sit in the little café and await my arrival. The boatyard would be full of bustle, with people bringing boats in and out. Even so, they might spot a strange man hanging about . . . I began to consider afresh. It was very early in the season. Might not the boatmen, the cleaners, the various staff who are always busy about the yard, notice a man waiting around but never actually taking a boat out? The very last thing Alan wanted was to attract attention, and there is nothing so calculated to achieve that as a man skulking around to no apparent purpose. Perhaps he didn't mean Stalham. Perhaps I was barking up the wrong tree entirely.

If I could only work out what he meant, there was still time to place my advert tomorrow so that it appeared on the morning of the sixth, but I couldn't signify agreement unless I was absolutely certain that I understood the bloody message.

Port of call. Port of call. I was sure now that it had something to do with boating holidays. Alan had always enjoyed messing about on the water and we had spent several holidays on canal boats and a couple on motor cruisers.

Last port of call. It wasn't a boatyard. That was where you went to give the boat back at the end of the holiday. It must have been the last place before that: the place where we had spent our last night afloat, prior to handing back the boat. Where? Where the hell had we stopped last of all?

There had been two separate holidays on the Broads: a long weekend, and a full week during which we had stopped at seemingly dozens of places, all of which had now merged into hazy recollections of wooden staithes and waterside pubs and herons – more herons than I had ever imagined existed – at every bend in the river.

Think, think. Forget the herons. Look at the road atlas – that will show the place names. I marched into the sitting room and cast an impatient eye across the book shelves which stood in the alcove under the stairs. Where was the big road atlas? I was pretty sure it hadn't been left in the car. I located the book on the bottom shelf and drew it out, carrying it back to the table where I could open the atlas right out at the page showing Norfolk and concentrate on the names of places which lay on the river. I knew the last port of call must have been somewhere not far from Stalham because you always had to get the boat back horribly early in the morning: so not Acle then, nor Ranworth, nor Potter Heigham, which I remembered because of the low bridge which we could only navigate with the aid of a pilot.

I traced the tiny blue thread which marked the river, a wiggling blue line labelled R Ant – rant was about the right word, I thought. Rant at the obscurity of Alan's message, combined with the paucity of my own memory. According to the map, Stalham wasn't even on the river, which was a bit confusing. I followed the river south with my finger – not an easy task on a map where roads predominated and every bit of space seemed to be cluttered with symbols for campsites, historic houses and gardens open to the public. Long-forgotten names rang distant bells. Thurne I remembered for its pub and windmill – we had stopped there at least twice, but surely not on our final evening, with so many miles of river still to go before we reached Stalham and the boatyards.

The most obvious place on the map was called Irstead. It was marked as a tiny riverside settlement, yet the name was entirely unfamiliar. Then I spotted the thinnest of blue lines, branching away to the left of the main river, and I remembered. That thinnest of blue lines was Lime Kiln Dyke, a narrow twisting channel lined by trees which led to a dead end where Neatishead staithe stood at right angles to the dyke. That had been our last port of call.

TWENTY-FOUR

Thoroughly absorbed in my clandestine world of cloak-and-dagger cryptic exchanges, I found it difficult to concentrate on anything else. It was almost a source of surprise to me, the way life in Lasthwaite went on just as usual, and on Thursday morning I was so preoccupied with ensuring that I got my confirmation of the rendezvous into the next day's paper, I had completely managed to forget about the Luke Robinson issue, and so was caught off guard when I encountered the Trollop in the upstairs corridor.

'I was coming to see you later,' she said, her tone half confrontational, half conspiratorial. 'To ask what you'd decided.'

I regarded her blankly. Then the penny dropped. 'I can't discuss it just now,' I said. 'You'll have to give me some time.'

She nodded and walked on, half as if this had been what she was expecting. I watched her disappearing down the stairs, struck dumb by my own words. Discuss it? Any idea of a *discussion* was absolute madness. There was nothing to discuss. I had to give her an official warning about reading a patient's records, instruct her not to mention anything more about Luke Robinson to anyone and put the file back where it belonged. Instead, I had promised her a 'discussion' and her nod had conveyed a suggestion of satisfaction. She thought I was on board with disclosure, or at the very least prepared to consider it.

As I walked back to my own office, I reflected again that she was prepared to risk her job for a point of principle, while mine was probably as good as forfeit already. Even so, I did what I could to cling on. It was easy to arrange some time off work in spite of the short notice. At morning break I told the doctors that one of my aunts had died. I said it was all very sudden, and that because the aunt had no children of her own and we were such a very small family, it had fallen to me to go south and make the necessary arrangements.

'Because it's a sudden death, it might be a bit complicated,' I said, mentally noting yet again what a plausible liar I had become. 'So I'm not really sure how long I shall have to be down there – probably a couple of days at least – but I will know better when I get there.'

None of them commented on the oddity of my never having mentioned this ailing relative before, or queried my pressing obligation to take charge of the funeral arrangements and sort out my aunt's affairs. Perhaps if I had been the sort of person forever seeking time off to bury grandmothers, an eyebrow or an objection might have been raised, but of course Susan McCarthy wasn't like that. She scarcely took all her holiday entitlement, never mind swinging the lead for sickness or family reasons. The doctors were all kindness and told me to take as long as I needed, and as word got round the other staff sidled up and said they were sorry to hear about my auntie and just to say the word if there was anything they could do.

I might not need to go, I told myself. Today might be the day when Alan turns up, or something happens to divert suspicion away from him. Even so I spent the afternoon wondering what I should take with me. Any form of identification to prove that I was Jennifer Reynolds was impossible – I had none by deliberate design. Susan McCarthy's driving licence went into the bag, although I hoped it wouldn't be necessary to actually show it to anyone. Clothes were another worry. I wasn't even sure how long I was going to be away because I still had no clear idea what giving myself up might entail. It would be awful if the police detained me and I ran out of clean knickers, and in any case I knew that my errand could not possibly be accomplished in a single day – it was too far from Lasthwaite to Neatishead and back – so overnight things would certainly be needed.

This in turn raised the question of where I would spend the night. Ought I to book ahead – find a suitable bed and breakfast somewhere in Norfolk? Then again, suppose we had to travel back to the Midlands – if we reported to the police in Norfolk, would they just hand us on to the relevant force? In that case an advance reservation might prove to be an expensive nuisance, so I decided that the question of where to spend the night could be resolved when I got down there. From what I could remember Norfolk was full of pubs, and it was early enough in the season to turn up on spec.

The biggest issue was Rob. If our world was about to be blown apart, at the very least I wanted to be the one to explain. He had called me once from the pay phone at the field centre, but I could barely hear him against a cacophony of high youthful voices, and every so often his words were drowned out completely by the rattle of coins dropping into something metallic close at hand. When I asked him what on earth was going on, he managed to tell me that the phone was immediately adjacent to the vending machines which sold drinks and confectionery, at which point his words were obscured as another series of coins cascaded down a metal chute and more voices piped up nearby. In such circumstances there was very little we could say to one another – conversations of an intimate or complex nature were definitely out.

'I'll ring you as soon as I get home,' he shouted.

I couldn't bear to think that this might be our final conversation before the dam broke and our relationship drowned amid the chaos wrought of my lies. He was due to return on the sixth but now Alan had named the sixth as the day for our meeting – it could hardly have fallen out worse. Rob wasn't likely to call from the field centre again, and even if he did that only resurrected the impossibility of trying to explain things over the phone.

Would he stand by me when I turned out to be a liar and a cheat . . . deserter and deceiver of a previous spouse? If only I could cling to the wreckage a little longer; at least hold everything together long enough to tell him I was sorry. As my mind raced in circles, I still clung to the hope that everything would work itself out. Maybe I should just sit tight and do nothing?

Just before leaving work I extracted all the relevant reports from Luke Robinson's file and took them to the big photocopier which stood on the landing. No one was likely to question what I was doing, but even so I breathed a little easier when the task was accomplished without the appearance of any potential inquisitors. Back in my office, I replaced the originals in the file, which I then locked inside my desk drawer to guarantee its inaccessibility to any other self-appointed crusaders. I slid the copies I'd made into a blank manila envelope, which I carried openly out of the building, as coolly as if I purloined patient records every day of the week.

Hopes regarding the 'do nothing' option were further dashed by the nightly news, which brought confirmation that the police were continuing their fruitless investigation of Alan's garden. A brief flicker of excitement had run through the waiting media encampment a couple of days earlier when rumours of a find had reached them, but it soon died down again with the confirmation that the bones unearthed in Alan's flower beds belonged to a small animal – no doubt the remains of some long-forgotten pet buried there by previous occupants.

With no other discoveries in the garden and no fresh leads on Alan's whereabouts, the story had descended into that middle section of also-ran items which come before the silly story at the end: the one about the dog who has been skateboarding along a seaside promenade, or the batty old bloke who intends to push a doll's pram around Europe for charity. The always leave 'em laughing principle, I supposed, although I never felt much like laughing at the end of the bulletins myself.

The realization that I had to go through with meeting Alan the next day induced a similar state of disbelief to that which I had experienced when I originally left him. The same air of unreality overshadowed my preparations, which on one level seemed no more than playing a game, until having put one foot inexorably in front of the other, you find that the moment has come for the step from which there is no drawing back.

And what about Rob? I couldn't just go off without saying a word. The obvious solution was to leave a message at his cottage for him to find on his return. He had given me his spare front door key, so it would be easy enough for me to let myself in and leave a note for him – which was all very well, except for the fact that I had no idea what to write. I was determined to tell Rob the whole truth. I *owed* it to him to tell him the truth because love without complete honesty is no sort of love at all. At the same time if there was one thing I was sure about, it was the need to sit down with Rob and explain everything face-to-face – no letter or note was going to suffice – but with no hope of seeing him until after my rendezvous with Alan, there seemed little choice but to formulate some kind of interim message which accounted for my sudden absence.

The dead aunt story had been good enough for my colleagues, but Rob was going to know at once that the dead aunt was a phoney. I tried to think of something that was roughly comparable which did not involve yet more lies. I toyed with telling him that I had to go and sort out some 'family problems'. This had the attraction of being more than partly true, since Alan and I were, technically at least, still 'family', but it would surely puzzle Rob, who until now had thought me singularly bereft of family to have any problems which needed sorting out. There was also the risk that he could easily bump into someone who *had* bought into the dead aunt story, at which point he might blurt out, unthinking, that I didn't have any aunts to bury, leaving me with a lot of explaining to do on my return to work. The last thing I needed just now was problems for taking time off under false pretences. (Oh, really? What was one more misdemeanour on a very long list?) Whichever way I looked at it, the hole I had been steadily excavating for myself these past few years had turned into a bottomless pit.

In the midst of all this, one tiny rainbow shone on the far distant horizon, for a meeting with Alan opened up new possibilities. If Alan agreed to a divorce that would free me to marry again: I could revert to my single name, or maybe even change my name officially to Susan McCarthy. I could be a legitimate person again. There must be ways of doing these things and although I didn't know what was entailed, if Rob was on my side I might at least be brave enough to ask the right questions.

I was getting quite carried away with this hazy, optimistic future in which everything was straightened out following the rendezvous at our Last Port of Call, when I abruptly remembered all the other sink holes that littered the path ahead. Better try to focus on one step at a time, which meant formulating the message for Rob to find when he got home. I made numerous false starts, covering sheaves of paper in hopeless drafts as I discovered that the more I tried to say, the more I needed to say, in order to explain what I had said already. I eventually opted for brevity. The final version was not particularly satisfactory, but it was the best I could do.

> *Dear Rob,*
> *I have to go away on a very private matter, but I promise I will explain everything as soon I see you again. I have told everyone at work that one of my aunts has died and I have to go and sort things out. Please don't let anyone know that this isn't true.*
> *I love you.*
> *Sue*

I wrote out a fair copy, then drove to his cottage with the note lying beside me on the passenger seat. The sky was tinged with sunset pinks and golds, and the birds were offering up a hymn to the beauty of the English countryside. As I walked up his garden path not a vehicle was audible, not a sound betrayed the century as the twentieth.

I had hardly ever been inside Rob's cottage when he wasn't there, and I let myself in rather hesitantly, stepping quietly as though to avoid waking sleepers. The sun had been shining steadily all day, warming the sitting room, drawing out the smells of dust and books accentuating some lingering scent of aromatic candles, which reminded me of a church in which the incense of many services still lingers long after the congregation has gone. I placed the note where he couldn't miss it, on the pine table in the centre of the living room atop a small pile of post, which I had picked up and carried in from the doormat.

His presence was strong inside the house. Just being surrounded by his things brought him closer. I lingered, drinking in the sensation, casting around for excuses to prolong my stay. I crossed the room and straightened the curtains, glancing out of the window as I did so. The sky was losing its pinks now, shot across with the purplish greys that preceded dusk. The notion came into my mind that I was taking a last look round because I would never come here again. I had to fist tears out of my eyes and pull myself together.

Rob had left a sweater lying across the back of a chair by the door. I picked it up and put it to my face, feeling the thick, soft wool against my skin, inhaling the scent of him, his unique desirable sweetness, as fresh and strong as if he had only taken it off a moment before, but when something small fell from it I jumped back, thinking of spiders. The thing at my feet was not a spider, but a curl of paper – a refugee from some torn writing which had avoided destruction by clinging to a sleeve. It was only possible to make out one word: *Strangle*. It looked as if there had been another letter joined on to the *e*. Strangles, Strangled, Stranglers – that would be it. A list of tracks – wasn't Rob always humming *No More Heroes*? I tossed the little bit of paper at the fireplace, but it missed and fluttered back on to the rug as if determined to survive. I retrieved it and this time stood near enough to the fireplace to drop it directly inside the grate. It was only as I straightened up that I spotted an earring lying on the mantelshelf. It was one I had mislaid weeks before, which Rob had evidently found but forgotten to give back. I retrieved it and put it into my pocket.

Then I noticed something else on the shelf. Rob was far from the tidiest of mortals, so there were in fact a number of items which did not strictly belong there – a spare set of car keys, a two-pence piece, a rather grubby, much folded piece of lined paper, and underneath the paper a beer mat. He had obviously emptied his pockets on the way into or out of the house. It was not one of these items which had arrested my attention, however. The beer mat lay at a careless angle, part on, part off the shelf, not quite level thanks to there being another small object underneath it. A loop of silver chain hung over the edge of the shelf, offering a clue to the nature of the hidden article.

I picked up and unfolded the paper first, immediately recognizing the running order of a home-made car tape – a list of tracks which began with Talking Heads – *Psycho Killer* and

culminated in a torn corner alongside: *rs – No More Heroes.*
I smiled – Rob having a back-to-the-seventies moment. I
refolded the list and returned it to the shelf. The beer mat
I recognized as the one Rob had used to take down the phone
number of a lad in the pub who was willing to loan him a
strimmer for use in his garden. Though I barely touched the
beer mat, the movement disturbed the chain underneath so
that it slid to the floor in a single sinuous movement and lay
on the rug at my feet. I could see that it was a cheap necklace
of the kind currently favoured by the early teens; one of those
chains with a single initial suspended from it – a letter J.

I stared at the necklace for a long moment. For some reason
I found myself reluctant to pick it up, but of course I had to
– it must be picked up and put back exactly as it had been
before I disturbed it. I attempted to drape the necklace over
the edge of the shelf, in faithful imitation of the way it had
been originally, but the chain seemed to have a life of its own,
plunging treacherously to the floor like an escaping snake
every time I tried to balance the beer mat on top of it. After
three attempts, I pulled myself up short. What the hell was
the matter with me? Did I think I had to fool Rob into believing
that I had not seen the necklace? If Rob had been bothered
about me seeing the thing, would he have casually left it lying
about in his living room? There were at least two perfectly
innocent explanations for the necklace coming into his possession. He was a teacher, for goodness' sake. On the one hand,
he might have confiscated it from someone – there were strict
rules about wearing jewellery in school. On the other, it might
have been handed to him as lost property. In either case, he
had probably put it in his pocket and forgotten all about it,
along with the beer mat. No doubt he had intended to take it
straight back into school – just as he had planned to return
my earring. He taught dozens of girls whose names began
with J – Joannes, Jodies, Jessicas – it probably ran into three
figures.

The crash as something hit the window made me jump and
cry out. I turned instinctively to see what had made the noise,
discarding the troublesome necklace on the table alongside
my note before approaching the window to investigate. There

was a ghostly avian imprint in the centre of one pane. Probably a sparrow hawk misjudging his direction in pursuit of small prey. I peered out anxiously but there was no sign of a stunned bird lying on the ground outside.

'You're a fool,' I told myself. 'All this stuff with Alan is making you crazy, so that you're spooked by anything.'

I drove back to Heb's Cottage, had some supper and went to bed early, setting my alarm for six. By quarter to seven the next morning I was on my way, showered and breakfasted, with the road atlas on the passenger seat beside me and an overnight bag in the boot. For some reason I felt absurdly excited, like a child setting off on holiday, the cloudless blue sky no doubt adding to the illusion. The radio had not worked since an unfortunate accident to the aerial at a car wash in Richmond, so I put on an Abba tape and joined in with the vocals, filling the car with a loud, cheerful noise. The journey engendered an illusion of leaving all my problems behind. Alone in the car I could be in the moment – no need to pretend anything to anyone, be on the lookout for booby traps, or try to make decisions about the best thing to do.

There was relatively little traffic in the dale, but once I reached the A1 I stopped singing and had to concentrate. Heavy lorries charged south with scant respect for my little Fiesta, and it was not until I reached the junction with the M18 that things calmed down enough to leave me space for thoughts unconnected with the perils posed by my fellow motorists. It had all been very different in those far off days when Dad took the car out for 'a spin'. Rural roads had been virtually deserted then. His car had been his pride and joy: all polished and gleaming. Just like him in a way – always well turned out so that people noticed and admired the exterior and never wondered what exactly lay inside.

How faithfully I had imitated him, I thought, hiding behind an assumed identity – an act entirely alien to most people, but one which almost made kindred spirits of my father and me. He too had invented so much of himself – the man who espoused music he did not listen to and books he did not read. Had he really played cricket for his regiment and had 'a good war'? How were we to know? Then there was his marriage, that greatest lie of all: a pantomime played out before an audience who never suspected the existence of the packet he treasured for thirty years containing letters from the real love of his life, the mysterious Jean, who had gone away to teach in South Africa so many years ago.

A man who had kept everyone at a distance. Too late now to question whether my father's coldness and indifference had been no more than my just deserts. Had I not shunned him all through my teenage years, watching him with cold, suspicious eyes? And all for nothing. My father had never harmed any of those girls. I was as sure of that now as I had once been convinced of his guilt, for the night Antonia Bridgeman died my father was lying in a hospital bed, recovering from the first bout of surgery on his heart. In the years that followed several more girls had supposedly fallen victim to the mysterious Nicholsfield killer, and by that time my father was already dead. It was too late to turn the clock back, too late to make amends. Only a series of chance coincidences had forged a chain of suspicion in my mind. I could only pray that he had never guessed the direction my thoughts had taken. When I remembered my father now, he no longer appeared to be a figure of fear but rather a lonely, disappointed man, sitting at a roll-top desk, occasionally re-reading the letters from the one woman who had truly loved him. Perhaps it was this vision of my father which had persuaded me to drive south in the hope of saving another man from drowning in a well of false conclusions and misunderstandings. It was almost like making amends.

I had been driving for over two hours by the time I reached Newark, where I drew in at a service station for a coffee, but although the sun was still shining and the driving easy, the holiday feeling had gone, its place taken by a creeping list of uncertainties. Even the phrase 'Last Port of Call' had taken on a vaguely sinister aspect. There was an air of finality about it, suggestive of a doomed ocean liner equipped with a Grim Reaper at the gang plank, beckoning passengers aboard.

And then there was my growing dread of coming face-to-face with Alan. It was not going to be easy after a gap of more than six years. I reminded myself that I was strong and independent now – a very different, grown-up kind of person who was not obliged to fall in with his every suggestion. I had nothing to fear from him. Not, I hastened to assure myself, that I had ever been afraid of him in the past – not really afraid of him – just completely dominated, steamrollered, carried along by his certainties, unable to resist the tide.

Well, it was different now. I was different.

TWENTY-FIVE

I was feeling tired and travel-worn by the time I finally saw the sign which announced that I had crossed the county boundary and entered Norfolk. I pulled in at the next lay-by and consulted the map, noting that it was still about thirty miles to Neatishead, and not all of the route lay along dual carriageway. It was also a long time since breakfast and I decided that a revision of plans was called for. In the first place, I would find somewhere to stop for lunch and in the second, in spite of my previous reservations on the subject, I would find somewhere to stay the night. I would initiate contact with Alan and then, irrespective of whatever ideas he might have on the subject, I would enjoy a decent meal and a good night's sleep in a comfortable bed in preparation for what promised to be a difficult day ahead. One more night wouldn't make any difference and there was sure to be a place with vacancies on the road between Norwich and Wroxham: not only would it be sensible to have somewhere lined up, I could also take the opportunity to wash and change.

My first priority was easily accomplished. I had an indifferent sandwich at a roadside pub, followed by coffee but no pudding. Tonight, I thought, when I've met Alan and we've agreed on the best way forward, I'm going to have a really good meal somewhere with pudding afterwards.

The Norwich Ring Road was busier than I had anticipated and my order in the pub had been slow to arrive, so it was getting on for two o'clock by the time I took the turn for Wroxham. I spotted the sign soon afterwards: *The Sunset Motel – 2 miles on the left.* I left the main road, taking first one turn and then another down the side roads indicated by further brightly painted boards until I found myself driving along a narrow lane between high hedgerows. It already seemed a good deal further than two miles from the main road and an inauspicious location for a motel. I had just begun to conjure up mental images of the shower scene from *Psycho* when the hedges gave way to a huge open forecourt, surrounded on three sides by neat rows of white wooden chalets, each with primrose painted gables which joined to form a bright yellow chevron against the sky. The doors and window frames were all picked out in this same yellow, as was the sign on the single-storey office building at one end, where the word 'Reception' was set in blue letters against a setting sun, orange on the yellow background. The place looked surprisingly prosperous and other parked cars indicated that I was not the only guest.

Reception was deserted, but a single press on the bell summoned a short, plump woman, slightly older than myself, who said that yes, of course I could have a cabin for the night and would I please fill out a registration card.

'You're quite a long way off the main road for a motel,' I said as I printed my name and home address on the card.

'People said we were mad when we first started out,' said the woman. I could tell at once that it was something she often said, perhaps two or three times a day, in fact. 'But a lot of people like the quiet and once folks get to know you're here you get repeat visitors and recommendations. We've got a lot of regulars. Now then,' her tone became more businesslike, 'we can do a breakfast tray to your room if you want it. Cereals, juice, long-life milk, fresh bread roll, butter, jam and a piece of fruit. You've got the tea and coffee-making facilities in the cabin already, of course. Or, if you prefer, there's a very good café just back on the main road where they do a cooked breakfast that I'd be happy to recommend to anyone.'

I declined the in-house breakfast, paid in advance with my Barclaycard and was allocated the key to cabin number four. I moved my car across from Reception and unlocked the cabin door on to a pleasant room fulfilling all the usual expectations: en-suite bathroom with a good supply of towels, floral-patterned duvet on the bed, hanging space, a television and a bedside telephone, beside which a card bore the legend:

Dial 0 for Reception
Dial 9 for an outside line

National calls will be charged at normal rates
This telephone will not connect international calls

I unloaded my bag from the car, had a swift wash and exchanged my lightweight sweater for a warmer hooded top, vaguely registering that the large white logo proclaiming me a member of some fictitious sporting club was just the sort of thing Alan had always loathed. Well, tough luck – I had total control over my wardrobe these days, and a sale bargain was a sale bargain.

In spite of my efforts, I felt sweaty again as soon as I was dressed. The reality of an encounter with Alan could not be avoided for much longer. I tried to reassure myself that in such singular circumstances as these, anyone might feel nervous. There was something else, of course. Something at the back of my mind which I didn't really want to acknowledge – a rather startling truth. The thought of seeing Alan unexpectedly invoked a strong feeling of revulsion.

Suppose Alan was difficult. Suppose . . . It occurred to me then that with somewhere other than the car to leave my things, I had slightly improved my chances of keeping my new identity a secret. Alan did not need to know anything about Susan McCarthy – not at least until I had sounded him out and established exactly how the land lay. Police questions would have to be answered, of course, but we would probably be interviewed separately, and if I asked them not to reveal my name and address to Alan they would probably have to respect my wishes.

I took some notes and coins out of my purse and stuffed them well down into my jeans pocket. That way there was no need to take a handbag or a purse full of clues like credit cards, from which Alan might accidentally glimpse too much information. Just cash, car keys and the motel key would suffice for now.

I took a swift parting glance around the room. Time was ebbing away. Alan was waiting for me and I ought to make contact without wasting any more time, but then the telephone caught my eye. Rob was coming home today. They were supposed to be leaving the field centre around midday, which meant that he might conceivably be back at the cottage by early afternoon. I dialled nine for an outside line, then the area code followed by Rob's familiar number. My heart leapt when the phone stopped ringing, but it was only the answering machine.

'Hi, it's me,' I said, conscious that my voice sounded brittle, even as I attempted to register cheery. 'I hope everything went well with the trip. I'll be in touch again soon. Bye.'

As I got into the car I realized that I had forgotten to say 'I love you'. Too late now. *I Just Called To Say I Love You*. I hummed it as I manoeuvred the car out into the lane. It was one of those songs which I thought I knew but didn't, so I kept singing snatches and coming back to the chorus, until I was so irritated with myself that I had to banish the song by deliberately singing something else: something I did know.

We've Only Just Begun. I knew that one, of course. It was one of the Carpenters greatest hits. I was still singing it when I crossed the bridge at Wroxham, glimpsing the briefest shimmer of the river and the boats below. That was one of the things I remembered about the Broads. From the road you could hardly begin to guess about that world of water and reeds that stretched for mile upon mile, whereas once down there on the water you could go for days at a time and be scarcely aware of any cars at all. Roads were things glimpsed occasionally as you went under a bridge, belonging to an entirely different world.

In spite of looking out for it, I almost missed the turn for Neatishead and had to brake rather sharply, earning an angry reproach from the horn of a following motorist. My hands felt slippery on the steering wheel as I negotiated the lane. I came into the village suddenly – a tiny place which appeared to be utterly deserted. I couldn't immediately see anywhere to park, but eventually I found a space in a small area above the staithe. The question now was where on earth would I find Alan? Not in the little shop surely, and the pub was closed.

I walked from one end of the village street to the other, but no obvious solution presented itself. I wondered if Alan was watching from somewhere close by, concealed by the net curtains which hung in one of the cottage windows perhaps, making absolutely certain that I was alone before revealing himself. I glanced from side to side and over my shoulder. It was absurd, of course, because there was no one watching, but the thought of being under observation made me feel uncomfortable all the same. I glanced at my wrist to check the time, only to realize that I had forgotten to put my watch back on after my ablutions at the motel.

What if I was wrong about Neatishead after all? Or maybe Alan had taken Thursday's silence as a refusal. Perhaps replying on the day itself was too late? Could there have been some mistake resulting in the non-appearance of my message in today's edition? I had not thought to buy a paper and check that my confirmation was there.

It only remained for me to look out on to the staithe itself. I hesitated, doubting now that Alan would have come at all. As far as I could see there was no one there, not even a fisherman sitting hopefully on his creel, a sight I had assumed to be obligatory on every Norfolk staithe, as compulsory as the heron at each bend in the river. It was much quieter here than at most of the public landing places. Just a narrow harbour hemmed in by trees, which today still had plenty of mooring spaces available. There were a couple of yachts and three or four small cruisers tied up on either side of the dyke – fewer than half-a-dozen craft and all apparently deserted.

I had just decided that for want of any better ideas, I might as well walk to the end of the staithe and back, when a head and shoulders emerged from the cruiser moored at the farthest end. The figure silently raised its left arm and made a beckoning gesture. It was Alan.

I entertained a sudden, ludicrous desire to turn tail and run. It *was* ludicrous, of course, because I had not driven for most of the day only to run off when I was on the very point of achieving the purpose of my journey, so after the briefest hesitation I continued to approach the boat, neither slowing nor quickening my pace. This seemed to irritate Alan, who again beckoned urgently. As I got closer, I could see that he was looking uncharacteristically agitated. He did not smile or greet me, just watched me advance in silence.

The little cruiser was moored as if in readiness to head out of the dyke. Alan was standing in the rear cockpit and when I reached the stern of the boat he moved aside, making room for me to step aboard and go below, still looking grave and saying nothing. I accepted the unspoken invitation and stepped on to the deck, hesitating as I felt it move beneath me. It was a long time since I had been aboard a boat and I had forgotten that unnerving tilt as the thing dips to take account of one's weight.

'Are you alone?' His voice was low and urgent – ridiculously so, I thought, considering that there was clearly no one within sight or earshot.

I nodded, opening my mouth to give further confirmation, but he cut across me.

'How did you get here?'

'By car,' I said. 'It's parked just up there . . .'

'Which one is it?'

'The Fiesta. It's the only car up there.'

'Go below,' he said. 'I'll be back in a minute.' He made as if to get off the boat, then said, 'Where are the keys?'

It was such an unexpected question that it caught me off guard.

'Here,' I said, holding them out as visual proof.

He took them – snatched them, really.

'Hey . . .' I made a futile protesting noise.

'Go below,' he said again. 'I'll be back in a minute.'

He bounded on to the staithe in a single movement and strode briskly towards the parking area.

I don't know quite how I had envisaged my meeting with Alan, but this wasn't it. There was something suddenly absurd about the whole proceedings: the cloak-and-dagger code we had adopted to make the arrangements, the ridiculous furtive beckoning from the boat, and now Alan dashing off along the bank, presumably to make sure that there were no policemen hiding behind the waste bins at the end of the staithe. I was inclined to ignore his instruction to go below, but when I saw him returning – having evidently satisfied himself that I was indeed alone – I thought I might as well go down into the cabin.

It was one of those small cruisers which is steered from an

open rear cockpit. A set of short, steep steps descended from the cockpit into the main cabin, which occupied the whole central section of the boat, one of the very smallest of someone's hire fleet; just a fore cabin with two berths and an aft cabin bisected by a narrow central passageway with a table and bench seats on one side, and the sink, cooker and toilet cubicle crammed in on the other. There was probably no more than eight or ten feet separating the cockpit steps and the fore cabin door.

Once inside the boat I stood in this narrow central space, unsure what to do next. Behind me was the ladder down which I had come, ahead of me the closed door beyond which lay the sleeping compartment. I decided the only thing to do was sit down, so I took the seat facing the cockpit.

It was a shabby boat, obviously old, perhaps not even part of a hire fleet any more. I wondered if Alan had bought it. In the past he had sometimes talked about how nice it would be to have a boat of his own, although knowing Alan I would have expected something much smarter. Perhaps this was newly acquired and he intended to do it up? I noted the chips in the edge of the table – not the sort of thing Alan would be willing to live with for very long.

I'd assumed that he would come straight down into the cabin, but he didn't. I felt the slight lurch of the boat as he came aboard, but he failed to appear at the hatch. For a moment I was puzzled, but then I realized from the movements overhead that he must be rigging the awning which covered the rear cockpit. For a moment I wondered whether I ought to offer to help, then dismissed the idea. Of course I shouldn't help. It was nothing to do with me.

In fact the delay was irritating. There was no earthly need to rig the awning just now. It wasn't going to rain. It wasn't anywhere near getting dark. Then I remembered that it was customary to rig the awning before leaving the boat, and Alan must have naturally assumed that we would head off for the nearest police station right away, which made it a perfectly reasonable thing for him to be doing. I almost called out to disabuse him of the idea, but instead I pushed away my irritation and took in more of my surroundings while I waited. If it was Alan's own boat, he had done very little to personalize it. The crockery on the drainer was the same utilitarian smoked glass that I remembered from other hired boats. There was a television, a tiny one, on the small flat area to one side of the cooker. It was switched on too, which was surprising, because Alan had never been a big fan of television and certainly not daytime television. I recognized the programme as a rerun of an old American cop series, which I assumed he must have been watching to pass the time, sitting here in the cabin, wondering whether or not I was going to turn up.

I gradually became aware of other things too. There was a smell, like unwashed socks and greasy washing-up water. The boat must need airing, I thought. The windows were all closed and I somehow didn't like to open one. It seemed an impertinence on someone else's boat. I began to tap my fingers nervously against my kneecaps.

The floor of the cabin was below the water level, and on the side where I was sitting the cabin windows looked out just above the level of the bank, so that if anyone was walking along the seated occupants of the cabin would only see their feet, while they in turn could not see inside the boat, unless they actually knelt down on the ground. The window on the opposite side looked across the dyke to where a white yacht was moored with her awning rigged. There were no signs of life anywhere, not even swans or ducks on the lookout for leftover crusts.

Alan seemed to be taking an inordinately long time, but at last his feet appeared, followed by the rest of him, descending the five steps into the cabin. Once down he pulled the sliding hatch across and closed the door. There was something ominous in this. Something that made me feel claustrophobic. Closed windows, closed doors and this cramped, slightly smelly cabin with Alan in very close proximity.

'Would you like a cup of tea?'

I almost laughed with relief. That most civilized of gestures. Confronted by one's wife, who walked out without a word, and has been gone heaven knows where for the past six years, and what is virtually the first question you ask her? Would you like a cup of tea!

'Yes, please,' I said meekly.

He filled the kettle, lit the gas, reached into the caddy for two teabags which he put in the metal pot, got mugs and milk from the cupboard and fridge working in that precise, methodical, Alan-like way, all the time only inches away from me. I was very aware of this, strongly conscious that I did not want him to touch me, not even to accidentally brush against me. Hoping that he wouldn't notice, I slid further along the plastic covered seat, putting some extra inches between myself and the gangway.

'You knew where to come,' he said as he placed mugs on the draining board. It was not exactly a question or a statement.

'Not at first,' I said. 'But then I worked it out.'

'Clever of you.' It was not said kindly. I felt wounded and almost asked him what would have been the point of his message if I had not been able to work it out, but then I pulled myself up short, reminded myself that he had every justification to be angry. It was small wonder that he had appeared agitated when I first arrived. He was wanted for questioning in connection with a murder. Under such circumstances anyone might look agitated.

I waited for him to say something else, but he continued to stand alongside the cooker, waiting silently for the kettle to boil. It was unnerving. I wanted to break the silence, but I found that I didn't know what to say. I had been so sure that he would make the verbal running, but instead he was making tea. Then I got it. He's playing with me, I thought. Of course Alan will have plenty to say. This is Alan. He's just waiting for me to blurt out some half-cocked remark so that he can ridicule it. He wants a chance to cut me down to size. While his motivation was understandable, I wasn't going to give him the satisfaction, so I waited, matching his silence with my own.

The American detective had got his man and children's programmes were about to start. A smiling presenter was holding up home-made birthday cards, each of them incorporating photographs of the child whose birthday it was.

The kettle began to whistle, but was cut off short in a disappointed spitting noise when Alan lifted it off the gas and poured hot water into the teapot.

'Still milk, no sugar?'

'Thank you.'

He placed the two mugs on the table and sat down, facing me. I was horribly conscious that our knees must be almost touching under the table and I had a strong urge to put more space between us by moving still further along the bench, but since I couldn't do so without its being obvious, I stayed where I was. I put my fingers into the handle of the mug but made no move to drink. The tea would be too hot anyway.

Alan was looking straight at me, cool and contemptuous. 'Well,' he said. 'Aren't you going to tell me why you've come?'

I was taken completely aback. The purpose of my journey was obvious, surely?

'I . . . well . . . I . . .' I stammered in confusion, trying to find a way to start. 'I thought you would want me to come – to prove I'm alive.'

'And how much money did you think I'd give you? No, put it another way – how much money do you want?'

'Nothing.' I was both indignant and amazed. 'I don't want any money at all.'

He frowned slightly. 'Come now, Jenny,' he said after a short pause. 'No point in beating about the bush, is there? I mean let's face it, you haven't come back because you've suddenly realized you love dear old hubby so much that you just can't live without him?'

'No,' I said quietly. 'No, I haven't come back for that. In fact, I want to make it clear straightaway that I don't want to go back to our old life together. Once we've got this business sorted out we will both have to go our separate ways.'

It came to me while I was saying this that he had not returned my car keys. Nor had I seen him put them down anywhere. He must still have them in his pocket.

'Well, well,' he said. 'So that's the idea, is it? I pay up and you disappear into the sunset.'

'I don't know what you mean,' I said. 'I'm not asking you for money. I don't want your money. If it comes to that,' I added with a touch of proud defiance that I couldn't quite suppress, 'I don't need your money.'

He continued to look at me as if half puzzled, half amused.

'Well, what do you want then?'

'I want to get you off the hook,' I said. 'I mean, once the police realize that I haven't been murdered everything will be OK, won't it? You'll be able to go back home.'

He gave a short laugh. 'Do you know,' he said, 'that's what I first thought when I saw your message in the paper. Dear little Jenny, I thought, she's going to come back from the dead and get me off the hook, bless her.'

He picked up my hand and put it to his lips. It was a mocking, rather than affectionate gesture. Revolted, I pulled my hand away sharply.

He stopped smiling.

'Sorry,' I said instinctively, then wished I hadn't. Why should I be sorry? He had no right to touch me – none whatever. All those things I had once permitted (some of which now filled me with squeamish shame), all the things I had loathed, yet taken as part of what was expected in a normal sexual relationship, since I had known no other – all of that was in the past and I *never* had to do any of them ever again.

'It was a nice idea,' he said. 'Of course, it's all gone a bit awry now, hasn't it?'

'I don't see why,' I replied.

'Don't you watch television?' he asked.

We both glanced involuntarily at the TV, where cartoon characters were chasing each other noisily across the screen. The completely irrelevant thought ran through my mind that there seemed to be far more cartoons now than there had ever been when I was a child. It had all been puppets and classic serials then.

'Of course I watch television,' I said. 'Sometimes,' the intellectual snobbery I had inherited from my father made me add.

'But not today?'

'Of course not today. I've been on the road for most of it.'

'Where have you come from?'

I had not intended to tell him so much – not even in general terms – but he caught me unawares.

'Yorkshire,' I said.

'Aah.' He nodded as though this somehow clarified a

previously baffling issue, though I couldn't imagine what it might have been. 'And I suppose you didn't have the radio on in the car?'

'It's broken,' I replied, still not seeing his point at all.

'You've come a long way,' he said.

There seemed to be nothing to say in the face of that.

'And you did it out of the goodness of your heart,' there was absolutely no mistaking the sarcasm in his voice, 'with never a thought of what might be in it for you.'

'There's nothing in it for me,' I snapped. 'In fact, I stand to lose a very great deal.'

I was starting to lose patience with him now. It was all very well him being upset because I had put him in this predicament. He had every justification, but nevertheless, I could not help thinking that he might show just a little bit of gratitude. As he had said himself, if nothing else I had come a very long way.

'Not even if I were to go to prison?' he asked suddenly. 'Didn't it occur to you that you would get your hands on the house and the bank accounts?'

'No,' I almost shouted. 'No, it did not. And anyway, you won't go to prison.'

'They've decided it's you in that ditch,' he said. He was looking straight into my eyes as he said it, staring at me in a peculiar way. There was something about that stare which made me desperate to look away, but I was determined to face him out.

'That's ludicrous,' I said, trying to keep my voice steady. 'It's not me. There's nothing at all to say that it's me. They're just jumping to conclusions.'

'A necklace,' he said. 'There's a silver necklace with a locket, engraved with a letter J. They will have found photos of you wearing your locket. That will have been the thing that decided them.'

'Well, they'll just have to un-decide, won't they?' I said, making a passable show of confidence. 'Anyway, hundreds of women must have necklaces like that. They were all the rage when you bought mine for me.'

'Only if their initial was J,' he said.

I decided this pointless comment was best ignored. Half the females in England seemed to have names which began with a J – and made a point of wearing necklaces to proclaim the fact.

'We can convince them,' I said. 'Between us, we can explain it all. Then they will realize that they've made a mistake.'

He gave a sort of laugh, a strange noise cut short – not a happy sound. 'You really believe that, don't you? You didn't come here to blackmail me at all, did you? You're still the same old Jenny, cocooned in your own little world – utterly clueless.'

I felt my anger well up, but although I was conscious of my cheeks reddening, I managed to keep my voice level. 'How dare you,' I said. 'I came all this way to help you and all you can do is question my motives and call me stupid. If that's the way you feel, then as far as I'm concerned you're on your own. I'm leaving right now.'

'Oh no,' he said. 'I don't think so.'

TWENTY-SIX

I stood up.

It was intended to be a decisive movement, but the table was in the way so the movement ended in an undignified crabwise shuffle.

'You can't keep me here,' I said, wishing my voice carried rather more conviction.

He stood up too. It placed us only inches apart, my eyes not even on a level with his shoulder, so that I had to angle my neck to see his expression.

'Really?' He arched his eyebrows, regarding me with interest, rather as an older dog tolerates a puppy romping in front of his bone, ready to issue a warning growl if the upstart gets too close. 'And just how do you figure that? Think you could wrestle me to the ground, get your car keys and make off along the bank?'

I didn't say anything.

'Want to try it?'

I sat down again, unable to face his sneering expression, and tried to think clearly. Alan was right in as much that I had no realistic prospect of getting off the boat without his cooperation. He was obviously in a strange, dangerous mood. The last thing to do would be to antagonize him. For some reason he was holding me as a sort of hostage and I had to find a way to convince him that this wasn't a good idea.

I wondered if the ordeal of being wanted by the police had affected the balance of his mind. Not that amateur psychoanalysis was much help. The main thing was to stay calm and be patient. Somehow, I had to find a way of persuading him to let me go.

'I've got things to do,' he said abruptly. 'You'd better go into the fore cabin.'

'Alan,' I began. 'Alan, I don't understand why you won't let me go. Even if you don't want me to go to the police . . .'

I stopped short as he took hold of my arm, ready to drag me to my feet and propel me into the fore cabin.

'It's all right,' I said quickly, in what I hoped was a voice of calm reassurance. 'You don't have to pull me about. I'll go through into the other cabin.'

He removed his hand and I stood up slowly, careful to avoid any sudden moves which might rattle him, wriggled out from beside the table, opened the door and stepped into the fore cabin. He immediately shut the door behind me and I heard a noise, suggestive of a heavy object being dumped at the door's base. The door opened outwards into the main cabin and as there was no lock, I assumed that he must have put something there to obstruct my exit.

I found myself standing in a triangle of space between two berths which curved inwards to meet each other, following the lines of the boat so that tall people sleeping in them would have had to share their foot space. Now I was alone, I tried to think more clearly. Yelling for help I dismissed immediately, on the basis that there was little prospect of anyone hearing me – besides which, a yell would bring Alan crashing through from the main cabin long before it had the desired effect on any potential rescuers. Signalling from the cabin window was similarly a non-starter as there was no one to signal to.

Just then I heard the faint groan of the water pump. Damn, damn, damn! He had put me in the fore cabin while he used the loo. Why hadn't I anticipated that? I might just have managed to push my way past whatever he had put on the other side of the door and got up on to the deck before he realized what was happening. He couldn't have blocked the way with much more than a kitbag – none of the furniture was moveable. If I could only manage to make it off the boat, I could dash along the staithe and maybe get to the pub or the shop – some public place where help was on hand. Too late now, of course. I flopped down on the berth facing the bank, silently cursing myself for a slow-witted idiot.

The cabin windows were all the kind which have sliding top sections, not opening far enough to admit a cat, never mind facilitate the escape of a grown woman – not even a fairly small version like me. Time passed as I sat wondering if another opportunity would come my way, all the time listening for any movements on the other side of the door, but whatever sounds Alan made, they were overlaid by the incessant chatter of the television. Then I spotted the skylight. Not a skylight, I thought, but a hatch – that's what an opening in the deck of a boat was called. It was in the centre of the cabin roof, a small square aperture, covered by a wooden hatch secured with two small metal bolts. It was obviously there for ventilation rather than as a means of entry, because it was positioned above the point where the two bunks merged into one, and was clearly not big enough for a grown man to fit through. It would be big enough for a child, however, and just possibly for a small woman. It was surely worth a try.

Stop. Wait. Think it through. Don't rush at it. Don't mess it up and waste the chance. The first thing was to move into position carefully, not making any sudden movements which might literally rock the boat and lead to Alan getting curious about what I was doing. I needed to position myself directly under the opening, keeping my weight as central as possible while I undid the bolts, lifted the hatch, then levered myself up and squeezed through the gap. Once out on the cabin roof, my best plan would be speed; a flying leap on to the bank and then run like hell along the staithe to summon help. Alan having my car keys didn't matter. It was getting some back-up that counted.

In slow motion I inched along the bunk until I ran out of floor space. Then I gradually turned, moving like a run-down clockwork toy as I swivelled myself into a kneeling position at the point where the two berths became one. Here I steadied myself before reaching up to pull very gently at the bolt on the left-hand side. Nothing happened. It probably wasn't opened very often, maybe not since the previous summer. I tried wriggling the little knob on the end of the bolt, praying that it would not betray me with a sudden squeak, but it appeared to be stuck fast.

It was surprisingly difficult to work with my arms above my head. I brought my arms back down to chest level and massaged them in turn until I had restored the circulation, then I tried the bolt on the right side of the hatch. After a brief initial display of reluctance it yielded quietly, sliding free with a minimum of fuss. I tried an exploratory upward push and the hatch moved a few millimetres skyward before its progress was arrested by the other bolt. The small movement sent a gratifying puff of fresh air down on to my face.

Encouraged, I renewed my efforts on the other bolt.

'Please,' I said, silently. 'Oh, come on. Please.'

The boat lurched suddenly – not by much, but enough to throw me off balance for a second. Someone getting on board? Alan getting off? Whatever it was, it would provide a distraction from any noise the bolt might make. I took firm hold of the recalcitrant knob and hauled at it ferociously. It gave a jerk, leaving the bolt half in, half out.

Simultaneously, I saw Alan's feet passing the window and felt the boat dip towards the bank as he stepped back on deck. He said something, but I didn't catch it, and then there was the sound of some unmistakeably heavy object being placed on top of the hatch and his knuckles rapping, *tap, tap-tap* – a sarcastic little victory sign.

The bolt finally gave. I pushed again but it was useless. The hatch was rigidly held in place by some dead weight. I felt like bursting into tears, my frustration compounded by the realization that Alan had again left the way momentarily clear for me to try a dash through the cabin and I had again been too slow to realize and take my chance. I returned to my former position on the bunk, sunk in misery. Then I fell to reflecting on his timely interception of my escape. Had it been mere chance, or was he spying on me? I couldn't see how else he could have known what I was up to and the thought of an eye pressed to some hole in the bulkhead made me cringe. I hugged my arms around myself as if the little fore cabin had turned into a deep freezer.

With my watch still lying in the motel bathroom, I had no means of knowing what time it was. I wondered how long Alan proposed to keep me penned up in his boat and, more to the point, what his motive was for doing so. I tried to suppress a growing desire to use the toilet. It would be too humiliating to knock on the door and ask to use the lavatory, like a child seeking permission during class.

After what seemed like an interminable length of time, the distinctive thrum of an engine put me on alert. I knelt up on the bunk and watched through the windows as a huge orange and white cruiser came into view. There were several people moving about on her and I waited hopefully while the steersman worked his craft into a better position from which to effect the tight turn in from the dyke. I used the time to think of something which would be recognizable as an obvious yet silent distress signal; something which the incoming party would not mistake for the friendly waving which tends to go on between boats on the Broads.

It took them an age to manoeuvre the craft so that she was pointing up ready to enter the dyke. The steersman was standing in a sort of mini-greenhouse amidships, concentrating all his attention on not ramming the bank or the moored yachts. The rest of his crew were all looking ahead, working out which spot would be most favourable for mooring their huge charge. None of them ever looked directly at the small, shabby cruiser moored at the mouth of the dyke. The monster nosed slowly past, actually jostling one of our fenders, but no curious face looked out of their cabin windows and into mine. The orange stern slid out of sight and after a minute or two, the engine was silenced. I watched hopefully for some time after that, but there was no further sign of the newcomers.

I fell to wondering again about Alan's state of mind. Whatever happens, I told myself repeatedly, I must stay calm. Calm is infectious – I had heard that said once, at a training session during a workshop about dealing with patients in stressful situations, but it seemed fair to assume that it held good for potential madmen as well.

From beyond the cabin door I heard the distinctive theme tune of *Neighbours*. I wondered idly why Alan didn't turn the television off. Perhaps it masked the sound of what he was doing – whatever that might be.

Just as I heard the sound of another boat approaching, he finally opened the door. Perhaps the possibilities presented by these passing craft had occurred to him too. There is always an upsurge of activity at the staithes around teatime as people start looking for places to tie up for the night.

'Come on,' he said, holding the door open.

I obediently moved forward into the main cabin.

'There's more tea,' he said, 'and I've cut some sandwiches.'

Sure enough there was a little picnic laid out on the table. Sandwiches neatly cut into triangles, a small pork pie cut into quarters, and a plate on which half-a-dozen Jaffa Cakes had been arranged in a circle, each slightly overlapping its adjoining fellows.

'I need to go to the toilet,' I announced, not looking directly at him.

He stepped back towards the rear of the cabin, making room for me to access the toilet while taking care to keep himself between me and the exit into the cockpit.

Toilets on boats are always nasty in my opinion and this one smelt nastier than most. It was also horrible to think that Alan could hear me. If there was any contradiction in my embarrassment, bearing in mind that I had spent years of marital intimacy with Alan, it did not occur to me just then. I washed my hands, noticing how slowly the scummy water drained from the sink, so that it was only half gone when I emerged back into the main cabin, where Alan motioned me to sit down and we took up the positions we had occupied earlier.

I sipped my tea and tried to eat a sandwich. It seemed dangerously churlish to reject these peculiar notions of hospitality. Given a choice I would have preferred a Jaffa Cake, but even in these curious circumstances, the bad-mannered rejection of my host's sandwiches, the eating of cake before consumption of savouries was prohibited by the good manners drilled into me so long ago.

'Yorkshire,' said Alan, helping himself to a wedge of pork pie. 'Whereabouts in Yorkshire?'

'You don't need to know,' I said. 'Better not to, really. Best to go our own separate ways.'

He finished his mouthful of pork pie and took another bite.

'Why don't you give me my car keys and let me go?' I asked, aiming to hit a note approximating calmly reasonable rather than panic-stricken pleading. 'I won't tell anyone you're here. I won't mention it to a soul. No one knows who I am up in Yorkshire. Why don't you just let me go? We can pretend this never happened.'

I fervently hoped that my voice did not sound as frantic as I actually felt. It increasingly seemed to me that the act of imprisoning me in the fore cabin while preparing dainty sandwiches for my afternoon tea bore all the hallmarks of a maniac. Alan looked normal and rational enough, but these were not the acts of a rational man.

'Dear Jenny,' he said, speaking patiently, as does someone who must habitually deal with a retarded child. 'I am afraid there is not the slightest question of my letting you go anywhere.'

The short silence which followed this statement was broken by the strident notes of the introductory music which prefaced the six o'clock news. 'This is the six o'clock news from the BBC . . .'

It was the lead story. I could feel his eyes on me, watching me, as I in turn focused on the shot of the house we had once shared, while both of us intently followed the voice of the announcer: 'Earlier this afternoon, police confirmed that they have found a second body in the Nicholsfield house of horror . . .'

'A second body?' I repeated the words in a daze of disbelief.

'They found the first one this morning,' he said. 'They announced it on the midday news.'

The sensations of shock and fear hit me physically, like someone flinging a bucket of icy water over my head. I was past reasoning with him, no longer ashamed to plead.

'I honestly came here to try and help you, Alan,' I said. 'Please let me go. I'll agree to anything you want, but I beg of you to let me go.'

He silenced me with an angry gesture. It was apparent to me now why he kept the TV switched on. He wanted to hear the news and because I must at all costs avoid antagonizing him, this dangerous, murderous stranger to whom I had once belonged, I must sit quietly and was thereby forced to listen too.

It seemed that having finally exhausted their efforts in the garden, the police had turned their attention to the cellar, where they found the bodies buried under some concrete slabs. Together with the body in the ditch, which was believed to be Jennifer Reynolds, that made three known victims. Among these grisly remains the police had found similarities which linked them to several other murders. They were actively seeking Alan. They showed a picture of him and the announcer gravely cautioned viewers against approaching him, as he 'might be dangerous'.

In the midst of my horror, terror and blind fear, I noted in a strangely detached way how the British media manages to generate unintentional humour. *Might* be dangerous. How many women does someone have to murder before a general consensus is reached that he *is* dangerous? Oh yes, and don't approach him – as though someone spotting him in the street might amble up and say: 'Got the time, mate? Oh . . . and aren't you the chap who's wanted for all those murders?'

Don't approach him – well, I thought, I had done better than approach him. I had driven the length of the country to meet him. Alan had always believed me stupid and at that precise moment I would have been fully prepared to agree with him. For a second or two I was all but moved to hysterical laughter. This train of thought inspired one last bluff. If Alan thought I was stupid, he might just buy it.

'I always knew there was something scary about the cellar,' I faltered. 'Just think, those bodies must have been buried all the time we lived there, probably since the house was first built. It's an awful coincidence but it will sort itself out.'

He looked at me in a speculative yet contemptuous way.

'When did you cut your hair?' he asked.

It came to me then, in another of those cold waves of horror, that they had all had long hair – Marie Glover, Antonia Bridgeman, every mug shot of every victim showed long hair. Just like those sad-eyed Victorian girls who had watched from the walls of Alan's house as we climbed the stairs.

'As soon as I left,' I said.

'Pity,' he said.

'Alan,' I tried again. 'You used to love me . . . please let me go. I promise . . .'

'Promises, Jenny? What are promises? Didn't you promise to honour and obey me when we got married? Is this how you honour and obey me? By running off without a word? Even today, when all I asked you to do was sit in the other cabin for a while, what do I find? You try to undo the hatch and creep out while I wasn't looking. It doesn't sound to me as if your promises are worth very much.'

'I honestly never meant to do you any harm,' I said. 'I'm sorry I hurt you by running off the way I did . . .' But now I know why. Now I know why I was afraid to confront you – because somewhere, deep down in my subconscious, I must have known that you were very, very dangerous . . .

'Hurt me,' he interrupted with a cold laugh. 'My dear girl, don't flatter yourself. Oh, I don't say I didn't miss having you around. You were always an interesting pawn on the chessboard; a very enjoyable piece of the game . . .'

I gave an involuntary shiver of revulsion. A vision of Alan having me sit before the dressing-table mirror while he brushed my hair in the candlelight was suddenly transposed from something romantic into something vile.

'. . . but I think it's going a bit far to say that I was actually hurt,' he continued. 'If you want the truth, I was bloody scared. I had to report you missing, obviously, which drew a lot of attention I could have done without. Then of course, there was the worry that they might actually find you before I did. I thought I knew why you'd gone off, you see, and for a while I thought there was a chance you would spill the beans. But then, of course, you didn't, and as time went on I decided you weren't going to. I had to put up with the police sniffing around a few times, but nothing to really worry about, until they found Donna.'

'Donna?' The name escaped my dry lips as barely a whisper, but he heard it.

'The one in the ditch. The one with your necklace on. I liked to make use of the trinkets you left behind – it would have been such a pity to waste them. She was the same build, everything – obvious mistake, but it set them on the right track. Luckily I'd made a few preparations in advance. Didn't even have to go back to the house.'

I felt sick. My necklace, same build, everything.

'Then when you got in touch, I assumed that you had known all along and decided it was time to pop back into the picture, to see if you could turn things to your advantage.'

'I used to think it was my dad.'

'What?'

'I used to think it was my dad – the Nicholsfield . . .' I trailed off, unable to say the words.

'Your dad!' He was incredulous. 'Your dad wasn't capable of anything like that. He might have got his shoes dirty.'

'I never knew,' I said quietly. 'I never even considered . . .'

'Have a Jaffa Cake,' he said, pushing the plate towards me.

I covered my eyes with my hands and shook my head.

Please God, I thought, if there really is a God then please get me out of this nightmare.

Through my fingers I saw that he had begun to eat a Jaffa Cake as impassively as if it were the tea interval at a village cricket match, or the office coffee break on a very mundane working day.

We continued to sit on opposite sides of the cabin table, mostly in silence. The remaining sandwiches began to curl at the edges; the flesh of the pork pie lost its sheen and became a dull, dried-up pink. Alan watched the television in a desultory sort of way, occasionally making uncomplimentary comments.

'Thick as a brick,' he said of a quiz show contestant, and 'absolute crap' in response to something else.

I stayed silent, making no attempt to reply, all the time trying to suppress my increasing fear of what might be about to happen. I tried to think coherently, to formulate some kind of plan, but I couldn't think straight at all. Why, why, a thousand times why hadn't I left word at the cottage of where I was going? No one knew where I was. No one could possibly be expected to come to my rescue.

At one point I remembered that Alan had not asked me whether I had told anyone where I was going. Maybe the possibility that someone might come looking for me had not occurred to him. For a while, I toyed with the idea of pretending that someone was expecting me to rendezvous and would know where to come if I failed to return safely, but in the end I decided that initiating a pretence of this nature might do more harm than good, perhaps suggesting to Alan that there was imminent danger if we stayed where we were. After all, I thought, so long as we're here on the boat there is surely nothing much he can do to me. For the moment, my best plan – indeed my only plan – seemed to be to wait it out and see what he did next.

At dusk he drew the curtains and switched on the cabin lights, finally clearing the remnants of food from the table and washing up the cups and plates. It was some time since I had heard any approaching boats. Neatishead isn't one of the really popular stopping places. Once dusk fell I knew that no one else would be moving on the water.

We watched the nine o'clock news – he with apparent dispassionate interest, me with a kind of fascinated horror, still tinged with disbelief. 'Why?' I whispered, when the bulletin finally moved on to something else.

For a moment I thought he hadn't heard me, but then he fixed me with a stare that turned my heart to ice. 'Why? Why are there endless TV series about murders, cops, detectives, serial killers? Why do you think people watch them? Everyone has an appetite for murder, Jenny. I didn't watch, I took part. That's the difference between all the little plastic people sitting at home and a handful of real ones. Some people apply to go on game shows. I had a game show all of my own.'

He's mad, I thought. I couldn't bear to keep on looking at him, but when I lowered my eyes he took hold of my chin, jerking my head up so that I was forced to face him.

'Not all of them were willing to play by my rules.' He was watching me, enjoying the effect of his words. 'Some of them broke the rules and had to be punished. You should be punished, Jenny. You broke the rules of the game by running off. The trouble is . . .' he glanced around speculatively, before turning his eyes on me again, '. . . there's so little space in here and I don't have the right equipment. What a pity we can't pop down to the cellar for an hour or so. I do like to follow the proper procedures – it's deviation from the script that gets you into trouble in the end.'

It was dark outside now. The birds had stopped singing.

Alan released me and abruptly reached across to silence the television. It was suddenly so quiet in the cabin that I could hear myself breathing. He stood up and opened the tall cupboard opposite the toilet cubicle. For a minute or two I could hear him rummaging about, hidden behind the cupboard door. Then he shut the door and I saw that he had a knife in his hand.

TWENTY-SEVEN

The Alan who emerged from behind the cupboard door was like a different person. He'd already frightened me, but this was something more. A dark energy emanated from his body: a compelling force which froze resistance in its path. In a voice as taut as a wire, he said, 'We're leaving now and if you make a sound I'll cut your throat.'

He raised me up from the bench, gripping my left shoulder while holding the knife an inch or so in front of me, and pushed me towards the cabin steps. Silenced words of protest blocked my throat, bubbles of dissent which exploded in my air ways, forcing my breath out in gulps. I offered no resistance whatever. You don't antagonize a man who has a blade inches from your neck.

'Keep your hands by your sides,' he hissed as I fumbled for the handrails.

I complied as best I could, managing to clamber awkwardly up the steps into the cockpit, with Alan all the time attached at my shoulder, our bodies bumping awkwardly against one another. The deck tilted unnervingly as he moved me towards the stern of the boat, where there was a gap in the awning. After the light of the cabin my eyes were almost blind, but Alan seemed to know exactly where to put his feet. As we emerged into the open air I considered deliberately tumbling into the water, hoping that he would instinctively release his hold as we fell, but I was too slow and the moment had passed before I had time to think it through. He forced me to sidestep along the edge of the boat, then said quietly, 'Step forward on to the bank.'

When I hesitated, tentative in the darkness, he dug his nails viciously into my neck. 'Step on to the bank.'

I stepped blindly and felt relief of a kind as my feet encountered solid ground rather than thin air. He was right behind me. A momentary pause and then I was frogmarched along the path.

Lights glowed through cruiser curtains on the other side of the dyke and muffled laughter came from inside the boat, but there wasn't a soul out on deck or barbequing on the bank, and I knew that the single scream I would have time for guaranteed no help. My best hope must be that someone would come walking back to their boat from the inn.

We met no one.

At the car – my car – he held me close against the passenger side while he fumbled with the keys. Then in an apparent change of plan, he walked me round to the rear and opened the boot.

'Get in.'

'Oh no, please . . .' I glanced desperately up and down the lane, but it was utterly deserted.

He placed the cold blade against my throat and I was immediately still, scarcely breathing.

'Do you want to die?'

'No.' I whispered it.

'Are you going to get in the boot?'

'Yes.'

He withdrew the knife by a few inches and I climbed in as slowly as I dared, desperately hoping for a dog walker or someone en-route to the pub to appear, but no one came.

'Lie down.' The silvery blade was jabbed in my direction.

I tried to fold myself into the available space but it was like trying to play a deadly game of Twister, with some part of me always extruding beyond the confines of the boot, so that the rear hatch would not close. It occurred to me that while appearing to be cooperative, I could drag this process out indefinitely. It must have occurred to Alan too because he seemed to hesitate, then ordered me to get out again.

He slammed the rear hatch so hard that the bang echoed and re-echoed round my head. 'Get into the back.' He flung open the driver's door as he spoke, and stood aside for me to work the lever which moved the front seat.

My eyes had grown more accustomed to the dark by now, but in any case I knew just where to find it. Resistance was ruled out by the proximity of the knife, but just as I moved the seat forward I heard the sound of voices from the direction of the river. Someone was coming. I took a breath and attempted a scream, but Alan's free hand was across my mouth, stifling the cry before it was half out.

I tried to hang on to the doorframe, but he was much stronger than me and I was shoved head first into the back, ending up half on, half off the seat, my kneecaps taking the brunt of his shove, and my shoulders and arms wrenched painfully where I had attempted to cling on to the car.

At least my mouth was free again. 'Help me!' I yelled. 'Help me!'

Alan shoved the seat back into place, careless of the bits of me still in the way, leapt into the car and slammed the door behind him before I had time to gather enough breath to shout again. 'Keep quiet.' I could tell he was rattled. I heard him fumbling for the ignition as I drew in enough oxygen to scream again. It had a deafening impact within the car, but how far did it carry outside?

Had they heard me? Quickened their pace? It took barely half a minute to get from the boats to the parking area if only they got a move on. I knelt up in the seat, desperately peering into the dark for any signs of approach, hurrying figures or a moving torch beam. In the meantime, Alan had found the slot for the key and gunned the engine into life. We set off in a series of jerks which flung me to and fro across the seat while I screamed and screamed again, the sound reverberating round the interior of the car.

'Lie down,' he roared, but I ignored him. He couldn't attack me while he was driving. I stopped yelling but continued to gaze out of the rear window as we headed off through the village, ready to pound on the window and scream my head off again as soon as anyone came into view, but we did not see so much as a cat.

I needed to come up with another idea – and soon – but the only thing I could think of was to grab Alan round the throat, and I did not see how that would do any good. If he lost control of the car we could end up in a ditch, and if he was able to stop the car safely he might decide to silence me there and then. I swivelled into a sitting position so that I could see where we were going, but I soon lost any sense of direction because once out of the village Alan took a series of unlit lanes, driving at speed and grinding the gears. We had been travelling for some minutes when he unexpectedly turned off the road and drew up next to a large wooden building, which looked black in the beam of the car headlights.

He took the keys from the ignition, retrieved his knife from where it had been lying in the foot well on the passenger side, unfolded himself from behind the wheel and finally located the lever which jerked the driver's seat forward. 'Don't make a noise. Get out and do exactly as I tell you.' I noticed that although he had exhorted me to silence he wasn't bothering to keep his voice down. Wherever we were then, there was no help to be had within shouting distance.

In my mind I held on to Alan's question. 'Do you want to die?' he had asked me. This implied a choice, offered hope. It must mean that he wasn't going to kill me. It meant that he intended to set me free. He was going to release me at some out of the way place so that he could make his getaway. He wasn't going to kill me as he had killed the others. He still had feelings for me, still cared about me – at least a little. The same loyalty or decency, or whatever it was that had brought me hundreds of miles to help him was now compelling him to let me go. After all, if he had wanted to hurt me he had let plenty of opportunities go by already. He's going to let me live, I told myself. Oh, please God. Let me live.

It was not that I deliberately resisted Alan's instruction to get out of the car, but my body would not obey quickly enough and he was unwilling to wait. Holding the knife in his right hand, he used his left to drag me out. The car headlights were illuminating a section of the big building in front of us, but I sensed that there was a wide open space in the darkness to our rear. My legs were giving way but Alan did not require me to walk far.

'Up against the car,' he instructed, shoving me face first against the rear window, so that I felt the harsh cold of the night time metal through my clothes. There was a momentary pause – a faint chink like one stone moving against another – and then he grabbed my hands, pulling them behind me. I instinctively held them as far apart as possible while he tied my wrists.

He must have brought some sort of cord in the pocket of his trousers, and too late I realized that he must have put the knife down, because he could not have tied my hands while he was holding it. Again I cursed my slowness – another possible missed chance. But what could I have done against him with my legs so wobbly that I could hardly stand up? And anyway he was going to let me go. Hadn't he as good as said so?

I was aware suddenly, sickeningly, that he was lingering over the hand tying. When he was done he pressed hard against me, pinning me against the car with my hands forced against his crotch, his mouth obsequiously close to my ear.

'We could have had such fun together, poppet. I could have given you the full treatment, just like the others, but I'm afraid we just don't have the time.'

In that moment, I understood the fear and horror of all those other girls, because it was mine. In that moment, it was no longer possible to deceive myself any longer. I understood that he had no intention of letting me go.

He stepped back, retrieving the knife from the ground in a single movement and giving me a shove to indicate that I was to move around the vehicle.

'Get in.'

He opened the passenger door to its full extent and held it while I slid inside awkwardly. Then he leaned across me and fastened the seat belt, which seemed an extraordinary gesture under the circumstances. After that he bent down and put the knife on the ground again while he tied my ankles with another thin piece of rope. The interlude gave me time to contemplate my fate. Would I feel it when the knife went it? How quickly would it all be over?

I knew it was futile to attempt a head-on struggle with him. Instead, keeping my legs as still as I could, I began to covertly manoeuvre my hands behind me. In my first year at senior school there had been a craze for playing a game which involved Houdini-like escapes from hands bound by knotted school ties. The trick was to position the bonds against the slimmest part of one wrist, splaying out that hand while flattening the thumb of the other hand as much as possible and

gradually wriggling free. It was many years since I had
attempted anything of the kind and although the ropes around
my wrists were not particularly tight, the task was unquestion-
ably more difficult when restrained in the front seat of a car,
sweating and terrified.

Having bound my feet, Alan stood up and leaned over me.
I could hear him breathing hard and for a few seconds I entertained the strange thought that he was going to kiss me, but
instead he gave an abrupt, unnatural laugh. Then he took
something else from his pocket – not a rope, but something
which I initially mistook for a piece of rag. He leaned inside
the car again and in the split second before it engulfed my
head I realized it was a bag.

I tried to scream, but the bag instantly crowded into my
mouth. It was made from some kind of cloth, which meant
that I ought to be able to breathe, but I was convinced that it
would choke me. Every breath I took came up short against
the fabric and each time I exhaled clouds of hot air got trapped
against my face. I was aware that Alan had slammed the door,
walked around the car and climbed back in alongside me. He
started the engine again and I was jerked back into my seat
as he put the car in reverse, then forward as we changed
direction.

I had never realized how much we rely on sight to keep our
balance in a moving vehicle. As we sped onward my body
was subjected to the vagaries of every twist and turn in the
road. The seat belt kept me in place, but with my hands and
feet bound and no way of knowing what physical adjustments
to make, I was completely disorientated. The bag was made
of sufficiently thick material that even the glow of the headlights was eliminated. Trapped in this stifling blackness, I
gulped frantically, desperate to find air, convinced that I would
surely be suffocated.

On and on we went, Alan taking the snaking roads at speed
with every change of direction thrusting me one way and
another, thudding my left shoulder against the side of the
car or crushing my hands into the small of my back, each
involuntary movement emphasizing my helplessness. Dreadful
though this was, I tried to stem my increasing panic. I told

myself that there must be enough air to breathe; otherwise I would have already lost consciousness. A dead person's shoulder could not possibly hurt so much when it met the side panel of a Ford Fiesta. Against all the odds, I gradually managed to regain a measure of self-control. I tried to brace myself against the worst excesses of Alan's driving, but holding myself rigid was difficult and the motion of the car had already tossed me about so much that I had to fight off waves of nausea. If I was sick inside the bag I might choke on my own vomit.

In the loathsome blackness I lost all sense of time, had no idea how long or how far we had travelled. One of my knees was throbbing from some earlier encounter with a hard object. Motion sickness threatened to overwhelm me. It was becoming an act of physical concentration to keep myself from retching. My ears buzzed with the engine's intermittent groans and roars and my thoughts descended into a mere mantra. Please stop the car, please let me out.

Eventually I was aware of us slowing, then making a left-hand turn on to what must have been a rough track, for the car began jolting me abruptly from side to side, tumbling my head one way and another, until we finally came to a standstill. Alan turned off the engine and silence descended. Surely, this was in every sense the end of the road?

TWENTY-EIGHT

'Well, here we are at journey's end.' His voice startled me – low and conspiratorial, suggesting close proximity, his mouth perhaps no more than a couple of inches from my ear. It was the first time he had spoken since putting the bag over my head. Words normally associated with cheerful arrival now invoked terror.

'Please, Alan . . . I'll do anything . . .' My pleading was muffled by the thick cloth, and my voice so tremulous that I doubt he was able to make out the actual words.

'Do you know what, Jenny? This is all your fault – and do you know why? Trying to be too clever. That was your problem. I liked you so much better when you were stupid.'

I made some more desperate warbling noises, but he continued relentlessly.

'I would never have hurt you. I could have done, you know. Any time I wanted to. I could have taken you down to the cellar and dealt with you, the way I dealt with the rest of them . . .'

I began to whimper frantically, like a whipped dog. I did not want to know what he would have done to me. My mind had flown back to the time when I thought I heard a cat in the cellar. The thought that those sounds had been made by some terrified girl, probably bound and hooded as I was now, someone who had already suffered at Alan's hands and was very soon going to die, made me shake and retch. I remembered as if it were only yesterday his teasing suggestion that he ought to make me go down there and see for myself . . .

'It's no good crying, Jenny.' He was chiding me as one might a recalcitrant child. 'You've brought all this on yourself. If you had just left things as they were I don't suppose anyone would ever have connected that girl in the ditch to me. We could still have been together, enjoying our little holidays, playing our special bedroom games . . . You've disappointed me, you know. When you first came into my shop I could see you were just the type I liked. I thought about following you home in the rain, pulling up beside you and offering you a lift . . . but there was something different about you, so I asked you out to dinner instead. You were quite a project for me. I enjoyed dressing you up, pulling the strings and watching my little marionette dance . . .'

My whole body was vibrating with encroaching hysteria which clearly annoyed him, for his tone became sharper as he said, 'Oh, don't keep snivelling, for goodness' sake. I can't bear snivelling. It's against my rules and I punish snivellers severely. Some of the other girls were punished very severely indeed before I was finished with them, and you – you deserve it more than anyone, running off and bringing all this down on our heads. You've ruined everything, do you realize that?' His voice had risen but it quietened again, his tone becoming efficient, even businesslike. 'I always thought that if I ever had to do this, I would do it properly. You above all people know that I am a methodical man. I like to stick to my system. Knives are so messy, bloodstains always a nuisance – awkward to explain if you happen to meet anyone, and very difficult to remove from clothing.' He might have been complaining about the problem of wasps at a picnic. 'Strangling is neat and quick – over and done with in a matter of seconds, if you know what you're doing. I have always preferred to make a quick end, once I've finished. But that's too good for you, Jenny. You don't deserve to go quickly, so I've come up with a better idea for you. Something which will last a little longer but still not make a nasty mess of my jacket.'

Fear is a terrible thing. It takes a stranglehold on your body and your mind, driving out reason. I had sometimes heard people claim that they had been terrified out of their wits, but until then I had never understood what that really meant. I was in such a state that it took me a moment to realize he had stopped talking and was getting out of the car. Then I heard his door slam shut. I fell silent, frozen in my seat. This was it. I steeled myself for the moment when the door would open on my side of the car and he would drag me out, but moments passed and nothing happened.

It came to me that instead of wondering what was keeping Alan, I ought to be taking advantage of the hiatus. Attempting to free my hands had been impossible while the car was in motion, but now I leaned forward and tried again. As I concentrated on my hands, I was struck by the lack of any sound apart from the rasp of my own breathing against the hood. What was he doing out there? Then a new idea shrieked into my mind – hadn't he just told me that he had planned an infinitely worse fate for me than death by knife? While continuing to work my wrists against the rope, I strained my ears for the sound of him unscrewing the petrol cap, followed by the striking of a match. Instead, I heard the whole car give the faintest creak, then felt a sideways lurch to the left and a corrective sway to the right. I realized that he was pushing the car and I understood at once. He had left the handbrake off and was pushing my Fiesta until it reached the edge and fell . . . but the edge of what? A cliff, a quarry, a shaft? Whatever it was, I must get my hands free. If I could free my hands before we reached the edge I might just have time to open the door and throw myself out. That would still leave me at Alan's mercy, but just then it seemed better to focus on one problem at a time.

The rope seared painfully into my wrists but I ignored the burning in the certain hope that I was making progress. I had managed to work my bonds down until the plumpest part of my right hand was jammed between my left wrist and the knot. I knew that once I had got that far, given time I could gradually ease the right hand through – but how much time did I have? How many seconds before the car tipped forwards and hurled me into oblivion?

The angle of the car changed abruptly and I experienced the half second of terror which precedes an unknown death. I was expecting a long drop, but as the car nose-dived there was a simultaneous splash and water began to flood in. It had never occurred to me that Alan was about to dump me in the river. The shock of the water momentarily stopped me dead, while the car itself seemed to give a kind of groan – it was probably just the air rushing out, but it sounded like a dying creature who knows its end is near. I felt the car begin to sink

– a sensation akin to travelling in a very slow-moving lift – but the bonnet found the bottom almost immediately and then the vehicle levelled as if it had settled on flat ground.

It is possible that these sudden movements helped, or else that the horror of my situation gave added impetus to my efforts, for within those first confused seconds of feeling cold water pouring in around my feet, my hands came free. With loops of cord still dangling from one wrist, I automatically reached up and dragged off the hood. The surrounding blackness was unrelieved and, on finding myself no better able to see, the same blind panic took over. Then, in the midst of the blackness, I had a kind of vision. I saw the face of the man I loved walking into his cottage, picking up my note, and knew that I must fight for survival because I had everything to live for. Because I had Rob.

Though I could see nothing, my other senses told me that the water was gushing in fast. I had always thought of a closed car as a sealed object, imagining that if submerged it would fill very slowly, but instead I could feel icy water rising steadily, actually hear it spurting in somewhere close at hand.

Come on, I told myself. Your hands are free. You've got your chance. In the darkness I found it easier to close my eyes and let instinct take over, my fingers locating and releasing my seat belt as surely as if I had been in a parking space at Sainsbury's. From somewhere in the recesses of my mind, I dredged up the information that the car door would not open until the vehicle was full of water, when the pressure was equal inside and out. Inevitably then, there was going to come a moment when I would be completely submerged. The car would become a sealed, water-filled tank with me inside it and no air at all. Only then would I be able to open the door. I did not have long to consider the possibility. The water was already up to my chest. I must be ready. I pulled myself up so that I was crouching on the seat. My trussed ankles moved more easily than I had expected, helped perhaps by the rising water. My head was touching the car roof but the water almost immediately regained my chest. I slid my fingers down the window, finding the place where the glass ended and the plastic began, and started feeling for the door handle. I found the recess, then the handle itself, gripping it as the water reached my chin. I tried to choose the optimum second to take a breath, but I mistimed it and had to snap my mouth shut as the water engulfed my face, filling my nose and ears.

I began trying the door handle. My chest was tightening already, the need to breathe becoming ever more desperate. Then the door gave. It opened a few inches and stopped. I pushed it but it refused to move any further. My hands explored frantically, finding the edge of the door, the side of the car. The door had opened perhaps six inches. I pushed it again with all of my sapping strength, conscious of my chest burning, and the way the roaring in my ears increased.

Then I understood: something was stopping the door, some other submerged object on the bed of the river. Something strong and heavy and immoveable. All my cleverness, untying my hands, remembering about the door opening only when the pressure was equal – none of it had done any good. I was trapped and I would never see Rob again. In the end I was going to drown alone in the dark, my existence extinguished secretly, just as I had lived in secrecy for so long. A perverted destiny had overtaken me and I was surely going to die. For a split second I saw the face of Susan McCarthy, her suntanned features framed by her long black hair, the mole on her left cheek, round and dark like a beauty spot.

Then a voice – my subconscious, perhaps even the voice of Susan McCarthy herself, said, 'Use the other door, stupid.'

I twisted around in the water, navigating my progress by the dashboard and the steering wheel, fighting off the treacherous instinct to inhale, every movement now calling for an act of sheer will from my oxygen-starved body. My hands encountered the smooth glass of the driver's window, then the ledge of the door, and finally the door handle itself. I hooked the fingers of my right hand around the handle and tugged it, while pushing on the door with my left – my ears singing, waves of giddiness sweeping over me, scarcely hoping, scarcely believing, but the door gave and I felt it swing out in a wide arc, taking my arms and torso with it.

I dragged the rest of my body clear and, in spite of my trussed ankles, kicked myself to the surface where I breathed in great gulps of air which, far from bringing the expected relief, seared my lungs and made me choke. I found the roof of the car was alongside me and crawled on to it, finding that if I adopted a kneeling position my chest and shoulders were clear of the water. There I balanced myself against the gentle drag of the current, trying to catch my breath while the natural buoyancy of the water helped to keep me upright.

In spite of my miraculous emergence from the deep, I experienced little sense of relief. The water was bitterly cold, but while desperate to escape from the river, I was so physically spent that for a moment or two I could not bring myself to relinquish the support of the car roof and make for the bank.

My exhaustion was probably fortuitous, for it gave me time to think. Somewhere not far away was a dangerous man armed with a knife and quite possibly a torch as well. (It would be unlike Alan not to have thought of everything.) He had the advantage of being not only larger and physically stronger than I was, but also unencumbered by wet clothes and shoes – or indeed by having his feet tied together. My only advantage was the element of surprise. Alan thought I was at the bottom of the river. Whatever happened, he must be allowed to continue thinking that. I could not afford to shout for help, or make any sort of sound, because Alan must necessarily still be somewhere close by. I must have made a certain amount of noise when I broke the surface and scrambled on top of the Fiesta – he might even now be watching from the bank, biding his time and deciding what to do next, so I forced myself to ignore the treacherous instinct to get out of the water as fast as possible, tried to breathe silently but deeply, ignoring the penetrating cold and gathering my strength while I scanned the bank for any movement which might betray Alan's whereabouts. Would he have watched the car slide under the water, shone his torch beam over the surface to satisfy himself that the captain had indeed gone down with the ship, then immediately set off back to Neatishead? Or was he waiting silently on the bank in the dark, listening for any telltale splashes which would indicate that I had escaped from the watery grave he had planned for me? He had not bothered to tie me up very securely, but presumably he had not anticipated that I would manage to find my way out of the submerged vehicle. How long had it taken me to get free? How long would he have waited?

Another thing to remember was that he had no car. He was on foot, so even if he had turned away from the river the moment the Fiesta sank out of sight, it might be a while before he was completely out of earshot. Yet as minute after minute passed, I began to contemplate the fact that for the first time since getting aboard Alan's boat, circumstances might just have moved in my favour. Alan thought he had disposed of me. There was no reason for him to suppose that I would get free of the car. The element of surprise was mine, but even so I could not afford to take any risks – I must do nothing to draw attention to my presence. However desperate the cold, however sorry my physical state, I must not squander this opportunity.

I crouched on the smooth, slippery roof of the car and made myself count to one hundred, trying to retain my balance with the minimum of movement. The cold was well-nigh unbearable. My lower limbs first lost their feeling and were then attacked by the agonizing pain of cramp. I might have sobbed aloud except that I had to keep my teeth clamped together to stop them from chattering. As I counted silently, I stared into the darkness, watching for the slightest indication of a human presence on the bank.

When I had reached one hundred and still detected no sign of life, I used my arms to swim for dry land, still moving as quietly as I could. I figured that as Alan must be on the side of the river from which he had pushed the car into the water, it made sense to head for the opposite bank, but when I tried to reach it I encountered a seemingly impenetrable bed of reeds, so I turned reluctantly and swam back the way I had come, keeping my tethered feet well away from the reeds, terrified of the rope getting snagged on something in the dark. I have always been a strong swimmer but although it was probably a matter of little more than twenty feet from one side to the other, it felt like half a mile. With my heart pounding, my whole body seeming to vibrate with cold and fear, I found the bank and dragged myself on to it, half expecting to feel the grab of Alan's hands and the cold steel of his knife, but I was alone.

I twisted myself into a sitting position and attempted to get my breath back, wondering at the fact that being out of the water felt scarcely any better than being in it. In the darkness, with fingers so cold that they seemed to belong to someone else, I set about trying to free my ankles from the wet rope. I spent several minutes fumbling blindly with the wet knots, but it was absolutely hopeless. I couldn't even see if the limited movements I had obtained were actually doing harm or good. By now I was becoming desperate. I began to claw hysterically at the ropes, forgetting about the need for silence as I sobbed with frustration, but the frenzy only lasted for a moment before I pulled myself together. This would not do at all.

Dithering with cold and working by feel, I considered a new strategy, exploring the way the rope was bound around my ankles. Alan had wound it round three times before tying a knot. If I could only wriggle one of those loops down over my feet, the other two would follow without my having to untie them at all. Undoing the laces of my trainers by feel was awkward when they were soaking wet, but still proved much easier than tackling Alan's knots. After removing my trainers I eased all three loops of rope down as far as they would go, so that I could drag my jeans out from under them, thereby gaining precious millimetres. I peeled off my socks on the same principle, then pulled the two upper loops so tight that they bit into my flesh and threatened to cut the blood supply to my feet. The pain was intense, but I was rewarded by creating enough space to insert a finger between the bottom hank of rope and my ankle bone. Slowly but surely, I slid the rope down, feeling it shave my skin like a blunt razor blade. I manoeuvred the first loop over my heel while the other coils cut further into my ankles, but once I had one foot out the rest was comparatively easy. I kicked myself free from the final length of cord and hurled it to one side. The splash it made as it hit the water startled me – I had not intended to throw it so far or make such a noise. I waited for a moment or two, but when nothing happened I set about forcing my feet back into my wet socks and then into my trainers, which were still heavy with water. I found it surprisingly easy to secure the laces by feel alone.

I stood up slowly, helping myself off from the ground with both hands, taking time to regain my balance on uncertain feet and legs. It was a clear night with almost half a moon and, once I was standing up, I found that I could see a good deal more than had been visible at ground level. The riverbank was wide and flat, and it looked as if it might be possible to walk along it for some distance, though that was obviously not the way we had arrived in the car. A path beside the river might meander along for miles without bringing me in reach of any help, whereas the track we had driven along must lead to a road.

Hampered by my waterlogged clothes and shivering violently, I took a few squelching steps away from the water and made out an opening in the trees and bushes which ran parallel to the river. I tentatively picked my way towards it and found that I was indeed on some sort of track, leading away from the river. I put down an exploratory hand and encountered flattened earth in place of the short, springy grass which grew on the bank.

It was as I straightened up that I glimpsed the light. For a moment I thought it was my eyes playing tricks, but then I saw it again. A light meant that someone was awake, someone in a nearby house who would be able to help me. Then I realized that the light was moving. It was tiny not because it was a long way off but because it was a small single lamp coming towards me. The shout I had been about to utter died on my lips, for who was moving around at this time of night with only a single lamp to guide him?

TWENTY-NINE

L ike a rabbit caught in the glare of headlights I stood dazed and frozen, staring at the approaching menace. Then I realized that even before the little circle of light shone directly on me I would probably be visible as a silhouette, standing tall against the open space above the river. Hide – I had to find somewhere to hide.

I dropped to my knees and began to crawl. Loose gravel dug into my palms and knees, but then one of my hands registered the weedy margin of the hedgerow in the same moment that the other unexpectedly encountered thin air and I lost my balance, half rolling, half falling into a ditch – hardly that really – just a small depression between the track and the hedge, full of last year's dried-up leaves and iron-hard tree roots on to which I tumbled clumsily, only just managing to stifle an automatic yelp.

From somewhere not far above my head, my ears identified the distinctive swish of wheels, followed by the sound of a bicycle braking. No wonder the lamp had been moving so fast – appearing out of nowhere and the next moment all but upon me. I found that by leaning up on one elbow I could see out from my hiding place. I knew this must mean that I was dangerously exposed, but I was mesmerized, unable to look away. The cyclist had dismounted and was propping his machine against a bush, only yards from where I lay, at the point where the track opened on to the river bank. It was impossible to see much of the rider but I knew who it must be – and if I could see him then as soon as he turned around he would be able to see me. Even so, I didn't dare move. He was close enough to be alerted by the slightest rustle.

He produced a torch from his pocket and shone it on to the ground. What was he looking for? Had he dropped or forgotten something? A droplet of water ran down the side of my face and dripped silently into the leaf mould. He hadn't forgotten anything – not Alan. I felt that icy certainty run through me again. He had prepared every little thing in readiness for my arrival, right down to concealing a bicycle somewhere in the vicinity of the place he had identified in advance for my disposal, knowing that he would need a way to get back to his boat. The thought that he had planned so thoroughly for my disposal made me shake harder than ever – his efficiency was chilling. I wondered why he had not made absolutely sure, by killing me before I went into the river? Was it to try and make it look like some sort of an accident? Then I remembered what he had said about knives. Alan wasn't interested in making the thing look like an accident. He was only interested in evading capture. In the event that he encountered anyone on his ride back to Neatishead, he wouldn't want to look out of the ordinary. It might be a funny time to go out on a bike ride, but no doubt he would have a ready-made, plausible explanation for that. What he could not have easily explained would be blood-spattered clothing, or the scratched face he might have sustained in the course of a struggle.

And just to be absolutely sure that everything had gone to plan, he had stopped en route home to make doubly certain that I had not escaped. He knew that if I had managed to get out of the river I would be soaked – water would be cascading from my clothes, making damp patches, even puddles, wherever I moved. At any moment he would catch the sound of my panicky breathing, hear my wet clothes dripping. I wasn't even properly hidden. He would see me as soon as he played his torch along the track.

There was still a lot of water coming off my clothes, and I knew that my shoes must have exuded water at every step, but surely he would not be able to detect footprints on earth or grass – not by the light of a torch? But the place where I had sat to undo my feet – what if he put his hand down and felt the grass? And the rope? Rope floated. Would the cords which had bound me have disappeared downstream or had they fetched up against the reeds? Were they lying there now, snaking treacherously in the current, ready to give the game away?

He had been walking towards the river, shining the torch

in that direction, but now he turned back and I instinctively ducked my head, not wanting him to catch the pale disc of my face. He had already passed close by me once, so there must be a chance that he wouldn't see me unless he actually shone his torch directly into my hidey hole. If he did, then I must be ready for him. My hands explored for a stone heavy enough to inflict damage, but my fingers encountered only thin gravel and last year's dried-up leaves, which rustled dangerously at the slightest contact.

Then it happened. The torch beam dipped as he bent over and I sensed rather than saw the shape of him, feeling the ground. He might not be in the right spot . . . but then the torch jerked upwards and there was a new urgency to his movements. He began to sweep the beam from side to side until it hit me full in the eyes.

I scrambled to my knees, hauled myself out of the ditch and tried to dart away, but he was too quick, covering the ground in a couple of strides and managing to grab the shoulder of my sweatshirt. I tried to pull away, hoping the fabric would rip, but it held strong. As he raised the torch to strike me I twisted round to face him, working on instinct with no time to consider the odds or formulate a plan. I launched one fist at his head, while simultaneously kicking him as hard as I could, before again attempting to drag myself out of his grasp.

When Alan had embarked on his previous kidnappings he had probably perfected a method of taking his victims by surprise, perhaps immobilizing them before they had time to put up much of a fight. Determined resistance had not formed part of the 'script', and the blows seemed to take him by surprise. When he tried to bring the arm holding the torch across my neck, I ducked my head and bit him before grabbing the hand that still gripped the neck of my sweatshirt and attempting to prize it loose, while continuing to kick wildly at his legs.

Though he managed to land a blow to the side of my head which made it ring, I kept on fighting. It couldn't last, of course. He was bigger and stronger – altogether at an advantage – but then I lost my footing, stumbling and falling heavily, dragging him downwards so that he automatically relinquished his hold in order to save himself. I had fallen on to my front, but I rolled over and, as he attempted to regain his hold, I unleashed another almighty kick, sending the full force of my training shoe, heavy with water, in the direction of his head. He saw it coming and I only managed to connect with the hand holding the torch, but even so I heard him exclaim in pain. I took advantage of his instinctive recoil, catapulting my entire body away from him, hauling myself to my feet and setting off, back towards the river.

There was perhaps a full two or three second's grace before he took up pursuit. Maybe I hurt him badly enough to give him pause, but I believe he had dropped the torch and had to retrieve it. As he pursued me the beam became a wavering spotlight ahead of me, bisected by my own grey silhouette. I hurtled along the riverbank, expecting any moment to stumble and fall again, or else feel the renewed grip of his outstretched hand. Sheer terror gave an impetus to my sprint – I ran as I had never run before, several times almost losing my footing, my ears filled with the sound of him crashing along behind me and my own frantic breathing, ever more laboured, each lungful of air a little harder to come by than the last. The light from his torch and the sound of his progress told me that I was managing to maintain no more than half-a-dozen yards between us, and how long could I keep up this pace?

Then the path became firmer and steeper beneath my feet, and in the light provided by the torch I made out the shape of a bridge up ahead which the river went under but the path evidently did not. I knew better than to check and though the short slope to the bridge impeded my progress, it slowed his too. As I gained level ground again my trainers slapped against solid tarmac and I realized that I had reached a road. It wasn't wide and I cast around desperately, hoping for a house, a passing motorist, but there was nothing – only a moonlit country lane which vanished into the shadows in either direction. Which way should I run? Split seconds to make a decision – and then I made out a distinctive shape against the dark shimmer of the water on the furthest side of the bridge. I had not considered prolonging my flight alongside the river, but there, about twenty yards further upstream was a moored boat. And a boat meant people.

I hurled myself down the slope on the opposite side of the road, a helter-skelter descent, not slowing when I regained the bank.

'Help me,' I sobbed, even before I got level with the craft. 'Please, somebody, help.'

I was too breathless to yell effectively, but I jumped into the cockpit of the boat and began to bang on the cabin roof with my fists. 'Open up – please, help me. I've been attacked. Please, please help.'

Glancing back along the path, I was aware that the circle of light which marked the position of Alan's torch was a little fainter than it had been – perhaps the batteries were running down. He had followed me down from the road, but now he was waiting about halfway between the boat and the bridge, ready to scarper back to his bike the minute any lights showed behind the curtained windows of the vessel, but not a glimmer appeared – no voices, curious or irate, enquired as to the nature of the disturbance. No welcoming bark of a dog, not the slightest sound of any occupants stirring.

I hammered desperately on the roof again, making a noise fit to wake the dead, pleading with the occupants to let me in quickly, but of course there were no occupants. The boat had been left secured and empty for the night.

I was sobbing aloud with fear and disappointment. The conviction that there was no one aboard must have come to Alan at pretty much the exact moment as it did to me, for the torch advanced swiftly along the bank, the shape of its owner solidifying as he closed on the bow.

I was cornered. I should have tried to leap back on to the bank and run again, but I had hesitated too long. As he drew level with the cockpit I backed away, using my hands to check for an escape route. There was a narrow walkway running around the outside of the cabin and I clambered on to it, never taking my eyes off Alan. I began to sidestep towards the front of the boat, my balance precarious with my shoes damp and slippery, and my hands vainly seeking a hold on the smooth cabin roof.

Alan did not immediately attempt to follow me aboard,

perhaps reluctant to undertake a game of blindfold dodge around the side decks of an unfamiliar boat. Instead he remained on the bank, walking slowly enough to keep level with me, addressing me in a strangely calm voice.

'Why don't you come down from there, Jenny? Otherwise you may fall and hurt yourself.'

I continued to inch my way along, even though I knew it was pointless, because by the time I reached the bows he would be there to meet me.

'Now Jenny, don't be silly. You know you can't go anywhere. You were right, you know, when you said that I loved you once. And I could love you again. I could help you, Jenny. I could take care of you, like I used to. Why don't you come down from there before you slip and fall? We could go back to my boat and get you some nice warm clothes and a hot drink. We could talk about how to resolve things, just like you said.'

Don't listen. He's a madman. He tried to murder you.

'At least come down from that side deck. I know I frightened you, but your punishment's over now.' His voice was silky smooth, persuasive. A compelling voice I knew so well. 'I let you get away, don't you see? But it's all over now, sweetheart. Come back to the boat with me. You must be so cold – we don't want you catching a chill.'

When I still failed to reply, he climbed aboard the boat and stepped into the small well at the front, reaching out and offering me his hand, but I had already begun to shuffle back in the opposite direction, putting more than an arm's length between us.

'Take my hand. Come on, I'll help you down from there and then we'll get that wet top off and you can have my jacket.'

'You've got a knife,' I countered.

'Jenny, darling Jenny, didn't I tell you that I'm not a knife man? Here, let me show you.' He drew the knife from his pocket and shone the torch on to it, angling the beam so that I could see him drop the knife over the side. I heard it hit the water – there was no trickery. 'Now will you take my hand and let me help you down?'

'You also told me that you can kill a woman by strangling her – in seconds – with your bare hands.'

'For goodness' sake.' He gave a little laugh – it was the one he had habitually used when letting me know that he thought I was making a fuss out of nothing. 'I can't cut off my hands and throw them overboard now, can I? Why won't you trust me?' He was trying to keep up the calm, hypnotic voice, but I sensed an edge creeping into it. He knew that he had given up the knife for nothing, that I would not willingly surrender myself into his hands.

'I can't trust you,' I said, 'because you have already tried to kill me once tonight. But if you want to strike a deal, then why not this one? You leave me here and go – go right away – and then I'll make my way back home and say nothing which will help anyone find you. You asked me to trust you – why don't you trust me instead?'

I was expecting him to make some clever reply, but instead he made an impatient tsking sound that I recognized of old. It was a noise I associated with his minor displeasures – an antimacassar out of place kind of noise. To my surprise he stepped ashore and began to walk back along the bank. I stood watching him, optimism rising within me, for surely this was silent acquiescence? But he only went a matter of feet before stopping to bend over something on the bank. I strained to see what he was up to, but his shape was dark against the foliage which hemmed the riverside, and the torch was definitely not as bright as it had been. Then I realized that he must be doing something with one of the mooring ropes. What on earth? Was he planning to send me and my craft drifting down the river? What the hell would that achieve? He switched off the torch and I sensed him putting it into his pocket before he crouched down again. I heard him grunt with effort as he pulled out the mooring spike – someone had evidently hammered it well into the bank. It must have come free suddenly because I saw him lurch backwards before straightening up and hopping nimbly aboard the stern of the boat, which was already starting to swing out into the stream, pivoting on the remaining rope.

Then I understood. A mooring spike, particularly if it

happened to be a metal one, would make an excellent weapon, and he had put the torch away in order to give himself a free hand to hold on with. 'One hand for yourself, and one hand for the ship' – wasn't that the old maxim?

I began to shuffle back towards the bows again, reasoning that if he followed me, I might be able to work my way round to where the remaining line was still securing us to the bank, jump for it and flee for my life again. I didn't think I could run far, but maybe if I ran along the road I would come to a house or find somewhere to hide?

Then I realized that Alan wasn't so stupid as to follow me along the narrow side deck. Instead, he used the side deck as a stepping stone to climb on to the cabin roof, where he advanced steadily, his arm raised, ready to strike. In the instant that I saw him swing back the spike, an idea half formed in my mind and I acted on it, raising my arm instinctively to ward off the blow, then, as the spike connected, deliberately toppling backwards into the water. I steeled myself not to struggle, letting my body surface as naturally as possible and allowing the current to float me slowly back towards the bridge, reasoning that without his torch, Alan would be able to see little or nothing, knowing only that he had struck with sufficient force to knock me into the water.

He was quick to bring the torch back into play. I saw its beam cleaving the air, then its brightness was focused on me. I forced myself not to blink, kept my eyes open and my features rigid, concentrated on looking up at the sky, focusing on a particular cluster of stars. I couldn't be sure how much he could see by the light of that failing torch, but I knew that it would be difficult to keep it shining steadily on my face. I was moving and the boat was unsteady beneath him. What would he do next? Get off the boat and follow me, obviously. Try to keep level and hope that I would drift somewhere within his reach, so that he could check whether I was dead and if not, finish me off.

It took every atom of willpower to stay still and calm, but then I saw a dark shape looming over me, cutting off my group of stars. I was drifting under the bridge. If Alan wanted to go on following me, he would have to climb up one side of the road and down the other – and while he was doing that, he couldn't possibly see what I was up to.

When I judged that I had reached the centre of the bridge, I drew myself into a vertical position and began to tread water. I knew I had to be quick. I dragged my sweatshirt over my head and down my arms, gagging and spluttering as the operation took my head under water. I couldn't know whether my idea would work, but I pursued it because I had no better ones.

There had been no time limit imposed when we had contrived floats from our pyjama tops to earn our ASA swimming badges, and the school swimming pool was a million miles removed from a night-time river – but then again, I did not need to make a life saver as such, just something which would stay afloat for a while, with a semblance of solidity about it. I made no attempt to knot the sleeves – there was no time for that kind of fancy manoeuvre – but working by feel I found the waistband and held it open as wide as I could, drawing it to and fro to trap as much air as possible in the main body of the garment before sending it on its way.

The sweatshirt was barely out of my hands before I saw Alan's light again. From the angle of it I realized that he must be standing on the bridge, working the beam back and forth across the surface of the river. I watched as the pale circle criss-crossed the water until it fell upon an alien object, close under the further bank. It was my sweatshirt – the logo showing white against the darker fabric. If I was lucky, Alan would not immediately suspect that the top and its owner had parted company. The sweatshirt would work like one of those conjuring tricks where you think you see what you're expecting to see instead of what is really there. Was the torch emitting enough light to show exactly what was there? Or more crucially, what was not?

My panicky breathing seemed to echo around the stonework, filling the arch of the bridge with a contagion of fear. Surely Alan must be able to hear me? I saw the shaft of light flicker – it was definitely failing, but the batteries had not quite given out – and as the beam steadied to a sickly yellow I saw the lump in the water drift out of sight beyond a bed of reeds.

I heard Alan curse and then the torch beam vanished momentarily before reappearing as he descended from the bridge to
the level of the river. Every moment that Alan's interest was
retained by the sweatshirt bought me another yard. Now was
my chance, while he was hurrying in the opposite direction. A
couple of strokes brought me upstream of the bridge. I dragged
myself over the muddy bank, so burdened by the weight of
my clothing that at one point I almost slid back into the water,
but I grabbed frantically at weeds and tufts of grass, finally
hauling myself on to dry land. Once clear of the water I climbed
as silently as I could to the level of the road, trying to control
my chattering teeth. I crept to Alan's side of the bridge and
peered over it, but I could see nothing. Presumably he had
disappeared round a bend in the river, still in pursuit of the
sinking sweatshirt.

I set off along the road, managing only the briefest of jogs
before I slowed to a walk. My shoes slapped and squelched,
as if endeavouring to make the maximum amount of noise
possible. I momentarily considered getting rid of my troublesome footwear altogether, but the prospect of walking who
knew how far barefoot was not appealing. I was frozen,
terrified, my arm had begun to ache where Alan had made
contact with the mooring spike and my wet jeans chafed
mercilessly, but while every step seemed harder than the last,
I knew that I had to keep going. Against all the odds I was
still alive, and now I had to stay that way.

Alan was still nearby, and he had a torch to help him.
As soon as he got a half-decent look at the sweatshirt he
would know what I had done and start to search for me.
He would guess that I had taken to the road and he would
catch up with me again . . . an involuntary whimper escaped
into the night. I must not be caught again. I can't fight back,
I thought. I've got nothing left.

So think. Stop and think. Can't stop, mustn't stop. Mustn't
waste a second. He found you before because of the water
coming off your clothes, and you must be making footprints
on the tarmac now – a line of damp footprints which will
show up in the light of his torch, telling him exactly which
way to go. Get off the road, then. Walk on the grass verge.

He won't be able to track you on the verge – all grass verges feel damp at this time of night.

But he knows which direction you've gone in. He'll find the footprints and then he'll follow you along the road . . . I stopped dead and looked around. Thick hedges hemmed the lane to either side for as far as I could see ahead. There was nowhere to escape if Alan climbed back on to the road, then followed the trail I had left for him. Even if I took to the grass verge – far too redolent of night-time damp and cold to determine whether it had been traversed by a pair of wet trainers – Alan would still know which direction I was headed in and that I must be somewhere not far along the road.

The way to confound pursuit was to do the unexpected. If I had left a mass of watery clues leading in one direction, then what I needed to do now was backtrack the opposite way. Oh, no . . . no . . . not back towards the river . . . and Alan. Oh yes, persisted that wiser counsel. That's exactly what you have to do.

I reluctantly turned back the way I had come, picking my way along the verge, which was much harder going than the road – uneven, with unexpected dips and bramble cables waiting to trip the unwary. Every few feet I stopped to listen, because if Alan had discovered my subterfuge he might already be heading towards me, and if his torch had died on him then he too would be creeping along in the darkness. The usual night-time sounds, rustles in the hedgerow and the faraway call of a tawny owl increased the sense of menace with every step.

The moonlight had been dimmed by passing clouds and I was almost on top of the bridge before I realized it. I pulled up short and crouched behind the end of the stone parapet, raising my head by inches until I could see over the side and look down river to where I had last glimpsed Alan's torch beam in pursuit of my decoy. I strained to make out any sign of movement, but there was nothing to suggest the presence of another human being nearby.

I was just making up my mind that it was safe to cross the bridge when I picked up a different kind of noise – the distinctive chink of something metallic. As I stared into the blackness the sound came again and a moment later a bright light shone out, close to where I guessed my original struggle with Alan had taken place. He had returned to reclaim his bike. I had forgotten about the bike lamp. And now I had placed myself right back in the path of this latest searchlight. He had only got to climb up to the road, shine his lamp across the bridge and, unlike me, Alan was moving decisively. I watched in horror as the lamp came nearer, systematically illuminating bushes and other possible hidey holes along the riverside path while making all the time for the bridge. Before his torch gave out he must have seen enough to know that I wasn't dead in the water. He was back on the trail, angry and determined, and if I didn't do something – now and fast – then in a matter of moments we would be face-to-face again. I had to galvanize myself, sprint across the bridge and get away. And in that second it dawned on me that my plan to confuse pursuit by re-crossing the bridge was useless. There was no grass verge here. The road surface ran solidly from one side to the other, so if my shoes were still wet enough to leave marks – which they almost certainly were, since water still squelched out of them at every step – then Alan would see immediately which way I had really gone. Fear rose up my throat and threatened to choke me. I had gained a small advantage, only to deliver myself up to him barely ten minutes later.

'Trying to be too clever. That was your problem. I liked you so much better when you were stupid.'

And I was being an idiot now. Trembling here in full view when there must be somewhere to hide. At least give yourself a chance – don't let that treacherous panic take over like it nearly did before. OK, he would not leave an inch of road or riverbank uncombed until he had found me, but it was still likely that he would follow my initial tracks along the road, not suspecting I had doubled back (after all, who but an idiot *would* have doubled back?).

There was no path along this side of the river, but I made out the narrowest of gaps between the base of the stonework and the hedge and I fed myself into it, feet first, sliding and wriggling until I was completely through the hedge. The reeds grew thickly on this side of the river, but from my new position beside them I could still follow the loom of Alan's lamp as he ascended the embankment, then walked out on to the bridge, where the bottom of the beam was cut off by the solid line of the stonework. If he shone his light over the side, he would see me . . . but his attention seemed to be focused elsewhere. I watched the pattern of light change again as it came level with the hedge. How thick was the foliage? It had appeared solid to me, but maybe there would be gaps through which he could shine his light, revealing the miserable drowned rat skulking on the other side. Good grief, he could probably smell me – the stink of the river was rising steadily from my clothes. I held my breath, expecting discovery at any moment.

Alan did not interest himself in the hedge, however, because he must have spotted the evidence of my original flight, when muddy water had oozed and dripped so freely on to the surface of the lane. His tread quickened and the lamp moved on – he was taking the bait. I gave him long enough to cover a hundred yards, then clawed my way back through the gap between the bridge and the hedge to regain the road. Still on my knees I watched the lamp growing more distant. He was moving quickly, swinging his beam from side to side, scanning ahead, wondering how far I had got with my few minutes' start.

Any hesitation now would be fatal. I turned my back on him and crept across the bridge, then began to walk as fast as I could, trying to place my feet in a way which minimized the seal flipper slap of wet trainers on tarmac. I figured that the speed gained by sticking to the firm surface of the road outweighed the risk of leaving any watery clues. Besides which, the absence of tracks would not necessarily save me, because I guessed that when Alan did not find me in one direction, he might well try the other – perhaps using his bike to speed his progress – so the important thing now was for me to move fast.

To my left the hedge soon became scrubby and intermittent, but there were no trees, buildings or other potential hiding places in view. I considered the possibility of arming myself: a fallen branch or even a large stone might provide me with some sort of advantage, particularly if I heard Alan coming and was able to take him by surprise, but it wasn't light enough to make out any useful objects at the side of the road, even assuming they existed. I kept glancing over my shoulder but a curve in the road had cut off Alan's lamp and I saw nothing to indicate pursuit. Then I saw that there was a narrow lane going off to the left, overarched by trees. The way I had been following was hardly a main road, but this was no more than a single width track, heading into the darkness. Which way would Alan expect me to go? The wider road offered more likelihood of settlements, even the possibility of a passing car, whereas a narrow country lane was, quite apart from anything else, a darker, scarier prospect for a woman alone.

More scary than what lay behind me? I struck off to the left, briefly increasing my pace as if to underline my conviction. You're crazy, said the voice in my head. This is the road to nowhere. You've got no idea where you might be heading or how far away the next house is.

The lane weaved first one way and then the other, but after no more than a minute or two of walking, the trees gave way to a fence with a visible overhang of shadowy garden shrubs, behind which I could make out the unmistakable shape of a rooftop. As I drew level I could see it was a cottage, much like a house in a child's first drawing – a quartet of windows and a central front door. I felt like cheering.

I located the latch on the garden gate and hurried up the short path to the front door, where the knocker stood out as a darker shape against light paintwork. I worked the knocker vigorously and was appalled when the resultant racket echoed into the night, like someone sounding a bass drum. It was absurdly loud and my heart thundered in concert with it. Surely wherever Alan was, he must be able to hear it? God, a noise like that must be audible for miles around. I had to suppress the desire to shout up at the windows, to plead with the occupants to let me in quickly before Alan, alerted by the cacophony, emerged from out of the darkness to get me.

Nothing. I waited, not wanting to send that dreadful sound out into the night again. Still nothing. But perhaps the unseen occupants had been aroused, and were now sleepily waiting to see if the summons at their front door would be repeated? I had to risk it. I took hold of the knocker and desperately banged it up and down again. The result was a quartet of deafening impacts which died away into the night leaving an empty quiet, broken only by drips as my clothes continued to shed river water on to the front doorstep.

There was no one at home. It was like coming across a lifeboat after floundering alone in mid-Atlantic – only to find that the lifeboat has a hole in it and sinks before your eyes.

It was hard to turn my back on the building in which I had invested so much hope. I stood at the gate looking up and down the lane, but there was no other sign of human habitation. Rural Norfolk had apparently been depopulated for the night. There seemed to be only two people left in the entire county – the hunter and the hunted.

Then I saw it again. That will-'o-the-wisp of light flickering through the trees. The only other person left in Norfolk.

THIRTY

My hand had been reaching for the garden gate, but I drew back as if the latch had been electrified. I didn't even consider some coincidental passing stranger. The sound of me hammering on the door had carried through the night and brought Alan – who must have drawn a blank in one direction and returned to try the other – straight down the leafy lane like an iron filing to a magnet. He would know exactly what that noise betokened and once he reached the cottage and found it in darkness he would realize that this latest bid for assistance had failed and that I could not be far away.

I doubted that I could outrun him, but I thought the building itself might offer a hiding place – maybe there was an unlocked shed, or an outhouse whose door I could barricade from the inside so that it appeared to be locked. I hurried up the path and headed round the side of the building. There was no shed or outhouse, only a greenhouse – a hiding place wrought entirely of glass. The sight of it almost engendered hysteria, so that I nearly laughed out loud. The plants in the small back garden were all of modest height. To complete this self-selected trap, the garden appeared to be surrounded by a head-high wall, impossible to climb.

The greenhouse door stood ajar and seemed to represent my only hope. As I slipped inside I heard the sound of the garden gate from the other side of the house and knew that Alan had entered the garden. The greenhouse evidently doubled as a shed, for the floor was a booby trap of pots and garden implements, any one of which would betray me if I inadvertently toppled it.

'Jenn-eee . . .' The call startled me. Alan repeated it, his sing-song voice loud enough to carry some distance. 'I know you're in here, Jenny.'

I watched until the telltale glow of his cycle lamp began to appear around the far corner of the cottage then darted partway from the greenhouse to the opposite end of the cottage, heedless of trampling the flower beds. I stopped before I reached the corner, watching to see him emerge in person, but the light was dazzling after so long in the dark, and I could see nothing of the man who held it. He played the beam around the garden and I was off again like a shot the moment it reached me. Had he managed to get a look at me or not? I pulled up short as I rounded the side of the building, flattening myself against the wall.

Whether or not he had seen me, he had certainly heard me, as I now heard him approaching with a brisk, heavy tread, his arrival preceded by a ray of light, its shape and brightness helping me anticipate the exact moment to swing the thin wooden handle of whatever tool I had taken from the greenhouse. It wasn't heavy enough to be a spade, or unwieldy enough for a rake, but I felt it jar in my hands as it connected, and he cried out and stumbled forward.

I had never before exacted violence on anyone, but I made up for it now: striking him again before he had time for evasive action, again as he seemed to fold at the knees, and inflicting a further blow when he hit the ground. At that moment I had no thought in my head but to stop him dead – and if dead was the way he ended up, I have to own that in those frantic seconds I did not care.

His lamp, miraculously still alight, had slipped out of his hand and rolled a couple of feet away. Still gripping my weapon, I retrieved it and turned its brightness on the prone form of my estranged husband. In doing so I caught a momentary look at the object in my hand and identified it as a hoe. When I focused the light on his head I could see a trickle of blood on one temple, where the business end of my improvised weapon had connected. I was just contemplating the possibility that I might have killed him when he made a faint sound, halfway between a grunt and a moan. Not dead then. I backtracked to the greenhouse and played the light across the workbench, where my hunch was rewarded by a small skein of garden twine, tucked into an empty plastic flower pot. He moaned again as I dragged his ankles together and wrapped the thin green string around them, knotting the two ends neatly. There wasn't enough to bind his arms, but I figured that did not really matter. The restriction I had placed upon his legs would buy me time, so that I could put some distance between us while he was no more than semi-conscious and in no condition to follow anyone anywhere.

For a brief moment I considered putting the matter beyond doubt, but I couldn't do it. Instead I turned and walked away, Alan's cycle lamp in one hand and the stolen garden hoe in the other. I let myself out of the gate, retraced my steps along the tree-lined lane, then walked purposefully down the road, my progress surer with the aid of a light to help me. I was bruised, aching with cold, my breath coming in little sobs, but I knew that every road must lead somewhere eventually, and the creak of a branch or the cry of a fox held no fears for me now, because even if every hobgoblin in East Anglia were dancing at my heels, I knew that, for the moment at least, one particular evil was not, and every yard I put between us made it that much less likely he would find me.

What would Alan do when he recovered enough to disentangle his feet? He wouldn't know how much of a start I had got, or which direction I had gone in, and now that he no longer had the advantage of a light it did not matter if my sodden clothes and shoes were still shedding water at a rate to betray my every footfall. Every choice of direction doubled the odds against Alan's being able to pursue me any further, and he would realize that once I found someone to help me, it was game over. He couldn't afford to scour the countryside indefinitely. It would soon become imperative for him to return to his boat and get the hell out of it before I raised the alarm.

I had no way to gauge the passage of time, but after a while I found myself at a cross roads. To my annoyance there was not so much as an old-fashioned finger post to suggest a direction. I tried to believe that the distance to the next human habitation was measured in mere fractions of a mile, rather than the five or six which it might easily be. It would be all too easy to despair. As if being frozen and exhausted were not enough, there was the thought that I might end up wandering in circles around the Norfolk countryside, always choosing the direction which took me away from help rather than towards it – or, worse, into the path of Alan's route back to his boat.

I made my choice then plodded steadily onward, trying to kid myself that the effort was making me feel warmer. After a time I finally emerged on to a wider road – left or right? I gambled left and within a matter of yards I detected the glow of artificial lights and the outline of roofs against the sky. Surely they couldn't all be empty holiday lets? I was too tired to feel elation, but I quickened my pace until the bend in the road opened out so that I could see a row of cottages with cars parked outside, and beyond them a pub whose frontage was illuminated by a couple of spotlights. A few yards on from the pub there was a chequered rectangle of light betokening a phone box. I worked my hand down into my damp pocket, blessing the tightness of my jeans. The folded notes were soggy, but the coins together with my room key were still in place. I did not need to bang hopelessly on the doors of strangers. I could go into the phone box and dial 999.

It is strange the way your instincts play you false. I had somehow expected the interior of the phone box to be warmer than the night outside, which of course it wasn't. I was breathing hard as I lifted the receiver in readiness to dial and I paused for a moment to get my breath back and sort out what I was going to say. It was then that I saw the card. I had often seen them in call boxes in towns, but I never expected a taxi company to bother placing them in rural call boxes – then I remembered that I was close to the Norfolk Broads, where holidaymakers who had left their cars behind might sometimes be glad of a lift back to the river after indulging in a few drinks or a pub meal.

STAR TAXIS
24 HOURS A DAY
RADIO CONTROLLED CABS

A wild plan began to crystallize in my mind. I stood for several minutes with the receiver in my hand. Think it through, think it through.

I dialled the number of Star Taxis and gave them my location from the slip BT so helpfully puts in all their phone booths. (I had always wondered what kind of callers did not know their whereabouts, and now I knew.)

'We'll have a car there for you in about ten minutes,' said the voice on the other end of the line.

It was like a return to sanity, leaving behind the nightmare world of submerged cars and knife-wielding maniacs and abruptly stepping back into a life where one could calmly order up a taxi and have it there within ten minutes.

I waited what I judged to be about five minutes and then I rang the police. I gave the operator the number I was calling from, because I guessed that they could trace it in any case. In my best yokel accent, I said, 'This isn't a hoax, OK, it's really important. Alan Reynolds is in Norfolk. He's got a cruiser tied up at Neatishead staithe. It's the last boat you come to. I can't get involved or give my name, sorry.'

After hanging up I went to stand in the shadows by the corner of the pub, ready to hop back out of sight if a police car came by. I abandoned my garden hoe and Alan's cycle lamp in the lee of the building and, by way of an afterthought, I returned to the call box, retrieved the Star Taxis card and put it in my pocket. There was no need to make it too easy for anyone who might attempt to trace the identity of the anonymous caller – not that there was any particular reason why they should. It was Alan they wanted – who would care where the tip off came from? Even if they were curious about the source of the information, I reckoned the police would be unlikely to check what other calls had been made from the kiosk that night, probably assuming that the mystery informant had arrived and departed by car, choosing to ring from an isolated phone box rather than making a traceable call from their home.

I had barely been waiting another couple of minutes when a car did appear round the bend, but it was not a police car. It was a dark saloon with Star Taxis painted on the side. I leapt to the edge of the pavement, waving my arms.

The car pulled up and when the driver got out I saw that he was a young Asian man. He looked perplexed and when he spoke, I recognized a Brummie accent.

'Blimey,' he said. 'What's happened to you?'

I had my story ready. 'I've been in the river,' I said. 'It was a practical joke, and now my friends have left me stranded here. Can you take me to The Sunset Motel? I'm not sure of the exact address but it's just off the main road between Wroxham and Norwich.'

'I know where it is, but are you all right? I mean, you look in a bit of a state, you know?'

'I'm fine,' I said, wishing he would hurry up and let me get into the car. 'I just need to get back to where I'm staying. Get out of these things and get dry.'

He hesitated. 'Hadn't ought to let you in the car in that state,' he said. 'Got to think about me next fare getting into a wet seat. Don't worry,' he went on hurriedly, sensing my panic. 'I ain't gonna leave you here. Hang on a minute.'

He went to the boot of the car and returned with a couple of plastic supermarket carrier bags which he spread out on the front passenger seat.

'I don't normally take anyone in the front, unless it's a three or a four,' he said. 'You sit on them and we should be all right.'

Mumbling my gratitude, I positioned myself on the outspread bags and fastened my seat belt. The sudden memory of Alan leaning across and fastening another seat belt in another car made me feel so sick that I thought for a moment I would throw up.

My driver did not notice; he had already put the car into gear and set off, turning the heater right up, so that I almost sensed steam rising from my clothes.

'Hen night, is it?'

'Sorry – what?'

'Hen night – you know, getting married? Weekend away with the girls?'

'No, not a hen night,' I said. 'Just a joke that went too far.'

'People are getting dafter,' he said. 'Stag nights is the worst. Too many drinks, bridegroom finishes up starkers in the middle of the road . . .'

I liked you better when you were stupid. The words echoed around my head. Well, perhaps there was merit in being stupid when it kept you alive.

'. . . Well, I mean . . . it ain't funny, is it?'

'No,' I agreed, wriggling my toes inside the wet trainers and wishing the heat would penetrate them.

'Staying long, are you – at the motel?'

'No,' I said. 'Just a couple of nights.'

'Funny place to have a motel, all that way off the main road. Still, there's a lot of places out in the sticks that do well round here. The Parceval Hotel – right off the beaten track, they are. 'Course they've got a spa there and they do all those treatments . . .'

I could have given you the full treatment, just like all the others. Was that why I had survived in the end, because he favoured a particular method and simply had not had the time?

My driver must have seen me shudder because he said, 'Sorry I can't get it any warmer for you. I've got the heater on full.'

'I know. Thank you.' I must not start to cry, although his genuine concern and kindly chatter were as distressing in their way as if he had met me with barbed words or outright cruelty. After what I had just been through, the kindness of a stranger was oddly difficult to bear.

We turned on to the main road, passing a solitary car going in the opposite direction. Again I experienced that welcome sensation of returning to the normal world. My driver must have realized that I didn't want to talk and drove on without further attempts at conversation; an understanding rather than uncomfortable silence. At the motel I indicated to him where he should pull in, and said, 'I'm sorry. You'll have to wait a minute while I go inside to get some money.'

'That's all right, love.' He turned to face me and for the first time he grinned. 'I can see you're on the level.'

I retrieved my purse from inside the cabin, adding a generous tip to the fare, which elicited an even wider grin. Then I went inside, shut the cabin door and leaned against it, listening to the taxi's engine as it sped away down the deserted lane.

Everything was just as I had left it. My discarded jumper and my suitcase, carried inside at some distant point in another lifetime. I went into the bathroom and ran water over my hands. It took a while but eventually the water came through hot. My watch was sitting alongside the basin, still faithfully marking time as if nothing out of the ordinary had happened at all, but in the bright light of the bathroom the goosey skin of my arm bore a patch of purplish blue, too tender to touch. I peeled off my clothes, piling them into the washbasin before I got under the shower, where I stood for a long time under the cascade of hot water, absorbing the warmth into my body, shampooing the smell of rotted weeds from my hair.

I felt strangely light-headed as I watched Susan McCarthy in the mirror while she dried her hair. She looked calm and blessedly ordinary with her short damp hair and a nightshirt with a rabbit on the front. She climbed into the king-size bed, snuggled under the duvet and switched off the bedside light. The room was completely dark except for the digital clock at the bedside which glowed red: 2:47, 2:48, 2:49 . . .

Tomorrow I would report my car stolen. I could say that I went to bed and found the car gone when I got up next morning. It was unlikely that Alan would volunteer the information that he had put me in the river when they arrested him.

2:51, 2:52 . . .

Nothing to connect me with Alan.

2:53, 2:54 . . .

I can probably hire a car tomorrow, so that I can get home.

2:55, 2:56 . . .

When they find the car they'll probably assume it was dumped by joyriders. Even if they find the rope or my sweatshirt washed up on the bank they won't be able to make anything of it . . .

2:58, 2:59 . . .

Maybe once Alan has been arrested I could go to the police . . . explain . . . perhaps the authorities were more lenient if they thought you were on the run from a violent husband . . .

3:01, 3:02 . . .

With Alan safely locked away, maybe I could go back to being myself again – except that sometimes I wasn't sure who that really was.

THIRTY-ONE

Submerged in sleep, I thought at first that the knocking was part of a dream, but as my stupor began to recede I realized that it was an external noise rather than something within the confines of my head. I half opened my eyes, absorbing the fact that daylight was partially illuminating the room. I also remembered exactly where I was and what had brought me there, but I thrust all that to the back of my mind, because at that moment I wanted nothing more than to be allowed to re-engage with the comfortable oblivion of sleep.

The knocking came again, louder and more urgent than before, as if the person outside was thumping the door with a fist. Housekeeping, possibly? Had I slept too long, outstayed my allotted time? I checked the bedside clock and found that it was only twenty three minutes past eight. Not housekeeping, then. Alan. It could not be Alan. How could he have . . .

'Sue – Sue – are you in there?'

It was a man's voice – in fact, it sounded incredibly like Rob's voice, but that was ridiculous. Alan, then? No, it couldn't be Alan, because Alan would have called me Jenny. Even so, there was no way it could be Rob.

There was enough light penetrating around the edges of the curtains to tell me that it was bright sunlight outside. When the pummelling of the door recommenced, I staggered reluctantly out of bed. There was a security chain and I engaged it before opening the door a crack. 'Rob,' I gasped.

'Susan,' he said. 'Thank God. When the car wasn't here . . . Can I come in?'

'Of course.' I was fumble fingered in my haste to take the chain off, although I knew now that I was actually still asleep and in the middle of a dream. There did not seem any point in asking him what on earth he was doing there, because people don't need a reason for turning up in your dreams, they simply arrive in places where they could not possibly be, often performing some unlikely act before vanishing again as unexpectedly as they came. So instead of asking pointless questions or acting stunned, I stood back to let him into the cabin, noticing as I did that his eyes were bloodshot and he was unshaven.

The chill of the morning air on my bare legs felt authentic enough and when I absently ran a hand through my hair I could feel the unmistakable frizziness which came from going to bed before it was properly dry. The digital clock had moved on to register eight twenty five. It occurred to me that in order to have arrived at this time in the morning Rob must have driven for a good part of the night – something entirely consistent with his appearance. I noticed too that contrary to his usual practice, he made no attempt to kiss or hug me; instead he walked straight past me and sank down on the end of the bed as if he was deliberately keeping a distance between us.

'Thank God,' he said again. 'When I couldn't see your car I thought you might have done another runner.'

For a millisecond I almost embarked on a pretence of surprise at the car not being there. The lies came so automatically now, but then I stopped myself. The time for pretence and lying was over.

'How did you find me?' I asked.

'Your message,' he said. 'I read your note and guessed why you'd gone, but not where. Then I listened to the message you left on my machine yesterday afternoon. You were the last caller, so I dialled 1471 and got the number. I called here and a woman tried to put me through, but when you didn't answer she said your cabin lights were out and your car wasn't there, so she guessed you'd gone out. I tried again and again but by midnight you still hadn't called back and I didn't dare leave a message, in case you ran away again.'

'Ran away? What do you mean?'

'Ran away from me.'

The answer was so unexpected that it struck me dumb.

'I had to find you and tell you myself,' he said. 'They've arrested Luke Robinson for Julie Peacock's murder. Apparently he walked into the police station with his social worker and confessed. If you'd waited one more day you would have heard. It's all over the local news. I was afraid all along that you thought it was me and then yesterday . . .'

I thought of the un-posted manila envelope in my cottage. Now I would never have to send it and nor was there any risk of the Trollop losing her job. I pulled myself back into the moment. 'Of course I didn't think it was you. Never ever. Not for a moment.'

He regarded me doubtfully. 'You started to act differently after the murder,' he said. 'You got kind of . . . well . . . self-absorbed. As though you were thinking about something all the time – something that you couldn't share with me.'

'Never,' I repeated vehemently.

'But you left the necklace on the table, next to the note, where you knew I would see it.'

For a minute I couldn't think what he was talking about, then I said, 'Oh, that necklace. It fell off the mantelpiece. I must have left it on the table instead of putting it back. It wasn't deliberate.'

'A necklace with a J,' he said. 'J for Julie.'

'Or Jocelyn, or Jocasta, or whatever the girl you confiscated it from was called.'

For the first time the ghost of a smile flitted across his face. 'Actually it was Jasmin Ratcliffe, but when I got back and heard about those bodies on the news . . . I thought you must have thought history was repeating itself. That you'd fled from one murderer only to finish up with another one. I was shocked, of course, when I heard the news about the bodies in the house, but then everything kind of fell into place. I always knew you wouldn't have arranged to do a vanishing act without having a good reason.'

I stared at him. 'You knew? You knew that I was – am – Jennifer Reynolds? How long have you known?'

'For sure? Well, I always thought it was a bit odd that you . . . sort of had no real past. You never seemed to want to talk about your life before you came to Lasthwaite, but I didn't want to pressure you. I thought there must be some unhappy memories there. Then I saw a TV programme a few weeks back – you probably never watched it. It was all about missing people and when the pictures of Jennifer Reynolds came on I was pretty convinced that it was you, but I kept on thinking "no – it can't be". I was going to talk to you about it the next day, but then Julie Peacock was murdered, and suddenly it seemed like life was going crazy. A girl I know is murdered in the village and maybe the woman I love is living under an assumed name, all in the space of twenty-four hours? I thought I must be losing my mind. I started to doubt what I'd seen on television the night before, but then you mentioned that girl who was murdered – Antonia. That was what eventually clinched it. I've got an old mate from university – Ray – who works in the big newspaper library in London. You didn't give me much to go on, just the girl's first name, but Ray's brilliant at stuff like that. I asked him to look it up – I made up a reason for wanting to know. It took him a few days to get back to me, but he said it must be the Antonia Bridgeman case. Antonia Bridgeman was abducted and murdered in Nicholsfield – Jennifer Reynolds's home town. One coincidence too many.'

'But why didn't you say something once you knew for sure?'

'I came really close once or twice, but I was afraid of losing you. I was worried that if I tried to raise it with you it would frighten you off. I kept on trying to think of ways to let you know that I was OK with it – that it doesn't matter because I love you. I want you whether you're Susan or Jennifer. It's all the same to me. It's the person inside who counts.'

I found myself in his arms, laughing and crying at the same time. He knew. He had known for ages. That barrier between us ever since the programme was shown, the sense of things unsaid – we had both been avoiding the same thing, keeping the same secret.

After a few minutes, I said, 'I never knew about Alan. I must have been horribly stupid and blind.'

'When I heard about those bodies in the house, I thought you must have found out about him and that was why you ran away. I couldn't understand why you hadn't gone to the police, but I thought you must have been too scared or something.'

'The ridiculous thing is that I never suspected him at all – other people but not him.'

'Even though you lived in the same house?'

'He used to go away. Or at least I thought he did. When he was supposed to be travelling around, going to antique fairs and specialist auctions, I always stayed with my parents. That left him with the house to himself. I never liked being in that house by myself. It was a museum – a mausoleum, as it turned out. Alan must have got pretty good at covering up for himself before we got married. I was only ten when the first girl went missing, but Alan would have been eighteen by then. I was horribly stupid – I can see that now. Antonia Bridgeman should have been the key. We'd given her a lift home you see, one afternoon when it was raining. So Alan would have known when her lesson was each week and I suppose because she'd accepted a lift from him before she wouldn't have thought twice about getting in the car with him again.'

'Poor kid,' Rob said softly.

'I should have known, I really should, but I never cottoned on. When the police started looking for Alan, I felt responsible because I thought that if it hadn't been for me running off he wouldn't be a suspect. I thought I ought to help Alan get out of trouble, so I arranged to meet him . . .' Even as I spoke I wondered at Alan's plausibility, his unaccountable powers of persuasion. What was it that had made Marie Glover and the others climb into the car with him, transformed me into his biddable slave, or for that matter made it seem so impossible for me to leave him?

'You know where he is?' Rob sounded incredulous. He jumped up and strode the half-dozen steps it took to get across the room and back. 'Thank God I got down here before you met up with him.'

'But you didn't,' I said. 'I rendezvoused with him yesterday afternoon, as arranged. He was waiting for me on a boat at Neatishead.' I stopped and swallowed hard. Then I told him, as briefly and un-dramatically as I could about the trip to – and escape from – the bottom of the river, the confrontation in the garden, the long, lonely walk which had followed, my phone call to the police and my assumption that wounded though he was, Alan would eventually have made his way back to the boat.

Rob sat beside me, listening patiently with his arms around me. I was crying and shaking long before I reached the end of the tale, but he did not speak until I had finished.

'I'll kill him.' The intensity of his expression frightened me. 'Prison's too good for him. I feel as if I want to murder him with my bare hands for what he did to you.'

'No,' I said. 'The police will have him by now. We have to close the door on this and leave it for others to finish.'

THIRTY-TWO

I was wrong about the manner of the arrest. Alan never made it back to the boat. In one of those peculiar happenstances which ends so many manhunts, a lone motorist spotted Alan cycling without lights, and assumed from his unsteady progress that he was drunk. On reaching home a few minutes later she rang the police to report the incident and a patrol car went to investigate. They initially took Alan in for riding a cycle without lights and resisting arrest, but it did not take them long to discover what a big fish they had landed. It goes without saying that the whole business made headline news. (If any action was taken following the anonymous tip off, there was no public mention of it, and if the police ever tried to trace the caller, they did not succeed.) Alan was charged and remanded in custody – and while he languished in prison awaiting trial, the case vanished from the media and the public forgot about him for a while.

It was not so easy for me. That first night of deep, uninterrupted sleep had been wrought of sheer shock and exhaustion. Peace was far less easy to attain after that and the nights which followed were broken more often than not. I could no longer bring myself to sleep alone at the cottage or indeed anywhere else, and I often woke Rob, crying out or thrashing my way free of invisible bonds, fleeing imaginary pursuers. Sometimes I lay awake, haunted by the faces of the girls and women I had not saved, or straining to identify every nocturnal sound, wondering if Alan was really locked away, safe in his cell, or whether he had outwitted his guards and was even now effecting a stealthy entrance via a forced window. I did not doubt that Alan perceived me as the sole architect of his downfall. Retribution was only to be expected.

It was a year before Alan came up for trial. Suddenly he was all over the media again, with TV cameras showing the prison van as it left the court each day, pursued by hysterical members of the public who bypassed the police cordon to bang on the sides and scream abuse. His barrister tried an insanity plea, but the court wouldn't wear it. He was sentenced to life imprisonment, with the recommendation that life should mean life. He stood accused of a whole list of murders, but ultimately not with that of his wife. DNA testing proved conclusively that the body in the ditch belonged to a woman called Donna Mellor, who had been on the missing persons list for three years.

The authorities proved to be a good deal more discreet and sympathetic than I could ever have anticipated. Jennifer Reynolds's name was quietly removed from the charge sheet and the missing persons list, and a divorce petition severing the legal ties between Jennifer and Alan Reynolds went through soon after his conviction, unnoticed by the press.

The case against Luke Robinson was dealt with more quickly than the one against Alan. A juvenile at the time of the offence, he was detained at Her Majesty's pleasure. It raised barely a flicker in the national media, but in Lasthwaite the case was not so easily forgotten and seemed to cast a shadow over the dale for a lot of people. Several houses went up for sale and Rob was not the only teacher at the comp who decided to look for a new post. He was lucky enough to get a departmental headship at a good school in York, and we moved to live in a village a few miles north of the city.

I think the doctors were glad to see me go. After taking time off for the death of my aunt, I rather went to pieces. Things began to slip and to make matters worse, the practice had been rocked by a minor scandal while I was away dealing with my aunt's funeral arrangements, when Terry Millington became the source of a complaint from a patient (alleged drunkenness and inappropriate behaviour) which brought his placement in Lasthwaite to an abrupt end. I never heard what happened to him after that.

As I struggled to keep going at work, unable to explain what was wrong with me, even to kindly Dr Mac, who was my physician as well as my boss, I received support from an unexpected quarter, for the Trollop became my unofficial right-hand woman, ally and general saviour, whose willingness and cheery good humour averted several crises. I gradually realized that she thought I was in some way responsible for the arrest of Luke Robinson, but whenever I tried to disabuse her she always adopted a knowing grin and said, 'Aye, Susan. Mum's the word, eh?'

When it became obvious that I would be leaving, the Trollop expressed a willingness to undertake the qualifications she needed to fill my shoes. It seems that we all have hidden depths and the potential to surprise one another. Her real name is Kathy, and she continues to run Lasthwaite Health Centre with efficiency and flair.

Rob and I never got to Australia. The biological clock was ticking and we opted for children instead. We were married quietly, with his family in attendance, and I think his mother forgave us the hole-in-the-corner ceremony when we provided her so promptly with two grandchildren – Josh and Rachel. At the wedding itself there were a few sharp intakes of breath when the vicar appeared to make a mistake over my name, but afterwards Rob explained to everyone that I don't like Jennifer and prefer to be known as Susan – and Sue Dugdale it remains.

Every so often, news filtered back to us from Lasthwaite. Bob Fox died and Jim sold the farm and moved into a cottage next door to the pub, where he continued to appear each evening, complete with collar and tie, shiny cap and a wild-eyed sheepdog called Jep in constant attendance.

I tried not to look back, for there is no future in the past, but the long shadows cast by the murders haunted me all the same. Whenever there was some fresh appeal – another set of grieving parents at a press conference, seeking their vanished daughter or appealing for the evidence which would apprehend her killer, I thought of the parents of those other girls. Some people might think that I should have known – that I must have known. But I did not know and never guessed. In spite of which I repeatedly asked myself the question: could I have saved them?

Alan became the stalker I never quite saw. A figure lurking at the periphery of vision as I turned over apples in the green-grocers, his footsteps echoing behind me as I walked the

Labrador pup which Josh had demanded that we buy. When darkness fell, I imagined Alan silently unlatching the garden gate, stealing cat-footed towards the back door. Had I remembered to lock up? Dared I go and check? Or should I stay huddled on the sofa with my arms around my knees, listening for every sound, too scared to move until Rob returned from teaching his Tuesday night-school class? For a long time my sleeping hours were stalked by terrors best unnamed, and in that dangerous twilight between sleep and wakefulness I would often imagine that Alan had escaped. He was cunning and clever – he would surely find a way. Then I turned on the television news one night and learned that he was dead. He had hanged himself in his prison cell.

I never rejoiced that Alan had taken one more life, but when I dream now it is of Rob and our growing children – the four of us together, taking that dream holiday to Australia, playing on the beach and swimming in the sun.